The Cooking School Murders

"Never mind that this is a really neat mystery with a sleuth you will want to meet again, the recipe for green tomato pie alone makes it worth the price."

Publishers Weekly

Also by Virginia Rich
Published by Ballantine Books:

THE BAKED BEAN SUPPER MURDERS

Virginia Rich
The
Cooking
School
Murders

BALLANTINE BOOKS • NEW YORK

To L. D. R.
with thanks and love

Library of Congress Catalog Card Number: 81-22162

ISBN 0-345-32621-0

This edition published by arrangement with E. P. Dutton, Inc.

Manufactured in the United States of America

First Ballantine Books Edition: November 1983
Third Printing: December 1984

It was not quite daylight when Leonard Silsby left his apartment in the two-story yellow brick box called the Harrington Arms.

Leonard's wife, Babe, still slept, spread like a starfish on the double bed. Later, when the sun reached the bedroom window, the flowered sheets would bloom in improbable colors. Babe's hair would be bright gold and there would be violet streaks on her closed eyelids and a pinkish smear of lipstick across her open, heavily-breathing mouth.

Babe now stirred, and as he left, Leonard heard a cross, explosive sound. He moved quickly, eager to leave the stale odors of the night.

The radio, turned to WHO in Des Moines, had not wakened Babe. Leonard had heard the early weather report and had switched it off as soon as he knew there had been no frost in northwestern Iowa. The September warm spell would continue, just as he had predicted to the boys at the plant.

The morning was still. Leonard's long, rubbery nose sniffed the air keenly as he came out into the morning. He sniffed without realizing he was doing so, identifying each element of the fresh morning smells—a pungent reminder of late marigolds, of rotting leaves under the stiff, neat barberry plantings, of a distant skunk off toward the east of town, of the lingering whiff of diesel from a since-passed early truck. Leonard sniffed in the way of a native farm boy, slowly and with obvious enjoyment, testing and sampling the new day. Then, with his loose gait, moving like a limber, long-bodied spaniel, he moved quickly around the building to the parking lot in the back.

The sprawled body lay facedown, almost in his path as he began

1

to cross the lot to his car. At first he did not see the dark congealing pool in which it lay. It was the scent, not the sight, of blood that stopped him. The smell of death was there, even in that fresh, cool morning air. Frozen where he stood, he was instantly back in the old, recurring nightmare, the nightmare of Vietnam that Babe could only postpone in the bed of bright flowers. Leonard Silsby would never forget the smell of blood.

The growing light showed the dark, viscid pool, purple-black beneath the still body in its pale dress. Leonard remained motionless, his jungle-trained senses alert, ready for enemy attack.

Finally, deciding that there was no hidden threat among the few small cars in the parking lot, none behind the ragged syringa hedge beyond, he forced himself to return to the apartment. He knew that his call to the police would waken Babe, and he hoped she wouldn't be mad at being roused this early.

At the same time, two other quiet bodies were equally blind to the coming light of morning. One lay awkwardly on the floor of a closed garage, in which a motor turned and hummed. The other floated easily in a gentle current, held by a shining silken tether to an underwater snag.

Harrington, Iowa, population 4,785, center of a moderately prosperous farming community, focus of a moderately popular summer resort, home of quiet, respectable, hardworking, right-thinking citizens, was waking up to a new day.

It would be a very different kind of day from the one Mrs. Potter might have imagined on the previous evening when she left for the cooking school.

The parking lot of Dorrance High School had been only sparsely filled when Mrs. Potter and her nephew Gregory Andrews pulled into a parking space. A September sunset still lighted the northern

Iowa sky, and the innocent air held the heat of the early harvest day.

Good crops, good land, good people, she told herself. An open country and a place where everyone knew everyone else—his parentage, his business and hobbies, his skills and scandals, his weak points and his strong ones, and his place in the social hierarchy of the town.

Mrs. Potter had enjoyed the lovely two-mile lakeshore drive, winding between rows of maple trees still green and untouched by the first frost. As they had left the big turn-of-the century house at the western end of the lake, she had considered offering her guest the key and the driver's seat. In spite of his obviously adequate age and size (nearly thirty and a good six-two) he had looked so vague, so mildly helpless, so indifferent as they came out of the house that she had decided against it.

Greg was, she reminded herself, still recovering from the hepatitis which had interrupted his Stanford research job. Physically, he seemed to be gaining, and the generous high-protein meals she prepared for him were what his father, her brother Will, had requested. When Will brought Greg to her—emaciated, with dull blue eyes peering out through a thicket of drab blond hair and beard—it was with the hope that a few months of rest at Indian Point, "Grandpa's house," and of good Iowa food, would be restorative.

He had eaten tonight's early supper with gusto. There were thin pink slices of baked Iowa ham, a mellow succotash made with the last of the garden sweet corn and the first of the "shelly" beans, rich with butter and light cream and a sprinkle of freshly ground black pepper. In lieu of salad there was a dish of tart, chunky applesauce. (What a marvel that the old Wealthy apple tree in back of the barn was still bearing, after all these years of neglect. Wealthies were the best apples for sauce, Grandpa had always insisted.)

On the emotional side, Greg's progress did not seem so certain. Usually he was quiet and withdrawn, as tonight. At other times he would explode in an outpouring of speech, each thought in itself seeming rational and clear, but with such rapid juxtapositions and interpolations that she seldom was able, afterward, to remember just what he had said.

3

Mrs. Potter drove, and Greg sat silent beside her.

Other cars were coming in, and the space beside Mrs. Potter's neat brown Subaru was taken by a vintage Mercedes.

" 'Genia, my darling. And Greg, how are you, boy? All set for our fancy cooking stuff?" Tanned, trimly mustached, balding, yet almost as flat and lean as Gregory, MacKay Moore greeted Mrs. Potter warmly. A kiss on each cheek, she thought, just like the Europeans. Pleasant, but surely one side would be enough for a parking lot salute? Still, she was very fond of this handsome man and it was always flattering to be the object of his affectionate gallantry.

"Dear girl, you twisted quite a few arms to make up this class," he told her. "I know you promised this fellow Redmond that you'd get up an even dozen for him. But that's all right and the class was a great idea. I only wonder if I shouldn't be doing the teaching bit myself. Didn't you think those stuffed mushroom things of mine were something of a triumph Saturday night?"

"Superb, MacKay. Your credentials are solid, even though I always suspect Bertha has something to do with it."

MacKay squeezed her shoulders and bent his head to rest his nose briefly on her shining gray-blond head. "Maybe I've fudged a little," she continued, "in having Greg enroll, since Redmond did specify previous cooking experience. But since he's staying with me this fall—"

Greg's interruption was barely audible. "I'm certainly not in Mr. Moore's league, Aunt 'Genia."

"But you make a nice omelet, love, and anyone brought up at my dear late sister-in law's table couldn't help but know good food."

MacKay held her elbow as he pointed to an arriving car. "Ralph and Dottie. Guess they managed to change the night of their midweek Bible class, or whatever it is."

Again there was ritual kissing, and now there seemed to be even more warmth engendered. The wonderful Christian fervor of the newly reconverted, thought Mrs. Potter. Dottie's roundly curved backside, encased in a fitted white knit pantsuit, received an appreciative pat from MacKay, and Ralph DeWitt's hand, warm and moist, held her own somewhat longer than need be.

"Shall we go in?" Mrs. Potter felt uncomfortable in the role of

4

hostess at a session of Adult Continuing Education. Still, she knew she had her responsibilities. She had been the one to persuade the noted food columnist to teach the class, and the one to persuade the director of the public evening classes to try the experiment of a class in *haute cuisine,* or *nouvelle cuisine,* or whatever it was to be.

Mostly through old friends from her early school days when she and Greg's father had lived with their parents at Indian Point—the big, old shingled house on the lakeshore to which she had temporarily returned early this summer—she had managed at least, so she hoped, a promise of the requisite number of students.

A few more of these appeared in the now-growing line at the desk marked *Information Center* in the large, modern central hallway of the new school, a line seeking room numbers for classes in beginning golf, intermediate Spanish, the history of philosophy, woodworking, and for the class in gourmet cookery. Large decorative plants filled a center atrium. Any last glow of sunset through the skylight was lost in the clarity of the indirect lighting and the insistent demands of the modern paintings displayed on the walls.

A trophy case filled one wall, attesting to the victories of past Dorrance athletic teams over high schools in other northwest Iowa towns. Next to this, a chrome-edged bulletin board displayed a lavishly decorated and lettered sign:

CAR WASH   SATURDAY 11–5
SPONSORED BY THE CHEER LEADERS
BENNY'S SERVICE STATION $2.00

How I wanted to be a cheerleader, Mrs. Potter remembered with a pang. It had been no comfort at all to be able to spell.

She brightened, seeing another promised student in the line. Jack Vanderpool, like the DeWitts, had been a friend of her Harrington High School days. Jack, now prosperous in real estate and insurance, was always willing to support a worthwhile new community project, especially if he could see in it some possible business advantage.

With MacKay Moore, the DeWitts, Greg and herself, she counted, Jack made six.

And then Julie joined them. Apparently our arguments were successful, she thought, in persuading her that it would be easier to learn to cook than to suffer the depressing parade of incompetents in and out of the Hofmeyer kitchen. Harrington is not a place where you're going to find the kind of cook you expect, she and Lynette had told Julie. They had reminded her that the imports from Minneapolis, the nearest big city, had, to date, turned out to be as poor as the available local talent. In Julie's case, Mrs. Potter could only hope that James Redmond's stipulations about previous cooking experience would be overlooked. It was Julie's defiant boast that she was the only woman in the world who could not heat a TV dinner without burning it.

So Julie made seven. Tall, thin, her silver-beige hair beautifully streaked or frosted (or whatever Miss Bee does to it—Mrs. Potter made a note to ask about this), her makeup perfect, her evenly capped teeth gleaming, Julie looked marvelous as always. There was also, as always, a slightly vague look in her eyes, as there had been from the time of their childhood days together.

A faint fusel fragrance of vodka mingled with light floral perfumes as the two women embraced. Julie had, clearly, taken a last quick drink before leaving home.

Mrs. Potter turned back to the earlier arrival. "How are things with you, Jack," she asked in tones of sympathy, "and how is Marie today?"

"Pretty good day, thanks, Eugenia, pretty good day. She insisted that I come to this class, you know, even though we both wonder what this fellow Redmond really knows about nutrition."

"I know how important that is to you and Marie," Mrs. Potter countered quickly, "and I'm sure you and he will find a great deal of agreement in using fresh, natural foods." She must not let him back out. The count was still only seven. As she nodded her encouragement she felt a loose hairpin and poked it firmly back into her hair.

Jack Vanderpool's red-brown eyes narrowed in the thin, ascetic, pockmarked face. "We'll see. We'll see. Anyway I'm here to start out, although how often I can come will depend on how Marie is doing. Bad days and good days, you know."

Then, straightening, "But I know we can cure this thing com-

6

pletely with the right diet, and we're having great results now with fresh vegetable juices."

Well, perhaps it helps them both, Mrs. Potter reflected sadly. Supposedly inoperable, incurable, terminal—all of those bleak and hopeless words. Why *not* a mixture of carrot juice, a dash of the DeWitts' born-again fervor, and a pinch of flavor and garnishment from the school of the talented Redmond?

Down the wide hall, the seven enrollees walked together to the area designated *Homemaking*.

Mrs. Potter had not been in a high school home economics classroom since her own school days, more than forty years ago, as a student at the old Harrington High. There was little resemblance in what she remembered there to the newly built Dorrance High School, which had been named in honor of Harrington's first millionaire, maker of the now-famous Dorrance motor bicycles, or mopeds, and donor of the town's new athletic field and the Harrington Community Health Center.

The old school had been a three-story red-brick structure with a cupola on top, its fire escapes wonderful contraptions of metal tubes, through which one slid in glorious abandon (on the seat of one's black sateen bloomers) on school-scheduled practice runs from escape hatches on the upper floors. In summer, when the school building was closed, one climbed up from the bottom of the tube on sweaty bare feet or in sneakers, on all fours, in order to turn and slide down again with rapturous speed. It was at the near-dark top of the fire chute, Mrs. Potter remembered, that she had first been kissed by a boy, a quick surprising peck on the cheek. Her chief recollection of the event was that of an overpowering smell of hot sneakers.

The new school was one-storied, with a nearly flat roof. (I wonder why, she asked herself, in such a snowy part of the country?) It had big windows and well-placed outdoor plantings, paved walks and ramps, and there was a central inner courtyard.

Inside, the contrast with old Harrington High was equally remarkable. Mrs. Potter summoned memories of the drab old "domestic science" room. Desks with built-in sewing machines (old treadle machines adapted for electricity, she remembered) had been on one side, yes. A large U-shaped zinc-topped counter, on which there was a two-unit electric hot plate between each two students, faced the teacher's desk. There had been a few basic utensils in the wooden cupboards below—graniteware bowls, tin measuring spoons and cups.

She recalled learning to make *blanc mange*, which seemed a pretty fancy name for a pretty plain white cornstarch pudding. She remembered striped dish towels that had to be hand-soaped and rinsed and hung to dry at the end of each class. The teacher always called them "tea towels," which had sounded quite elegant, and she had insisted that a lowly dishrag should only be called a "dishcloth."

This must have been the same teacher who silenced and embarrassed the young Eugenia by saying, "Surely, dear, you don't call it *dried beef gravy*. You must learn to say creamed chipped beef."

I don't think I've said "dried beef gravy" again to this day, mused Mrs. Potter. Nor have I said "watter" since a kind college professor in Connecticut told me, quite gently, how "water" was pronounced outside the Midwest. Surely now, at sixty, I'm sufficiently secure to say what I like, but actually I *prefer* "creamed chipped beef" now, or "creamed chipped beast," as the children used to say when they were little, and the one word that jars on my ear now in Harrington is *"watter."*

Later, many times, Mrs. Potter tried to remember exactly who said what, who moved where, in that shining new chrome and orange Formica classroom.

When she and her party came in—Greg, MacKay Moore, Jack Vanderpool, the DeWitts, Julie Hofmeyer—they found Lynette Dorrance already in the room. Poised, assured, Lynette was standing center front near one of the small tables, each with three chairs, that faced what would be the instructor's table and demonstration area.

Lynette, old friend and playmate of Mrs. Potter's childhood.

Lynette, only daughter of tough, inventive and successful Roger Dorrance, who had founded Dorrance Manufacturing, and wife of Paul, her second cousin twice removed (Mrs. Potter could, quite naturally, trace the lineage of all the old families in Harrington) who now ran his late father-in-law's company with something less than the vigor of the founder, if indeed he ran it at all. There were those who insisted that Lynette made all the important decisions and that Paul was chiefly an errand boy.

Lynette, whatever her role in the family business, was the product of intensive self-discipline, apparent in every movement of her taut, compact body, in her perfectly-fitted, understated mode of dress, in the smooth curve of her only faintly graying dark hair. With great competence she directed most of Harrington's good works. Strong, determined Lynette.

Mrs. Potter had always admired Lynette's challenge to the boys of their high school days—from ice hockey, diving and speedboat racing to her unsqueamish skills in biology lab dissections. She knew of her later nerveless performance as a wartime hospital aide. Perhaps Lynette had inherited some of her father's ruthlessness as well as his strength: Mrs. Potter knew something of the part she had played in forcing a small Dorrance competitor into bankruptcy some few years back.

Lynette was here tonight, Mrs. Potter realized, not to learn to cook, something she did very competently. Nor was she here simply for entertainment, or even as a kindly response to the plea of an old friend. She was here to take her accustomed role—the leading role—in a new community project that she deemed worthwhile.

Mrs. Potter had not looked for Lynette's husband, Paul, to join the group, but she had hoped—indeed had expected—that their only son, Roger Two, would be there.

Roger Two (he had never been called anything else in Harrington) had grown from beautiful baby to teenage idol to rising young businessman. Now, at thirty-odd, he was reportedly on his way to becoming Harrington's newest millionaire (amazing that there now should be several), buying and selling, at what seemed to Mrs. Potter fantastic prices, parcels of the increasingly valuable farmland of northwestern Iowa.

Lynette had been one of the old friends who had kept up an annual newsy Christmas letter to Mrs. Potter through the years, long

9

after she had moved away. These had been full of seemingly off-hand bits of news about Roger Two. President of his class. Prizes for sailboat racing and waterskiing on their beloved Blue Lake. Phi Beta Kappa at the state university.

Now, still unmarried, Roger Two remained boyishly handsome, obviously devoted to his mother, and (thought Mrs. Potter, a bit unkindly) somewhat given to standing in carefully staged Praxitelean poses whenever given a suitable backdrop.

Roger Two was not in the classroom. This was disappointing, when Lynette had said that he had agreed to join the group.

In counting, however, Mrs. Potter found two bonus pupils. One was the young man who had come to work as houseman-cook for a Des Moines family of summer people. The Rummels' large, splendid new vacation house (what one would have called a cottage in the old days on Blue Lake) had been built beyond Indian Point on the western lakeshore. The only name she could remember was that his employers had, she thought, called him "Eddie-boy." He was staying on now as winter caretaker, she had been told, and he was here at the class, no doubt, to improve his professional skills. Small, fair, and *could* that be blue eye shadow?

"Good evening, Edward. So glad you can join us," she told him warmly.

Also here in a professional, skill-improving category, she concluded, was the home economics teacher of the Harrington Junior High School. Apparently many of the girls these days, and the boys as well, elected to study "Homemaking" at the ninth-grade level. Maybe this will get her a promotion or more pay, Mrs. Potter thought, or maybe she just likes to cook, as I do. All she knew of the young woman, however, was her name, Miss Versteeg. Possibly related to old Peter Versteeg, who used to have a farm north of town? Tall, heavy, square in shape, long blond braids pinned firmly around her head in an old-fashioned way, it was indeed likely that she was old Peter's granddaughter. Mrs. Potter had a vague memory of some early scandal.

And that made ten. Mrs. Potter was still counting anxiously when the door opened and in burst the missing Roger Two, golden suede sport coat matching his beautifully cut golden mane, hand in hand with a strikingly beautiful girl.

There were a number of things Mrs. Potter recalled clearly later.

Lynette, whom she knew so well, had briefly but visibly stiffened before she greeted the pair with an animated wave and a toss of her smooth dark head. She had then returned immediately to conversation with Julie, not motioning to the two newcomers to join them. In turn Julie's pale eyes had surveyed the pair briefly and, Mrs. Potter thought, coldly. She had nodded to Roger Two and had raised her lips in a tight little smile. With Lynette, she then turned and they seated themselves at the front center table, where they continued an audible discussion of the last playreading session of the Harrington Drama Society.

Miss Versteeg, perhaps taking it as her professional right, placed herself squarely on the third chair at their table, but not until she had taken time to study the newcomers with slow and appraising regard. After she was seated, the back of her fair-skinned neck showed a dull dark red below the gold coronet of braids, above the square and solid Versteeg shoulders.

The DeWitts had moved abruptly to the far side of the room and Jack Vanderpool as quickly joined them. The picture that came to Mrs. Potter's mind was that of three elderly spinsters, clutching their skirts and scurrying to a safe retreat from a whiff of brimstone.

She could not imagine why such a foolish idea suggested itself. There were no more secure pillars of Harrington life than these three: Jack Vanderpool, whose opinions were always heard with respect—moreover, the devoted husband of a dying wife, herself distinguished for her strength and generosity of spirit; Ralph De-Witt, prosperous owner of a small chain of appliance stores throughout the county, vice-chairman of the hospital board, the library board, and all those other boards in town of which Lynette, of course, was chairman; and finally Dottie, Ralph's wife, church organist, daughter of an old and well-to-do local farm family.

All three had been mighty forces in the town's Methodist church. Jack's allegiance was still unshaken, but the DeWitts recently had succumbed to the eloquence of a young fundamentalist preacher, a newcomer to the community, and had joined his active, growing fold.

Surely, Mrs. Potter told herself, there could be nothing in the arrival of an old friend's son—Roger Two, whom they had all known

11

from his birth—with a pretty young woman in tow, that could have occasioned such apparent consternation and flight.

MacKay, always quick to appreciate feminine beauty, had moved in directly with practiced ease, placing the newcomers at a vacant table beside him. Mrs. Potter could see his mustache quiver; his faintly protuberant brown eyes were shining with the challenge whose excitement was undimmed by his almost seventy years. "You'll have to share her with me, boy," he told Roger Two, placing the girl between them.

These small things Mrs. Potter was later able to remember— these, and the cool, level gaze with which the young woman had seemed to challenge each person in the room.

However, at the moment, her chief reaction had been simple relief. Now we're twelve, she thought, and I can relax. Why do I get myself into organizing things and then feeling so responsible? Gratefully she settled herself at a vacant table, motioning Edward (I *cannot* say Eddie-boy) and Greg to join her there. She murmured an introduction of first names, hoping to learn Edward's last at roll call, or whatever the initial procedure was to be.

Still no James Redmond in view. The wall clock showed a digital 6:57.

Mrs. Potter used those few minutes in open study of Roger Two's beautiful companion, or as open as she thought she could manage without appearing to do so. (Mrs. Potter was frequently mistaken about achieving that balance. What she considered covert surveillance was, friends told her, often nothing less than downright staring.)

The girl was not as young as she had thought. Perhaps she might be thirty, or even a little more, rather than the twenty she had first seemed to be. She was beautiful, whatever her age, in a spectacular way. A gorgeous figure, no other word for it, wearing an elegant, simple off-white dress that was a perfect foil for Roger Two's golden suede jacket. Beautiful legs (MacKay dropped his silver pen, Mrs. Potter noted, to check on this) and high-heeled thin sandals. The dress, the silky legs, the feminine shoes, all were in contrast to the light-colored pantsuits and fashionable, but heavier, footwear of Dottie DeWitt, Miss Versteeg, and even Lynette Dorrance.

Julie's blond linen rather measures up, thought Mrs. Potter. It

12

did not occur to her to consider her own cool, shirtlike blue chambray, her own still-slim smooth and tanned bare legs, her venerable spectator pumps. Mrs. Potter had ceased to think of her own clothes, hair, or house furnishings in terms of fashion. At sixty, after Lew's death, she had declared to herself that all three of these—the furnishings of her several houses; the arrangement of her long gray-blond hair in a simple bun at the back (professing to be grateful to nature for doing the frosting, thus sparing her Julie's periodic ordeals, whatever they were); and her collection of simple and, as much as possible, timeless clothes—were pretty much settled. From now on in she would waste very little time on any of them except for occasional necessary household or wardrobe replacements.

She watched as the young woman turned to listen to Roger Two, then to respond with animation to a remark of MacKay's. Warm olive skin tones, dark eyes, a glorious flash of white teeth, lustrous dark hair moving like a shining black waterfall as she turned first to one man and then to the other.

And a really good perfume. The scent drifted back to Mrs. Potter's table and Edward sniffed appreciatively. As she looked at him, she thought he looked a little pinched, a little older than she had first guessed when he entered the room. Greg did not appear to notice the fragrance, but sat examining his own long, thin hands and fingers.

Lynette and Julie continued vivacious conversation, still ignoring the new arrivals after the first waved greeting. Miss Versteeg sat at stolid attention, apparently not expecting to join the talk of the other two at their shared front table.

That much Mrs. Potter could recall when she searched her memory later for the beginning of the fateful first cooking class. Roger Two's arrival with a beautiful stranger had caused a stir. However, surely the most important event was to be the entrance of the star, the instructor, the famous cook and writer, James Redmond.

At exactly seven, a bell sounded from somewhere down the long, white-floored hall. The classroom door opened and the star of the evening made his way quickly to the large table at the head of the room. In his hand was a small black leather satchel.

James Redmond was perhaps fifty-five, of average height, neither lean nor plump. His hairline was receding, but the smoothly-combed cap which remained was coal black. His eyes were a surprisingly light clear blue, under black brows, and his skin was only faintly tanned from his summer on Blue Lake. Mrs. Potter had decided at their first meeting that he was probably a dark Scandinavian, possibly of Danish descent, but whether she thought this because of his appearance or because of something in his careful manner of speech, she could not say.

He had been on the lake for the season, staying as a guest of Chicago summer people in their small guest cottage. He had come first (it was said) for a period of rest after illness and overwork. Now, in the fall, he remained because (again, it was said) he liked the place and found its quiet and beauty conducive to the writing of a new cookbook.

Mrs. Potter had first met him when the Chicago neighbors, the Hannons, had invited a few local people to meet their distinguished summer guest. She had found him strangely attractive, with his smooth skin, his suggestion of strength under a cool formality. They had talked of food and of Chicago. Presently the noise and chatter of the cocktail party surrounding them had seemed oppressive, and she had left the party early, albeit deciding that she must have a small dinner party very soon for the Hannons and their interesting friend.

The next day her hostess had telephoned to announce that while Mr. Redmond had very much enjoyed meeting Harrington people, his recent illness and the demands of his writing would prevent his going out. Therefore he would be unable to see any of the charming local citizens again, and thank you so much for coming yesterday.

Mrs. Potter and those others who had been asked to meet the writer had expressed a bit of surprise to each other, and perhaps a bit of pique as well at having been so summarily dismissed. Then they had almost completely forgotten about him.

It had been near the end of the summer, when the Dorrances, the DeWitts, MacKay Moore, Julie Hofmeyer and her youthful-looking husband, Harold, always known as Hoddy, were together with Mrs. Potter one evening at Indian Point, that Mrs. Potter had the inspiration of proposing the cooking class.

After that, with her usual energy and self-imposed sense of purpose, she went on to approach first the author-cook himself, and then the local superintendent of education. The result, finally was this evening's class.

What a lot of doing it took, Mrs. Potter reflected. Both sides required so much persuading. First she had to promise, personally, that she could produce twelve students. Mr. Redmond had stipulated that as a minimum number, and at four times the usual adult education class fee. This was necessary, he affirmed, because of the cost of the materials he would require for his demonstrations, and also because of his substantial international reputation. Next, she had to assure the Harrington school superintendent of how much goodwill and prestige the new class would engender, and just which leading citizens were interested in the idea. With her final argument—possible support for future school bond issues from these influential members of the community—she was able to secure his agreement.

Why did I do it? she wondered. Not just that I found this man Redmond oddly interesting. It's really because I hope he can teach me how to make French bread. As simple as that.

I'm a fair country cook, she admitted to herself, even though I am easily overwhelmed by the demands and the calories of true *haute cuisine*. But one thing I keep trying to master, and so far in vain, is good French bread. To be honest, I wouldn't care so much if I could only buy it in Harrington, or at home at the ranch, or at the cottage in Maine. However, if I choose not to live in range of a good *boulan-*

15

gerie (and she saw no likelihood that she would ever again do so), I really ought to learn to bake a proper French loaf on my own.

Mr. Redmond, at the table in front, had opened his black satchel. Slowly, almost reverently, he laid out a graduated series of dully gleaming dark-handled knives, each of which he unwrapped carefully from a folded square of dark green flannel. Then from the refrigerator behind him he brought out several plastic bags of celery and other vegetables; a small platter on which, under clear plastic, appeared to be several uncooked whole chicken breasts; finally a much larger platter bearing a whole baked ham, handsomely glazed and garnished.

''Good evening,'' he began, in a high, tight voice.

Good heavens, the man is nervous. In fact, Mrs. Potter thought, everybody here is nervous. Greg is trying not to bite his fingernails, and on the other side of me Edward is twisting a gold signet ring. Lynette's gestures are much too animated, Julie keeps reaching down for the big straw bag on the floor beside her, not taking out the cigarette I know she wants. MacKay is too keyed up, even for him, the dear old tomcat, about the new girl. Ralph is holding Dottie's hand and putting his shoulder between her and the rest of the room.

What's the matter around here?

The instructor's tight voice rose to a slightly higher pitch. ''First I shall ask each of you to stand and say your name. This will help me to know you and will serve as an introduction to the other members of the class, if you do not already know each other.''

I don't believe he's ever done this before, Mrs. Potter thought. In spite of those newspaper columns, all those magazine articles and interviews, those well-known high-priced cookbooks, this man is not quite sure of what he's doing.

Lynette's self-assurance was another matter. She rose first and faced the class. "Mrs. Paul Dorrance," she said clearly, secure in the knowledge that it was her duty as well as her prerogative to be first in all things in Harrington, Iowa.

Miss Versteeg's name was Varlene. (Of course, breathed Mrs. Potter, remembering the original Varlene for whom she must have been named. I should have known.)

Eddie-boy was John Edward Casaday.

The beautiful newcomer with Roger Two, her soft, breathless voice almost a whisper, was Jacquelyn Morsback. Everyone in the room watched and listened intently as she spoke.

With the almost inaudible murmur of "Greg Andrews," the roll was considered complete. At that moment a thirteenth voice announced itself in a husky, almost harsh, low tone, from the rear of the classroom.

"I'm Charlie Ragsdale, and I enrolled at the last minute. Will you have room for me?"

All heads swiveled to the speaker standing near a back table. Blond hair cut haphazardly, faded blue jeans, open-necked yellow shirt, turquoise and silver rings on one tanned hand, brown sandals on bare, tanned feet. A unisex costume, but unmistakably a young woman inside.

Mrs. Potter recognized the speaker at once as another Harrington returnee, although of a younger generation than her own. Charlotte Ragsdale, she quickly reckoned, must be in her late twenties. She was the daughter of old friends, former editors and publishers of the Harrington *Herald-Gazette*. She had gone away to college somewhere, Mrs. Potter remembered, then to art school, and had returned after her parents' deaths to live in the family homestead.

Lynette had been speaking of Charlotte recently, and of her newly successful business of designing greeting cards. Her trademark was a delightful tomboyish character named Debby, Lynette had said. Having seen some of the Debby illustrations—Debby climbing a tree, Debby swinging a baseball bat, Debby riding a bicycle no-hands—Mrs. Potter now noted their resemblance to Charlie, Debby's creator.

"Well, yes, ah, Miss, ah Ragsdale. We will be pleased to make room for you. Providing, of course, that you do, as do these others, begin with a certain proficiency and a degree of sophistication in the kitchen. You do know something about cooking?"

17

"I've done it for years," was the cheerful, harsh-toned response. "My mother wasn't well most of my growing up, and my father liked to eat. Also to hunt and fish. From the time I can remember I've cleaned and cooked the fish and game. For everything else, he just handed me copies of Escoffier and Rombauer and said, '*Get cracking.*' "

"Well, ah, that certainly sounds satisfactory, and we welcome you to the class. You have, of course, paid your fee?"

Preliminaries out of the way, the lesson began. At each class, Mr. Redmond explained, he would demonstrate some special culinary techniques. He would prepare certain dishes, either wholly or in part, depending on the time the session would permit. He hoped that they would come prepared to take notes.

Maybe that high, flat voice is the reason he hasn't been on television, at least to my knowledge, Mrs. Potter thought. He certainly lacks the color that would make a successful performer.

"For tonight," he continued, his voice now sounding more assured, "I want to instruct you in the care and use of proper kitchen knives. I want to show you my personal collection, and I want to show you how to use them so quickly and well that you will have no need for any of those expensive chopping and cutting machines. In my opinion most of these are simply unneeded and high-priced gadgets to make room for and to maintain."

Cheers for my boy, thought Mrs. Potter, whose kitchen philosophy was in total agreement. She despised most of those contrivances, chiefly electrically powered, that found their way into her kitchen, either by well-meant gifts or by her own weak-willed succumbence to the wiles of advertising. Each year there was a new, revolutionary (or worse, *improved*) indispensable device, and each year more such items left her kitchen for the repair shop, for the Goodwill, or, in desperation, for the trash barrel.

One after another, Mr. Redmond held up his knives. The first was his ten-inch chef's knife, the blade quite broad at the handle, then tapering to the point. "This is the knife to use for slicing, dicing and mincing," he proclaimed. "Let me show you how to use it." He looked searchingly around the classroom.

All at once, the careful, slightly pompous diction changed, in a way both startling and even embarrassing to his audience. In a queer half-giggling high-pitched voice, he began to lisp. "Alwath remember, firtht thing, *good cookth* thcrub their handth!"

Somewhere in the room there was a short, gasping sound, as if someone had begun, then suppressed, a cough. Or was it a laugh?

With this cue, the class decided that the only possible polite response was a brief murmur of forced laughter.

Fortunately the speaker's obvious and awkward attempt at humor did not continue. He retired to one of the gleaming stainless-steel sinks in the area behind his table and washed with thorough precision, not wetting his starched striped shirt cuffs.

"And now I will demonstrate." No sign of the high, foolish baby voice returned, then or later.

Lynette rose to her feet. "To see a little more clearly, Mr. Redmond, don't you think we should ask those in the rear to come forward and stand around your table?" It was less question than command.

On her side of the room, Mrs. Potter watched Roger Two and MacKay move to the front with the beautiful newcomer between them, each with a hand on a slim, rounded elbow. Edward excused himself as he crossed in front of Mrs. Potter to stand next to Roger Two, and she saw him raise his fingers in a little half-wave which Roger Two did not appear to notice. Greg hung back until an encouraging gesture brought him to her side. The newest student, Charlie Ragsdale, circled the room from the back to stand beside the DeWitts and Jack Vanderpool.

From the plastic bags, carrots, onions, parsley, celery spilled onto the demonstration table. "Hold the point on the board, so, then rock the blade up and down rapidly. . . ."

Neat slices, minced bits, julienne strips, thin slivers of the various vegetables blossomed in tidy piles on the board. The knife blade continued, rapid and inexorable, beneath the steady right hand as the foodstuffs were advanced quickly and precisely by the apparently fearless left.

Mrs. Potter noticed that Greg, apparently no longer reluctant to join the group of watchers, appeared fascinated, almost mesmerized, as he watched the flashing knife.

"Next I will show you the slicing blade, which also is a long one, ten inches. This has a much narrower and more flexible blade. It is used to slice turkey, roasts, and the like. Let me show you how I carve a baked ham.''

He carves beautifully, thought Mrs. Potter, but then probably so does every man in the room, and undoubtedly most of the women as well. Certainly Dottie DeWitt, who had grown up on her family's big farm south of town, would be able not only to carve a ham but to cut up an entire hog at butchering time, hams, bacon and all, right down to chopping the head and neck bones into the right size to cook for those small last succulent bits of meat that would make the cold jellied head cheese.

Even Greg, at tonight's early supper, had shown a left-handed proficiency at carving, which pleased her. Lew had carved splendidly, with great panache (as did MacKay), but Mrs. Potter herself managed only passably, and only when there was no one else to call upon.

I don't think I've ever seen Jack Vanderpool carve, she thought. Did he and Marie ever have people to dinner, even before she was ill? Perhaps not. As she glanced at the long, thin-skinned face, the reddish flush just below the surface promising at any moment to match the sandy red at the high, receding hairline, Mrs. Potter observed an unbelievable, but unmistakable, gesture of Jack's large bony hand. He was most definitely holding up two fingers, and his eyebrows were lifted in a definite question.

Question to whom? Mrs. Potter turned her head quickly and saw the new girl, the beautiful Miss Morsback, answer with a tiny smile and nod.

Frowning slightly, Mrs. Potter returned her attention to Mr. Redmond's hands, flexible, smooth and deft. His left little finger stuck out just a bit, as if it had been broken and badly set, but this in no way seemed to hamper the efficiency of his movements.

The next knife was an eight-inch carving knife for steaks and fowl, its blade both shorter and narrower than the chef's knife of the first demonstration. Mrs. Potter noticed that Varlene, the young schoolteacher, had moved to one side, where she seemed to be studying the slim figure in white between Roger Two and MacKay. Mrs. Potter watched her smooth her square, capable hands down over the pale blue tunic top of her pantsuit, then reach behind to tug the back of the top down firmly over her sturdy hips. As she noticed Mrs. Potter glance in her direction, Varlene's Dresden coloring again burned with the same dark, unbecoming red that had suffused the back of her neck as she sat down at the beginning of the class.

Mrs. Potter looked away hurriedly, in time to see the instructor hold up what was the favorite and most used knife in her own kitchen.

This—the thin, sharp six-inch French boning knife—is actually the one I use for almost everything, she thought. Mr. Redmond extolled its virtues for filleting fish, for boning, for trimming meat for stew.

With the thin blade shining, he approached a small platter of uncooked chicken.

Julie, beside Lynette at the front of the room, reached down for her straw handbag and made a willowy retreat through the group on her way to the door.

"We'll excuse Mrs. Hofmeyer for a minute," Lynette assured the instructor easily. "She'll be right back."

Lynette knows as well as I do, Mrs. Potter thought, that Julie is not going to stand there and watch anything resembling raw meat being cut up before her eyes. Lynette and young Eugenia had always been the ones to rescue her from rain-washed earthworms on the sidewalk, from an unexpected rush of tadpoles in the spring freshets of Little Blue Inlet, from the sight of her own blood in a tiny scrape or cut. Naturally, Julie would step outside for a moment, and also naturally, there would be a fresh whiff of fusel fragrance surrounding her when she returned.

The skinning and boning of the chicken breasts was accomplished with skill and speed. As he held up two smooth pale ovals, chicken breasts ready for cooking, the instructor looked again at the members of the class assembled around him, his attention now on the faces rather than on the meat and bones on his cutting board.

Again, his voice seemed strained. "Will you all now please take your seats?" He turned his back for a moment.

As they filed back to the small tables, Mrs. Potter saw that Ralph DeWitt's gray crew cut was inclined protectively over his wife's pink-blond head, and one massive shoulder arched around her like a shield.

The teacher turned back to his class. "Later I will give you a recipe for a favorite Oriental dish. It was chosen for its simplicity,

21

since tonight's class is intended to be an exercise in knives and cutting techniques rather than in cooking procedures. We will sample this dish later.''

Most recipes for chicken breasts, he told them, begin with browning the fillets in butter or oil. Recently he had found interest in new dishes based on a delicious and much lower-calorie technique.

The breasts can be poached, he declared, rather than sautéed. Using stock, wine, or other liquid, they will cook very quickly. In as little as ten or fifteen minutes they will be tender and opaque, ready for a flavorsome coating, or ''napping'' with some sort of sauce, or for combination with other ingredients in a special dish.

''My assignment for you for next week is to show how imaginative you can be. Practice skinning and boning some chicken breasts in the easy way I have shown you, and cook them by poaching in whatever liquid you choose.''

For the first time his voice held a touch of warmth. ''Then experiment with a special dish of your own, using the poached breasts. I shall not expect you to bring the results of your experiments, but we will share and discuss your inspirations next Thursday evening.''

The last knife of the collection was a small four-inch paring knife, with which Mr. Redmond quickly reduced a lemon to a stack of paper-thin slices, right to the very end. There seemed a constant threat, never realized, to the quick left hand, always just a fraction away from the fast-moving razor-sharp blade.

As he continued with the small knife, radishes became roses, turnip and carrot slices turned into daisies, celery strips became tiny spreading fans, tomato skins rosy dahlias. Fluted mushroom caps drew respectful applause from those in the class who knew how much practice was required for their perfection.

''Now, before I discuss what to look for in choosing good knives, and how to care for them,'' said Mr. Redmond, ''I want to ask how many of you have a good set of knives, similar to these, in your own kitchens?''

Not at all to Mrs. Potter's surprise, almost every hand in the room was raised. Julie Hofmeyer probably doesn't even know, she thought, but her claim is doubtlessly honest, if only to appease a demanding succession of cooks hired and fired in her kitchen. MacKay is a splendid chef for dramatic party dishes, and his kitchen is well equipped. Both of the DeWitts love to cook and eat, and their kitchen lacks nothing in expensive and modern tools. Jack Vanderpool certainly must have good knives, with all those health foods and fresh things he prepares. And Eddie-boy, forgive me, John Edward Casaday, works in a well-kept house and presumably there are proper tools for his job. Lynette is an excellent and efficient cook. Of course the Dorrance knives must be the best.

Miss Versteeg had not raised her hand. The junior high school knives were probably not too good, and her teacher's salary might not cover what could be a considerable initial investment. Greg's hands remained on the table, where he had continued to watch them closely throughout most of the lesson. Roger Two raised a well-manicured hand. Jacquelyn Morsback did not. Mrs. Potter did not turn to see how the greeting card artist behind her was signaling.

"Excellent, excellent." Their instructor seemed to be satisfied with the showing.

The class went on. How to buy knives? Simple, buy the best. Stainless steel looks handsome, but old-fashioned tempered steel retains its edge and can be kept sharp forever. (Heads around the room nodded in agreement. The man is sound.)

To her mild surprise, Mrs. Potter found that Edward, at her left, was taking careful notes. *How to buy knives,* he was writing in a neat round backhand. She read the words "shoulder, deep enough," "tang secured in handle," "triple rivets or permanent bonding," and something about heft and balance.

Up front she noticed that Miss Versteeg also was taking studious notes, and across the room Ralph DeWitt had an open notebook in front of him and a thin, sleek gold pen in his large fist. All of them taking notes on knife care. Dull knives are dangerous. Sharpen with butcher's steel at a twenty-degree angle. Don't wash in dishwasher. Wipe clean after every use and put back in rack at once.

Mrs. Potter reflected on what had seemed to her an advance in knife storage, and such a simple one that she wondered why it hadn't been thought of before. A newish auxiliary set of thin vanadium steel knives, which she liked for certain slicing tasks, had a small open cross stamped out of each blade, about an inch down from the tip. Thus each knife could be hung up safely and quickly by slipping this small cruciform opening over the matching screwhead on the rack. As she thought about it, she realized that this

23

wouldn't work with her favorite steel blades, all of which blossomed in her favor as they began to lose steel to the continuing toll of years of sharpening. As each old knife grew shorter, its blade narrower, even inwardly scalloped, as were many of those in Grandma's old kitchen, it became nicer to hold, more skillful in its work. Any cutout in such a blade would mean its discard just as it was reaching its best, sharpest, most useful stage.

The lecture drew to a close. Mr. Redmond lovingly rewrapped his knives, each in its flannel square, and replaced them in the black satchel. He cleared away the neat piles of cut-up vegetables and fruits, and Mrs. Potter nodded approvingly to see these go into separate plastic bags and not into the trash. Cooking demonstrations often seemed so wasteful. The entire ham went into a large covered oval and the chicken fillets—and yes, even the chicken bones and scraps—went into separate bags.

This is a man who is not going to waste food, she thought, quite in keeping with his attitude on tuition fees, which had shown a very respectful attitude toward money as well. (At the same time, she wondered why they should be paying to watch a man wrap up his food scraps.)

Anyway, it would be fun to try to devise a new recipe for poached chicken breasts and to hear other people's ideas.

"And now for this evening's recipe. As you know, there are many excellent dishes to be made with breasts of chicken, or *suprêmes de volaille*. Tonight's recipe was given to me by a well-known international hostess, one of whose parties I wrote about in a recent magazine article. I hope you will enjoy sampling it."

The directions were simple indeed. The chicken, in a shallow baking dish, had been sprinkled lavishly with a mixture of white wine and soy sauce to which a little brown sugar had been added, then topped with a light grating of fresh gingerroot. After several hours, it was baked, in its marinade, covered, for 45 minutes at 325 degrees.

"In case you are wondering," the instructor said, "I bought this fresh gingerroot in a Harrington market." He held up a long, smooth-branched pale brown root for their inspection. "With the growing interest in Chinese cookery, it is increasingly easy to obtain this in most parts of the country. Lacking the fresh root, you could use a piece or two of preserved ginger, first washing off

24

some of its coating of dried sugar or syrup. You will find that the marinade gives the chicken a lovely rich brown color and that the spicy flavors permeate the delicate meat.

"To complement these rich and spicy fillets, let me suggest appropriate accompaniments. I like to serve with this a cold platter centered by a mound of well-drained, well-chilled, briefly cooked fresh green peas. I cook these quickly in boiling water only a minute or two longer than the blanching stage, then drain them, cover them with ice water, adding a few extra ice cubes for good measure, and I hold them in the refrigerator until draining them at serving time. Around the edge of the platter, I arrange small stuffed whole tomatoes. After I have skinned, seeded, and drained these, I fill them with a mixture of diced ripe avocado, homemade mayonnaise and sliced water chestnuts."

A small baking dish was then brought out of the oven and its contents divided into a morsel apiece for each member of the class. Using tiny paper plates and plastic forks, people murmured "delicious" and "how simple." Mrs. Potter made mental note of the suggested accompaniments, the chilled peas and stuffed tomatoes, which seemed important (and missing) orchestration.

The class was over. Mr. Redmond assured them of his satisfaction in the local sales of his latest cookbook. "I bid you all good-night," he said stiffly, "and I look forward to seeing you all here promptly at seven, all thirteen of you, next week on Thursday."

Before that night was over, the class membership was to be tragically reduced.

The class broke up rapidly. Mr. Redmond remained at his desk, still gathering his tools and supplies. MacKay and Miss Morsback drew aside for a few moments of conversation, then turned—she to join Roger Two and he to bid Mrs. Potter a quick and affectionate good-night. He'd like to ask her for a nightcap at the Blue Lake

Inn, he said, but unfortunately he had to hurry home to await an important phone call.

The others had already moved into and down the wide hall with only brief good-nights, which seemed surprising. Mrs. Potter had assumed there would be something of an exchange of opinions on the first session once they were out the door, and certainly that everyone would want to meet, and admire at closer range, Roger Two's beautiful companion.

After her own words of welcome to the two, and her cordial self-introduction to Miss Morsback (learning that she preferred Jackie to Jacquelyn), Mrs. Potter thanked Mr. Redmond for the good sense of his lecture on knives. He seemed now even more tense and constrained than during the class, and she left quickly after a brief good-night.

Roger Two and Jackie were still in the hall outside as she and Gregory left, and were concluding what sounded like a mild argument. "But I came in my own car, darling, and I'm going straight back to the apartment in it. Really *can't* see you until tomorrow, darling. *Really* can't." The pair followed the others down the hall and out the big front doors into the night.

Slightly behind them, Mrs. Potter paused and spoke to her nephew. "I'm going to stop at the director's office, love, just to tell him that the new class started off nicely. Since it's a nice night, would you rather wait for me outside? I'll only be a minute."

The Director of Continuing Education was alone in his office to the left of the information desk, and his door was open. He and Mrs. Potter greeted each other cordially, as childhood friends. Do you suppose he remembers the old fire escape, she wondered with mild amusement, and what does *he* think about when he smells hot sneakers?

Their conversation was brief, amiable, and nonreminiscent. Mrs. Potter reported that the quota for the new class had not only been met, but had been oversubscribed by one. She recounted the names, most of them as familiar to the director as to her. Perhaps he knew some of them even better, for unlike her, after college he had returned to their home town as a teacher. Later he had become the high school principal, and now, in a prelude to retirement, he remained as head of the new department of adult education.

It could not have been more than ten minutes later, she thought, perhaps five, when she left his office. Instead of leaving directly by the front door of the school, however, she elected to make her way to the parking lot through the paved passages and plantings of the center courtyard.

The fragrance and warmth of the late September evening were welcome after the antiseptic chill of the director's office, with its modern white plastic furniture, its large plastic potted plants, its chrome and glass coffee table. The moon had not yet risen, and the sky was now almost dark. There was, however, light from the windows of the still occupied classrooms fronting the inner courtyard, and she made her way easily along the wide walkways and between the areas of greenery.

As she rounded what appeared to be a handsome large juniper, her eye caught a flash of white, scudding out of sight behind brick planting walls and more shrubbery before she could be quite sure she had seen it. A daring young junior out to meet what in Mrs. Potter's youth would have been called "her fellow"? A blowing sheet of paper in the evening breeze? More likely faulty vision, she decided. She'd remember to make a date with the Tucson ophthalmologist in December when she returned to the ranch.

Greg was waiting at the parking space, and he seemed even more withdrawn than usual. Her few questions met with courteous but noncommittal reply. Did he think the young woman with Roger Two was a knockout? Yes (hesitantly). And yes, maybe Edward Casaday was wearing blue eye shadow, but this was spoken in a tone implying "doesn't everybody?"

Mrs. Potter gave up further attempts at conversation and devoted her attention to driving. It would be nice to have someone else do the driving at night, she thought. The lights in town seemed glaring, and as they left town for the drive around the north side of the lake toward Indian Point, the roadside reflectors were disconcerting. I definitely must see Dr. Prentiss when I get home, she reminded herself.

They approached what Mrs. Potter still called "the new bridge," although it had been built in the late forties. The Bridge, the *real* bridge of her childhood, spanned the same narrow body of water about a half mile to the north. This channel, called Little Blue Inlet, fed into Blue Lake itself from the much smaller, somewhat marshy lake (mostly unloved except by the duck hunters of

27

the fall) known as Little Blue. The old bridge remained, a sturdy narrow concrete hump, a favorite fishing place for generations of Harrington children, reachable by a crumbling old macadam road seldom used except in hunting season.

There was a sudden glare of headlights as another car approached. "That was MacKay, I'm sure of it," she said with surprise, "and he's heading back into town!"

Another *yes* from Greg, but with a little more animation this time. "You're right, Aunt 'Genia. That was MacKay's Mercedes, the only one in Harrington."

Greg had volunteered a whole sentence. By dint of what few questions she could think of about the Mercedes' qualities, age, fuel consumption—and then, divinely inspired, a request to have Greg explain just what "250 SE" really meant—Mrs. Potter was able to stir up a conversation which proceeded almost brightly all the way back to the big shingled house at the end of the lake.

Indian Point was where Eugenia and her brother, Will, had grown up, their parents having moved out from town to stay there at Grandma's first illness. To please the grandparents, to look after them, and also because they loved the house and its place at the western end of the lake, the family had remained there.

Now, with Grandma and Grandpa gone, and after her parents' deaths as well, the previous year, Mrs. Potter had returned to the old place to decide about its eventual disposal.

By the terms of her parents' will, the house was hers. Brother Will, Greg's father, had received a small office building and some business lots in Harrington, and each of them felt that the bequests had been both fair and sensible, since either could take full responsibility for any decision to keep, rent, or sell his separate inheritance.

They had always referred to the place simply as Indian Point. Perhaps Grandpa had found an arrowhead or two when the foundations were dug for the commodious cellar, although it would be hard to find any given section of northwest Iowa land without its quota of arrowheads and Indian history. The "Point" was only a suggestion of a geographic feature, being simply the meeting of two gentle scallops of gravel beach in front of the house. Still, Indian Point it had been, from the time Grandpa retired from actual farming, at a gentlemanly forty or so, to "move to town." Hard

28

work on his own first homestead land, as a young man newly out of Ohio, had given him his start. Only once did the young Eugenia remember his telling about the long trip west, he and his twin brother walking barefoot all the long summer miles beside the family wagon and team of oxen. He told her, almost shyly, of their pride when the twins, by working on the first main building of the new land-grant college at Ames, were able to buy for their father the first team of horses he ever owned. From farming his homestead, Grandpa had gone on with astute judgment to buy more land, to lease out other rich Iowa farms. Eventually, and at what now seemed a remarkably early age, he had built his modest mansion, and he spent the rest of his long years taking his ease there, finding his chief entertainment in chivying his various farm tenants throughout the county.

The house itself made its only concessions to cottagehood by its location on the lakeshore and by the fact that it was clad in dark, weathered shingles. Periodically each side had been reshingled down through the years, as weathering turned that area too pulpy, black and even mossy on the tree-shaded side facing the south lawn.

Not even this infrequent maintenance had been performed in past years, however, so even before she arrived to take up summer residence this year, Mrs. Potter had arranged for the entire house to be reshingled. For the first time this had been done with new cedar shingles hand-dipped in a bleaching stain before they were put in place. No matter what I decide to do with the place, she had thought, it deserves to be taken care of.

The chemical was just beginning to show its effect now, and the big old house, its ornate cupola, the long back kitchen wing, were beginning to show the first signs of the soft silver hue that each year now would, instead of darkening, only become more beautiful.

The big porch, facing east toward the lake and south toward the shady lawn, had been newly screened, as had the little open porch on the second floor, under the elegant cone of its cupola roof. (Grandma used to dry apples there, she suddenly remembered— lovely leathery brown slices drying in the morning sun on suspended sheets of clean white cotton.)

Other than these exterior repairs, Mrs. Potter had so far done nothing about the house, and she had not completely made up her mind to put the place up for sale, even though she realized it was the sensible thing to do. Lakefront lots were bringing unbelievable prices these days. Grandpa always had been a man to spot a good buy, but even he could never have guessed what his thirty-odd-acre "homeplace" would be worth now.

Maybe the place would sell even better with the old house and barn simply torn down and taken away. How many vacation condominiums, which seemed to be the popular thing around the more built-up south side of the lake, could be put on thirty acres of lakefront?

At any rate, Mrs. Potter had come back to Harrington for the summer, to her dear old home town—county seat, farming center, summer lake resort. Her reason had been, ostensibly, to decide about the house. In part, she had wanted to get away from the ranch in Arizona for a time as well, much as she loved the place. It was all at once too lonely without Lew's homecomings to look forward to.

I was always either getting ready for him to come home or getting over it once he left, she thought, with the now-familiar little wrench of pain.

As she and Greg now returned from the school, they parked the small station wagon in the old barn which had been built for horses and carriage, for the sled-runged cutter, for the two milk cows of earlier days. So far she had done nothing about restoring the old structure, which seemed, on the surface, structurally sound. It was mostly empty now except for small scurryings in the dark loft overhead, where the old playhouse used to be, where she and Julie and Lynette (and whoever else was in their favor at the moment) had spent their Saturday mornings. The barn was full enough with memories of Grandpa in his big, old open touring car, the first Cadillac in the county, always driving in the center of the road, his modest speed steady and unswerving, one hand ready on the horn. Grandpa drove as if he'd taken his highway instruction classes at Toad Hall, Will said.

Mrs. Potter and Greg circled the house from the back, in order to enter at the front door. The new shingles had an almost luminous glow in the light of the rising September moon, and the path of its reflection was a silver band across the water.

"I do like a house to face east," Mrs. Potter confided. "Watching the moon rise over the lake has always seemed magical to me. And I really like the reflections in the eastern sky at sunset—all those soft hues of violet and apricot and pale green—better than facing the color and dazzle in the west."

How ridiculous, she told herself. Just as you get the boy talking for the first time about something that interests him, like cars, you put him off with boring remarks about moons and sunsets.

To her surprise, Greg responded seriously. "You're right, Aunt 'Genia. Back home in California we always liked best to face the mountains instead of the ocean for sunset. Mom would have agreed with you."

They entered the unlocked front door, switched on lights in the front hall (the moose head over the hat rack really has begun to look moth-eaten, they agreed), then moved by unspoken agreement through the dining room with its shining parquetry floors and its small green marble fireplace, through the long pantry, and into the big old-fashioned kitchen.

We could just as well have come in this way, Mrs. Potter said but one always has to have one look at the lake before coming in, no matter what time of day or night. Either door would have been unlocked. It had not been until after her parents' deaths that the family lawyer had learned, to his dismay, that there were no keys to be found. In Mrs. Potter's memory, no door in the house had ever been locked and she saw no reason to make any change now. If there had been keys, they were long lost. A new owner could call in the locksmith when the time came.

Greg's fifth meal of the day was the present concern. Frequent meals and high-protein foods—these, with rest, were the chief prescriptions for his convalescence.

"More ham, love? We have some of Bertha's little homemade rolls in the bread box—does that sound good?"

Greg carved more thin pink curls of the cold ham, quite as deftly, she assured him, as James Redmond could have done, and in even thinner slices. He tucked these into the buttered small rolls, added a few slivers of good rat cheese, and finished each with a dab of the special hot tarragon mustard sauce Lynette had brought them the previous week. On the side, he set out a glass and a

31

pitcher of milk and a small bowl of the applesauce from the old Wealthies.

Then came the cookies, made from Grandma's old recipe. Thin, dark, only slightly sweet, these were molasses spice cookies, each big circle spread lightly with a creamy icing. Grandma never used butter for this, simply mixing confectioners' sugar with a bit of heavy cream, adding a drop of vanilla and a quick grating of fresh orange peel if an orange was handy.

"Nobody today would *believe* that cream, Greg. You had to use a silver knife to scoop it out of the glass jar. The owner of the dairy himself delivered it, from a shiny little black wagon pulled by a horse. His was the last of the horse-drawn delivery carts I can remember, and it was wonderful fun for your father and me in the winter. Mr. Bjerke used to wait for us to put on our skis and let us tie on to the back of the wagon when it was snowy. Then he'd pull us all over town. *Skijoring,* he called it."

Greg seemed more interested in selecting a ripe pear from the wooden bowl on the kitchen table, and in cutting a bit more cheese to go with it.

Well, we did have a good conversation in the car, she thought, and now it's time for bed. He really needs ten hours a night now, and there's a new mystery waiting on my bedside table.

There was no good-night ring from the telephone on that same table. MacKay usually called before bedtime, to exchange news of the day or to share amiable gossip if they had attended the same event or gathering, as they frequently did.

Maybe he'll call in the morning, she thought, or there will be one of his inimitable little notes tucked in the mailbox tomorrow—if only to say why he'd been going back into town as she and Greg were driving home.

The call, when it came about eight the next morning, was not from MacKay.

"This is Pete Felderkamp, Chief of Police." The first words were spoken strongly.

Then, a little less firmly, the voice went on. "You know me, Mrs. Potter. Remember you went to high school with Dad?"

The man's voice steadied. "Well, it's this way, Mrs. Potter. It looks like we've got a pretty bad mess on our hands. Can I come over and talk to you about it?"

Young Pete Felderkamp (Arnold is his real name, Mrs. Potter knew, just as his father, also Pete, had been christened) arrived ten minutes later in the Harrington police car. With him were his deputies, Cary and Gary, the Hayenga twins.

Mrs. Potter and Gregory were awaiting them on the big screened porch, coffee and more of the molasses cookies ready. If you know that someone is coming to see you in Harrington, for almost any reason, even to hook up a new telephone or to fix the washing machine, you automatically set out coffee cups and percolator.

"You remember Pete," Mrs. Potter had reminded Greg before they came. "Tall, good-looking, about your age, came into the market that dark rainy morning last week to tell us that the car lights were on? And Cary and Gary? Named for Cary Grant and Gary Cooper, of course, since their mother—Delma Truckemiller she was then—used to sell tickets at the Bijou."

Greg nodded vague assent.

"Hayenga is one of those Dutch names you had so much trouble with when you first got here," Mrs. Potter continued. "It's not pronounced like, well, *syringa,* the shrub, as you thought when you first saw it in the paper. Just remember it sounds more like *'high 'n' gay'.*"

"Sounds a bit questionable for police officers, Aunt 'Genia."

First sign of humor in the boy. And he used to be such a funny little boy. Maybe this is a sign he's getting well, she thought. She rescued a fallen hairpin from the wicker table and unbuttoned her light sweater in the warmth of the morning sun.

Three solidly handsome Hollanders—Pete dark and ruddy, the twins classic Dutch, pink-cheeked and blond—marched heavily up the wide front steps.

"Well, this is just awful, Mrs. Potter," the young police chief greeted her. "There's been a murder in town. A girl got stabbed to

33

death right in the parking lot behind her apartment. You know the Arms, there on Fifth Street? Stabbed to death was what she was, right there beside her car.''

"That's dreadful, Pete, and what a shock it must be for you. Have you ever had a murder in town before?''

"Never did, Mrs. Potter. There was a bad shooting back in my dad's time, maybe you remember? Old man Versteeg shot his daughter and her boyfriend right after prayer meeting? Killed him, crippled her, is what he did. But this one is my first and I've been chief now for going on four years.''

"I'm so sorry, Pete. Will you have some coffee, and you too, Cary and Gary? What can we possibly do to help you?''

Greg spoke up hesitantly. "Who was the girl, do you know? I can't imagine how Aunt 'Genia, Mrs. Potter that is, could help.''

"Well, the book says first you talk to close friends and the people who saw the victim last. So I called Charlie Ragsdale, because everybody knows the two of them used to be real close friends. She didn't have much to offer, but she told me about this cooking class last night and said you'd be the one to know who all was there. That's the reason we came here.''

Pete turned and stood, coffee cup in hand, staring at the lake. "After that, the best idea the boys and I have got so far is to go out and have a look at that hippie joint. You know, the commune thing that's beyond you out on the dirt road west.''

"You mean to say the girl was someone at our class last night?''

The twins vied to answer, in alternating sentences.

"Yes'm. Jackie Morsback.''

"Name of Jacquelyn, really, but she liked Jackie.''

"Prettiest girl you ever saw.''

"New in town, but friendly. Real friendly.''

"Used to stay with Charlie at the old Ragsdale place before they had a row, everybody says, so she moved to the Arms.''

"Prettiest girl you ever saw. Not so young, maybe, but pretty.''

The chief turned and the twins fell silent. "Mrs. Potter, did you know her well? You look kind of white, and Greg here doesn't shape up much better.''

"Oh, dear. Poor Pete. And poor beautiful Jackie.'' Mrs. Potter sat down in an old wicker chair. "I agree with the twins—she was one of the prettiest girls you ever saw.''

34

No one spoke, and she continued. "But I don't imagine that Greg and I can be of much help to you. We met her for the first time last evening, you see, when she came with Roger Two to the cooking school class at the new high school."

"Yes. Roger Two. Charlie told me about him and we already went out to see him. Talked with him and his mother and father, too, and they all said she left the school by herself in her own car, is what she did."

"I think that's right, Pete, don't you agree, Greg? We heard her tell Roger Two she had to leave, that she had her own car, and that she'd see him the next day. Wasn't that right, Greg?'

Greg's "Yeah, I guess so," was almost too low to be heard.

"You know, Pete, I don't think anyone, other than Charlie Ragsdale apparently, and Roger Two, is likely to have known her before." Mrs. Potter quickly recited the names of the enrollees in the class.

"Oh, sure, I bet all those people knew Jackie. Maybe some of them kind of knew her on the side, if you'll excuse me for saying so, Mrs. Potter, but they knew her. She's been around town here for most all summer."

Pete turned to the twins. "You write those names down now, boys, and we'll make the rounds later."

Greg spoke up suddenly. "Just how did it happen, and when?"

"Some kind of sharp knife, and somebody who knew how to use it. Body bled like a stuck pig, if you'll pardon the expression and that's just the way she was killed. Jugular slashed once from left to right, it looked like. I think whoever did it grabbed her from behind with his left arm, like this" (Pete demonstrated on the nearest twin) "and then just slit her throat with one swipe with his right." Pete's sigh was uneven.

For a moment Mrs. Potter glimpsed a memory of an earlier Pete, a boy determined not to cry over a run-over puppy. Of gentle Pete senior, who with his high school sweetheart—later wife, and mother of the present Pete—had been among the friends of her Harrington growing up. The older Pete had become town marshal (no chief, no deputies in those days) and Varlene, pretty, animated, "peppy" was the word for it then, had become the popular and competent town clerk. So popular, in fact, that a good number of girl babies in the county were named for her. Varlene Versteeg. Of course, I should have known, Mrs. Potter told herself again.

Pete was speaking, apparently in response to another question from Greg. "Last night about eleven, at least that's what Doc thinks. Anyway everybody at the Arms was already in for the night, they say. There's only the six apartments there, you know. Nobody saw anything, nobody heard much. It's a pretty quiet place and they all go to bed early."

Pete paused. "Anyway there's no way they could have seen or heard much. Jackie's apartment is on the ground floor, the old super's apartment is what it was, and it's got a separate back entrance."

There was another pause. "It was just about six in the morning when Leonard Silsby came out and saw her. He lives there—foreman on the early shift at Dorrance's is what he is. When he came out to get in his car, well, there she was."

"Right beside her car."

"Dead, all right, on her face in all that blood."

"No sign of the knife, though."

"We looked all over."

The twins fell silent as Pete raised a large finger.

"Let's go see those hippies, boys. I've been suspecting something fishy out there."

Then, to Mrs. Potter, "We're really awful sorry to have bothered you about all this. I guess I just needed to talk to somebody for a minute and get up steam to tackle this thing, that's all. Thanks for the coffee."

The Harrington police car wheeled in a fine spin of gravel and headed for the dirt road northwest.

"I'm sure they will do all right," she reassured herself and Greg, "but isn't it dreadful to think that beautiful young woman is dead? How could something like this happen here in Harrington?"

Greg had no answer, but helped himself to another cookie and poured the rest of the coffee cream into his milk glass.

"A sharp knife, Pete said. Isn't that an irony of fate, when the class last night was all about knives?" she continued. "I wish MacKay would call. He's never up before nine, but it's past that now and I'd really like to talk with him."

The telephone rang, but it was not MacKay.

"Mrs. Potter, this is Bertha. *Bertha*, you know, at Mr. Moore's. I just got here and I tried to call Pete Felderkamp. Is he still there at your place?"

The flat, faintly Germanic voice of MacKay's housekeeper went on without inflection. "Mr. Moore isn't here, Mrs. Potter, but the car it sounds like it's running in the garage, and I think there's something wrong."

"What is it, Aunt 'Genia? Please sit down. Are you ill? What can I get you?" Greg's concern was in contrast to his customary air of apathy.

"It's MacKay, love. I don't know. . . . I hope I'm wrong, but that was Bertha on the phone, and I'm afraid something dreadful may have happened there."

She rose, now with quick determination. "We can get there faster than calling anyone else. Could you drive?"

The little car whirled out of the barn, down the quiet lakeshore road, under thin and competent hands. "It'll be all right, Aunt 'Genia. Whatever it is, we'll take care of it."

Even with Greg's unexpected support at the wheel, Mrs. Potter's thoughts were in turmoil.

MacKay, nothing could happen to MacKay. MacKay was indestructible. Gallant, courtly MacKay, with his twitching mustache and his shining, eager brown eyes, his lean, tanned face and balding head, his body taut, erect, well dressed. Irrelevantly she wondered about that impeccable tailoring, about who pressed those creases, who shined those well-polished English shoes. Bertha, no doubt.

She had known MacKay for more than twenty years, during her visits home to see her parents; had met him first, as she remembered, at Lynette and Paul Dorrance's. At that time he had been a newcomer to Harrington and to Blue Lake. But, as Paul said, he had seemed to fit in from the first, enjoying the hunting, fishing and boating that were the favorite diversions of what Mrs. Potter still thought of as "the gang."

Now it seemed he had been a part of that group from the beginning, even though no one had known him or anything about him when he first arrived. He had apparently retired from business, or from whatever pursuit provided the generous way of life he enjoyed. Most people assumed that he had simply inherited money, as they assumed that he had been previously married and tragically widowed. These were assumptions he did not contradict.

Immediately upon coming to Harrington, he had bought the old Taylor place, adjoining Indian Point but out of sight beyond the next cove and nearly a mile closer to town. He had demolished the ramshackle old house and barn, which had been set far back from the water, and had built, after the style of a famous architect of the period, a modern house of stone and wood, almost overhanging the shore of Blue Lake itself.

MacKay spent part of each year traveling. "I'm the widow's delight," he had assured her, on the cruise ships, on the long, expensive trips which were a part of his usual winter schedule. This year it was to be a new trip, to China, where he had not been before, and he was looking forward to it. However there was time for the fall hunting—and for the fall cooking class—before his cruise ship embarked.

On ship or shore, MacKay was in constant, ardent pursuit of every attractive woman, young or old, on the scene. This seemed a harmless habit, a personal entertainment, that most of his targets appeared to find flattering. At home he was an easy and frequent host at his own small dinner parties, and a fair cook as well, often with Bertha functioning smoothly and silently in the background. Sometimes, recalling that Bertha had been in her school class—was it in junior high or even before that?—Mrs. Potter would try to engage her in conversation, either about food or about the old days in Harrington. Bertha would look up, her eyes piercingly blue in that dark Germanic face, but her answers would be little more than a grunt.

One evening the previous week, Mrs. Potter and MacKay had shared a drink on the deck, enjoying the end of the day and the deepening color of the water. Bertha had brought out a wedge of ripe Brie, she remembered, then had disappeared with only a nod to acknowledge her greeting.

That was when MacKay had reported to her, with some amusement, that their friends were prophesying their marriage.

"It's all over town," he told her, "so I've decided to propose and make an honest woman of you at last. The ring is all ready—a nice whopping big old blue sapphire with diamonds that was my grandmother's. I'm going to get it out of the safe deposit box tomorrow. How about it? Think you'd like that?"

"Don't be silly," she had replied. "You know neither of us wants to get married again. How about just inviting me to go with you on next year's cruise instead? Now don't look worried. Not this year—I've got Greg with me. But someplace nice and romantic like the Dalmatian coast sometime?"

They both had smiled. It had been wonderful to have someone to flirt with again.

As the little car turned into the gravel driveway, she realized that her thoughts of MacKay were like small hard stones, plunked one by one into the clear blue water of the lake before them. They had all been in the past tense, all dropping from sight with dreadful certainty.

Now, she told herself, you must put that idea away, and firmly. Talk to Greg. Greet Bertha, waiting for them at the front door, seemingly imperturbable as always, her black hair as always smoothly arranged, her tall, generous frame neatly uniformed in pink-striped cotton.

With Greg, she followed Bertha through the house and kitchen to the closed door leading down to the attached garage.

Greg stopped them suddenly. "I'm going in there, low and fast," he said. "I'll raise the doors. You two stay back until I give the word."

Then came the sight that she had feared, in some way had known, from the moment of Bertha's call—the sight of the body slumped on the garage concrete, behind the car, almost directly in front of the deadly purr of the exhaust. Both front doors of the old Mercedes were open. Its vintage motor was still running quietly.

Greg turned off the motor, and in the fresh air of the morning he motioned to Mrs. Potter and the housekeeper to join him in the open doorway.

"Looks as if he'd been trying to reach the garage doors to open them, but I'm afraid he was too late," Greg said, as he bent over the still body. "He passed out and fell here. That's the way it looks to me."

"Is it too late?" Mrs. Potter knelt beside Greg, hesitating to touch the still form.

"Let's get him out on the lawn in the air and maybe we can bring him back." Greg began to lift MacKay's body. "I'm afraid I'm not strong enough. I'll need your help, Bertha."

"Is it too late?" Mrs. Potter asked again. "Can you do something?" Even as she spoke Greg began emergency respiration. When he began to tire, Bertha, strong and capable, took over, although Greg was shaking his head despairingly as he gave her directions.

As Greg and Bertha took turns bending over MacKay's quiet body, she herself put in a quick and surprisingly incisive call to the doctor, giving him all the information—the running motor, the closed garage, the location of the house.

Doc's reply was brisk. "Well, I know where MacKay lives, 'Genia, for Pete's sake."

For Pete's sake, for Pete's sake.

That reminded her what she must do now, although she did not like the sound of it. She must call Pete, Pete Felderkamp, of course. But he had gone off to see about that girl's murder, and anyway what could he do now?

Reluctantly she dialed the police number, gave her name, and reported the information about the accident. This time she was not able to state the facts quite so clearly and quickly as she had recited them to Doc Winkelman.

It seemed a very long time before the ambulance arrived. Mrs. Potter walked back and forth on the well-raked driveway, watching Greg and Bertha as they worked, still hoping to restore breath and heartbeat to the prone body on the green lawn. She felt unable to offer either assistance or encouragement.

She walked into the garage. Everything here was neat and shipshape. Garden tools hung in shining order. Cases of mineral water were stacked on a two-wheeled hand truck, ready for return. A comfortable cord of split firewood ranged along an inner wall. An inside stairway on the left led up to what she knew was Bertha's room, on those occasions when she spent the night here instead of returning to the house in town she shared with her sisters and brother.

She noticed a hairpin on the clean wooden step leading up from the garage to the kitchen. Absently she thrust it back into the bun of her hair, then further straightened her appearance by rebuttoning the thin yellow sweater she had put on earlier.

It seemed forever. She tried to think about Doc Winkelman, whose father had been the "Uncle Doc" of her own childhood ailments.

The senior Dr. Winkelman had come to Harrington about the time Grandpa gave up active farming and built the house at Indian Point. Uncle Doc sat in the pew behind the Andrews family in church, she remembered, and he wore a black skullcap which he unfolded from his pocket as soon as he was seated, fitting it carefully to his bald and bony head. To her knowledge, no one had ever questioned his reason for doing so. One did not challenge the dignified behavior of the town's only doctor.

What would it have been like, she wondered, to come west to a raw prairie town at the turn of the century if you were a young Jewish doctor? Even now, there was probably no synagogue within fifty miles. Uncle Doc, she thought, had worshiped as best he could, and who could do better than that?

Still the ambulance had not come.

She waited. It was five minutes, perhaps just a little more, when it pulled into the driveway. Doc was in the front seat beside the driver. When it turned abruptly back toward town, Doc was in back, doing something—she hoped he was doing something—to MacKay.

The ambulance had been out of the driveway and on its way into town only seconds before the police car pulled in from the opposite direction.

"We got your message on the radio," Pete was shouting as he ran toward the open garage doors. "What's happened? Where's MacKay?"

At once Pete was back at the wheel of the car. "You stay here now, boys," he ordered the twins. "First I want exact markings, as close as Greg and the ladies can show you, of where Mr. Moore was lying in the garage. And don't move a thing. Next, go over the whole house with Mrs. Potter and Bertha. They'll know if there's anything that looks funny."

Before he pulled away for the hospital, he leaned out to give further instructions. "Remember to make notes, now, and don't you get out of reach of that phone."

The twins were moving from side to side, like boxers in a ring.

"Radio got us just as we left the hippies' place."

"Nobody there, though. Old man Swenson, owns the place, moved back in two weeks ago, and the whole gang cleared out."

"Headed up someplace near the Sioux reservation in South Dakota, he thought they did."

"So nothing doing there, Pete says."

"Wish there had been. We sure would like to catch a ritual killer."

"Maybe even a whole *schmier* of them, chicks and all."

Greg, as Pete had done earlier, lifted a mildly authoritative finger.

With Bertha leading the way, her air of authority increasing, the five went into the garage.

Yes, Greg said, both front doors had been open that way when they went in, and he had been the only person to touch the car when he reached in to turn off the ignition. MacKay's body had been slanted *so,* they all confirmed, lying half on its side, the left hand outstretched, on the floor almost behind the now-silenced exhaust of the motor.

"Anybody see this before?" One of the twins pointed to a short, round piece of iron pipe lying on the floor at the far side of the garage. Bertha said it was probably a piece left over from a length of pipe Mr. Moore had put up along the end of the garage for a clothes pole. They all looked at the rack and at the neatly hung fishing waders, hunting jackets and windbreakers whose hangers it supported. Bertha said that little piece, only three inches or so

42

long, had to be cut off so the rack would fit the space. She didn't know how she'd missed it when she swept up after Mr. Moore finished the job.

They completed their tour of the garage, now harmless in the morning sunlight, then moved as a group to the front door of the house. Entering the hallway with its polished flagstone floor, they began a slow tour. The twins, each with notebook in hand, entered notes (presumably identical) on the proceedings. Simultaneously it occurred to them to issue a warning about fingerprints, and the other three at once self-consciously clasped their two hands together.

We look like a procession of supplicants, thought Mrs. Potter. It would be better if we were on our knees as well. When will we hear from the hospital?

First they went to MacKay's own quarters, a half level up from the living area of the house. The big bedroom had been half-cantilevered out from the building, forming a waterfront deck and terrace below, with a magnificent view of the lake in three directions.

Blue Lake that morning lived up to its name. One of the southernmost of the chain of glacial lakes spilling down through Minnesota and into northern Iowa, Blue Lake was considered (at least locally—Mrs. Potter had never found this in any authoritative geographical reference) to be one of the few true blue-water lakes in the world. An exclusive category, people always added, that included Switzerland's Lake Lucerne. The September morning sky was clear azure; the unruffled water a deeper, serene reflection of the same pure blue.

Bed not slept in. The twins took notes busily as Bertha made her comments. Bathroom tidy. However, as she remarked, Mr. Moore was not one to leave his things in a mess. He always hung up his towels nice and square, didn't leave toothpaste froth in the washbowl, always put his things away. Still, she could bet on it, he hadn't been up here last night after she had prepared his early dinner, cleaned up and left the house.

That was when he'd gone to the new class to learn more about cooking, as if between the two of them—Mr. Moore that is, and herself—they couldn't cook about anything they wanted to already.

43

Bertha's repeated opinion, as they came down the wide half-flight to the main floor of the house: MacKay had not gone up to his personal quarters once he came home from the high school.

There seemed nothing unusual, nothing out of place in the wide front hall, in the first-floor guest bedroom and its large, deeply carpeted bathroom. The great living room, its floor-to-ceiling windows looking south onto the water, seemed equally undisturbed. There had been three lamps on in that room when she arrived this morning, Bertha remembered, but she had automatically turned them off and had begun her usual "flaxing around" before she realized that anything was amiss in the household.

In the study, however, on the north, or driveway, side of the house (the undisturbed dining room was its opposite number, on the lake side), there, finally, was the heartrending clue they had been dreading to find. The lamp on the big desk glowed pale in the morning sunlight. The desk chair was shoved back, having caught and rumpled the edge of a small richly-colored Oriental rug.

On the polished desktop was a single sheet of beige notepaper, monogrammed in brown. How many wildly affectionate notes had been written there, Mrs. Potter thought, in MacKay's distinctive hand, and how often she had enjoyed, had been amused by, the frequent ones addressed to her.

There was nothing amusing about the words on the sheet in front of them now, but the message began, definitely and shockingly, with her name. One of the twins leaned forward, without touching desk or paper, and read the note to them aloud, squinting slightly in his attempt to make out every word.

" *'Genia darling,*" it began.

The other twin whistled brief surprise.

"Will you ever be able to forgive me? By the time this reaches you, you will know about Jackie. News travels fast in Harrington, as you and I have good reason to know.

"What I had to do tonight was terrible beyond belief. What I have to do now will be easier. When it's all over, I hope I can count on you to understand.

"After all you and I have meant to each other, always remember that I am

Yours, MacKay"

The handwriting, unmistakably his, was like the man himself: masculine, extravagant, assertive.

There was a postscript, the writing clearly the same except that the letters seemed less certain.

"Good-night, my dearest 'Genia. I will be thinking of the Dalmatian coast when I put out the light at last."

Mrs. Potter steadied herself against a high-backed wing chair. Without seeing, she stared at the note, at the polished desktop, at a stack of memo pads initialed *MM*, at the brown felt-tip pen with which the letter had been written, at a nearby holder of sharpened pencils with an opened brown leather-covered telephone book alongside. She looked at the pale glow of the table lamp, which MacKay had not put out after all.

Her eyes then returned to the letter, so like in form and appearance to others written to her from the same desk, in the same distinctive hand, over the years.

Could this letter, this innocently abject note of apology and affection, be saying something else? Mrs. Potter shivered in her thin sweater. Could this be an unthinkable, damning link between Jackie Morsback and MacKay Moore, between the horrible bloody killing in the parking lot of the Harrington Arms and the quiet, deadly, unending hum of the motor in MacKay's garage?

Of course not. How could MacKay be involved in the death of a young woman with whom he could at most have spent only a few minutes in private conversation at the end of the cooking class? The only mystery was why he had been returning to town so quickly the previous evening, when he had said he had to go home to wait for a phone call. There was no reason for him to make up a story for her, of all people.

As if in partial answer (or had she spoken her questions aloud?) Bertha was speaking. That girl, that Jackie, she told them, had been at the house here for dinner with Mr. Moore twice in the last two weeks, just the two of them. And she knew for a fact that Mr. Moore had met her at the bar at the Inn last night after the class.

Bertha spoke without emotion, stating facts. Jackie had phoned him the minute he got home—before she, Bertha, could even ask him about the cooking—and he turned right around again and went out to meet her. That was just before she herself went home and spent the rest of the evening, what there was of it, with Alice.

Greg touched her shoulder gently and Mrs. Potter's gaze again included her nephew, the indomitable Bertha, and the still busily writing Hayenga twins. "We should see the kitchen, too, don't you think," he asked, "and leave everything just as it is right here?"

Nodding, dumb, she followed the others to the big, well-furnished kitchen, with its great stone fireplace and the gleam of polished old pine. In the last twenty years or so of her visits home, she had shared many small dinners, mostly foursomes, at that comfortable and welcoming table. Bertha's dark presence would have been banished to her quarters above or to the Walters' family house in town. There might be snow or rain sheeting down on the lake outside. There was warm firelight and splendid savory aromas filling the room, good drink, pleasant talk. Sometimes in the past year it had been just the two of them, she and MacKay. Those were the times, she thought, he should have shown her that ring.

This has to be a bad dream, she told herself. Even Greg appeared to be frozen, staring straight ahead at the colorful Spanish tiles on the walls above the big stainless sink and at the well-kept chopping board beside it.

Oh. As he turned, she saw the object of his intent gaze—the large wall-mounted wooden knife rack above that section of the counter. *Oh.* Perhaps the twins would not notice, or would not perceive the immediate significance if they did. Bertha would certainly see soon, if not right away.

To Mrs. Potter, and obviously to Greg, the sight was a billboard. The third knife from the end—the small, thin, murderously sharp French boning knife, she knew it must be—was missing.

The telephone rang and they all moved suddenly. It was closest to hand for Mrs. Potter and she took it automatically. At last there were the words she had known would come, and had dreaded so desperately to hear. MacKay was gone, beyond any hope of return, had been gone long before Greg opened the doors of the garage.

"I'm sorry, but I'm going home. Bertha, you've got your car and can get back to town? Twins, tell Pete to call me later if he wants me. Will you drive me, please, Greg?"

They drove home without speaking, the picture of the empty third slot in the knife rack repeating itself before Mrs. Potter's eyes as she leaned back against the leather seat.

The old house seemed very quiet in the bright September sunlight when Greg and Mrs. Potter returned. It did not remain quiet very long. From then until dusk, there were telephone calls to take and to make. There were friends stopping by for friendly purposes and others in semiofficial capacity as well.

Mrs. Potter was to go through this day, in between callers, attending to the routine duties of the household in a state almost devoid of feeling. Occasionally she wished that the day were over, so that she could go to her room to cry. There were tears to be shed for the beautiful stranger, and most of all for dear, vain, gallant MacKay. There was need to think about whatever dark thread might have joined the two of them in death.

The first thing, however, was concern for her convalescent guest. "It's really time for you to have some food, Greg." She tried to rally herself. "Now, what sounds good?"

Greg seemed stronger, more in focus, than he had been since his arrival at Indian Point, as if his role, taking action as he had at the scene of the tragedy, had given him new purpose. "Don't you think about it, Aunt 'Genia. An omelet is just the ticket, and I'll make one for myself and have it on the table on the back porch. Will you join me there if I make a pot of tea for you, too?"

She had barely settled herself there with him on the shady screened porch, away from the late morning sun, when the first of the telephone calls began.

There were, in close sequence:

Number one, Lynette. All of the Dorrances were shocked and saddened by the news, and of course she was speaking for both Paul and Roger Two as well. First the death of that unfortunate young woman (after this, she made no further mention of Jackie) and then the dreadful blow of MacKay's death. Please tell her everything, every single thing.

47

Mrs. Potter managed a brief outline of the facts, saying only that Bertha had called, that she and Greg had driven there immediately, that MacKay's body had been in the garage with the car motor running, that Doc had come in the ambulance.

She did not mention the general surface scanning of the house with the twins and Greg and Bertha. She did not speak of finding the note, of Bertha's assertion that MacKay had known the girl before the cooking class. Least of all did she speak of the horror of the empty knife slot in the kitchen. This last detail she was trying to stifle even in her own thoughts. The other facts would be known soon enough, not only to the Dorrances but to all of Harrington as well.

Lynette, used to taking charge, began with practical matters. None of *them* knew any relatives of MacKay's. Did 'Genia? Vanderkoop and Vanderkoop were his lawyers here in town, Lynette thought, and they undoubtedly would know who should be notified. About funeral arrangements, did 'Genia have any thoughts about that? Did the prayer book have anything to say about services in case of a suicide? Lynette would call the rector at once and get this straight.

She ended by asking Mrs. Potter and Greg to come have a quiet family dinner with them, an invitation which was declined with thanks.

Well, yes, maybe Sunday supper instead, Mrs. Potter then agreed, and again thanks. Could they talk about it tomorrow?

Telephone call number two, Pete Felderkamp. He wanted to say many, many thanks for her help to the twins in going over Mr. Moore's house, and was she all right? He wanted to tell her how sorry he was about Mr. Moore, knowing he had been such a good friend of hers and all. He hated to bother her, but could she and Greg stop at the courthouse tomorrow afternoon, Saturday, about two? He'd need statements from them, but it could just as well wait until then since he guessed she was pretty much done in right now.

Call number three was from Julie. Hoddy had just phoned her from the office with this absolutely shattering news. All she knew was that MacKay had been killed in a car accident or something. Whatever had happened?

Again Mrs. Potter provided a bare outline of the circumstances of MacKay's death.

Julie could not be more utterly, completely devastated. She would take a couple of tranquilizers at once. (Mrs. Potter hoped she would not follow them with vodka, but did not say so.) 'Genia must tell her—how in the world would they all manage without MacKay? Without the only presentable, attractive single man in the county?

And had 'Genia heard the other awful news Hoddy had told her when he called? That black-haired Jackie Morsback—you know, the one everybody made such a fuss over when she came in with Roger Two last night—did 'Genia know she used to be a *very dear* friend of Charlie Ragsdale's, even lived there with her for a couple of months before they had a lovers' tiff or whatever you'd call it? And since then had been seen with every married man in town, except Hoddy and (possibly) Paul Dorrance? Well, Hoddy said she's been shot or stabbed or something. Heaven knows who could have done it, but really it might have been *anybody*, man *or* woman, from the reports that have been going around.

And did 'Genia think this might be the end of the cooking school now, with two of the members out of the running?

Mrs. Potter was suddenly furious. "Julia Janice Vermeer, I'm ashamed of you. A stranger in town has been murdered, and one of our best friends has died in some kind of miserable accident. We can't talk about cooking schools!"

Julie was quick to apologize, as she always had been as a little girl, when at one early stage in their lives she and Lynette and Eugenia were an inseparable trio. Julie, then Julia, never wanted anyone to be angry with her. It was enough that Grandmother Vermeer, with whom she lived, appeared to exist in a state of cold bad temper with the world at all times. Julia had a real store-bought dolls' house, Julia had a pony, Julia's dolls had handmade clothes with buttons that unbuttoned and real leather shoes. But the three of them never went to the Vermeers' house to play after school or on Saturday morning.

That big, dark red house in town had been home to Julie since childhood. Mrs. Potter remembered Grandpa saying something about the "old harridan" and about her "running off the whole pinch-faced tribe" of her family with her coldness and her stingi-

49

ness. That apparently had included Julia's mother, of whom nothing was ever mentioned.

However, the "miserly stinginess" Grandpa had deplored was never evidenced in Julia's upbringing. Julia had Blue Lake's first sailboat. Julia's clothes were bought, expensively, in two trips a year to Marshall Field's in Chicago. Julia went to an eastern boarding school for her last two high school years, while the rest of them, even Lynette, finished at Harrington High. And after college, Julia, now Julie, most surprisingly came home to live again with Grandmother Vermeer in the big old house.

Julie's present apologies continued. She hadn't meant to be unfeeling, and of course MacKay had become nearly as dear to her as were 'Genia and Lynette and Paul and all the old gang. And Hoddy felt the same way, although he hadn't been a member of the old gang either, of course.

Mrs. Potter remembered Julie's years following her return to the dark red house, so carefully screened from outside view and sunlight by tall, closely planted evergreens and heavy shrubbery. Each time on her own visits home, she had found Julie initiating some new cultural activity in the life of Harrington. There was the book review group, the music appreciation study club, the new playreading society. There were always trips to Iowa City, Minneapolis or Omaha (with a small group of faithful followers) to view the museums, to hear concerts or opera. Each time Mrs. Potter returned she found Grandmother Vermeer further removed into her own small, cold world of disapproval and Julie taller, thinner, a more uncertain focus in her big blue eyes.

When had Hoddy first come to town? Could it be as long as twenty-five years ago? It was, she thought, about the same time MacKay had also appeared out of the blue, so to speak, both of them to become, solidly and quickly, part of the social fabric of the community.

Hoddy had looked then, as she remembered him, like a junior wrestling champion. Or perhaps even more like a cheerful Eskimo, as if his smiling square, dark face should be framed in a parka ruff of wolverine.

Two qualities were greatly in his favor, in addition to the primary one, which was that he was *there*.

The first was his unsnubbable supply of good humor, which refused to be intimidated by the heavy atmosphere of Vermeer money and disapproval. He admired Julie's cultural pursuits, although he took part in none of them. He walked Grandmother Vermeer's unpleasant small dogs and appeared to enjoy them.

The second was that he obviously had plenty of money, which engendered Grandmother Vermeer's grudging respect. In fact, as Mrs. Potter remembered it, she had pressed even more money upon the newlyweds, as the then forty-year-old Julie had admitted to her, after Hoddy had bought the grain elevator. These added funds later helped to establish the meat-packing plant which was now proving so successful.

It was on Vermeer land, the long-undeveloped shoreland of the far western end of the lake, that the Pink House had been built for the newly married Hofmeyers. The big formal house, vaguely French, was where the three of them spent their summers. Each fall they moved back, with some ceremony and a great deal of packing up, into the old red mansion in town.

"Of course, yes, I understand." As she had, since they were six or seven, Mrs. Potter now found herself comforting Julie for a rebuff she had brought upon herself in the first place. They all knew Julie had her problems. Drinking, for one.

There was another, more basic one, she had suspected for several years. Julie had once showed her a small collection of poems she had written, which she thought she might have privately printed. These had not seemed very good to Mrs. Potter, and she was relieved when Julie abandoned the idea, but she remembered one of them. Entitled "Ice Maiden," it began:

> *Frozen lips waiting for the warmth of your kiss,*
> *Frozen limbs awaiting the heat of your embrace—*

Hoddy might be faithful, given to lavish praise of his wife, might present a sports-loving, hard-drinking, club-joining, pipe-smoking, ever-smiling manly image to the world of Harrington. It seemed that he also might have some fundamental shortcomings as a husband.

It was possible, too, that Julie had heard what Mrs. Potter had been told confidentially by a mutual friend a few days earlier. It seemed that faithful Hoddy had been seen at Ruppert's drugstore counter twice recently having midmorning coffee in the company of a gorgeous brunette. If so, more trouble was brewing here.

Mrs. Potter returned with a start, as Julie's voice continued at the other end of the line. "Oh, yes, Julia, the class. The class. Let's wait until next week to decide, shall we?"

Julie agreed. It wasn't that she was all that keen about learning to cook, anyway, as 'Genia and Lynette should remember. She just wanted to go on record right now that they certainly ought to demand their money back if the class broke up.

Finally, good-bye; but would she and Greg like to come over for a drink before dinner? Hoddy had some visiting firemen in town, people from Ottumwa, to see the new packing plant, staying at the Inn of course. They were going to have drinks at the house, then take them out to the new steak place. Well, maybe dinner some night next week, then. Eddie was going to come to work for them now. Eddie-what's-his-name, *you* know, 'Genia, and it's going to be heaven to have someone in the kitchen again. Let's talk again tomorrow and set a night next week?

Mrs. Potter hung up the phone, her neck muscles stiff and tense, and escaped gratefully to the garden at the south of the house, to sit in the sun and look, unseeing, at the shadows under the big maples and at the clear blue of the lake under the late morning sun.

It was nearly noon when Greg came to find her. "So sorry to break in on you, Aunt 'Genia, but this call is from Charlotte Ragsdale. You remember, that beautiful girl who came in late to the class last night? She seems awfully eager to talk with you, and I told her I'd see if you felt like coming to the phone."

So, morning call number four was Charlie Ragsdale. *Beautiful girl?* she asked herself.

"I apologize for calling you today, Mrs. Potter," came the oddly scratchy voice. "This is a nightmare day for you, I know, and in a way it is for me, too. But could I see you?"

"Could it wait for tomorrow, my dear, or the first of the week?"

"Tomorrow would be all right, I guess, Mrs. Potter, but it's terribly important to me and I hate to put it off any longer. Could I stop by sometime tomorrow afternoon?"

"Charlie dear, Pete Felderkamp wants me to come into town tomorrow about two, about something at the courthouse. What if I

52

came by your house after that, instead of your coming here, say between three or four? And may I bring my nephew Greg with me? It's such a help to have him drive when everything is so sad and confused."

After that, Greg and Mrs. Potter returned to the still-cool and pleasant back porch for a quickly assembled lunch. A big pot of end-of-the-garden soup had been made earlier in the week, and now awaited only reheating. There were additions of cheese and a slice of cold leftover pot roast for Greg, to continue stoking his thin frame with the necessary extra protein. For them both, there were thick-sliced homemade whole wheat bread with butter and crabapple jelly and tall glasses of cold buttermilk. They ate almost ravenously, in silence.

The quiet was broken by the sound of a heavy car pulling to a halt in the driveway to the barn. Jack Vanderpool approached them quickly, bounding on the soles of his striped running shoes, his thin skin translucent in the midday light, his long, sharp nose and high forehead perpetually red from the sun, his fiery red-brown eyes alert.

It was hard to reconcile this thin, ascetic-looking man (he has the look of a holy martyr, Mrs. Potter thought warily) with her high school memories of the young Jack. Of all people, he was the boy *no* one's mother would let her go to the Bijou with (even though the Vanderpools were among the town's leading families) after a certain report of his goings-on there in the back row with some girl from out of town. The annual, the *Harrington Hullaba-loo,* awarded him "Don Juan of the Senior Class" status, and he was revered as a font of knowledge for untutored freshmen, eager to get the facts of life straight at last.

Now she greeted him with apprehension. "You've heard, Jack? You know about MacKay and about that poor girl who came to the class last night with Roger Two? But then I guess you knew her too? I can see you've heard the whole wretched miserable business. Can you believe it, Jack, here in Harrington?"

"I must say I hardly knew Jackie—that poor unfortunate young woman, that is to say—and that's not why I'm here, Eugenia. What I am upset about, and Marie is too, is our friend MacKay. I hear you were there at the house early this morning. What in Sam Hill is going on?"

"First, let's have a glass of iced tea," Mrs. Potter suggested. "You look hot, Jack, and we can move to the front porch now, where there should be a nice breeze from the lake."

Greg, again with newfound energy, mustered ice, tall glasses, a pot of freshly made strong tea, and even three thin slices of lemon.

How dreadful, thought Mrs. Potter. Am I going to think about those knives for the rest of my days? Thin, thin slices of lemon under a dexterous blade, smooth, flexible hands with a crooked little finger? An empty slot in a knife rack in MacKay's beautiful, friendly kitchen?

"To come to the point, Eugenia," began Jack, appearing to sense that her thoughts had wandered, "to come to the point. I am told you and Greg were at MacKay's house when his body was found this morning, and I want you to tell me everything that happened."

Mrs. Potter repeated her honest, but limited, account of the morning's happenings: Bertha's call, the finding of MacKay's body in the garage, Doc Winkelman's response to her call, Pete Felderkamp's arrival with the twins.

"Yes, yes, I know all that," he interrupted a bit impatiently. "What I need to know is, did you see anything out of the way? Was there a note, was there anything that made you think, well, that MacKay had done away with himself?"

"Jack, I really think you'll have to ask Pete about this, or maybe Doc." Mrs. Potter was polite but firm. "Have you talked to Pete?"

"Naturally I have, but he's not saying much. Close-mouthed Dutchman, just like his father was. What you don't understand, Eugenia, is that I *need* to know about every single detail." Jack took a long swallow of iced tea, then continued.

"Let me explain why. MacKay was insured with one of my companies. I was his insurance broker, get it? He had a policy that is not going to pay off if it was a suicide. I've got to know. I'm one of the 500 Club, Eugenia, the top life insurance club in the whole country, and I've got to know these things."

"Pete and Doc will tell you everything, Jack, the minute they have anything to report. I know they will. Now tell us, please, how is Marie today?"

She paused, then added, "Lynette is eager to learn if MacKay had any family that ought to be notified. Maybe you'd know about this, and would you be good enough to tell her? And she just called me back about something else. She is concerned about who has information to write up the obituary piece for the *Herald-Gazette*. You know Lynette—she has to get everybody organized. Nobody seems to know just where MacKay was born, anything about his family or what he did before he came here. We all knew him so well, but they can't seem to locate those kinds of facts.''

''All I know is that his insurance beneficiaries are local charities,'' Jack said. ''Local boys' club, that sort of thing. I haven't an idea who'll get the house or his money. Expect he's made some provision for Bertha—not that she wouldn't be able to look after herself, but she's been with him for some years now. I assume there's plenty of mazoola, even with the way he's been throwing it around for the last twenty years.''

Jack rose to leave, reluctantly. ''Sure you don't know anything that would help to give a reading on this, Eugenia? No signs either of suicide or foul play?''

As he bounded back to his car, Jack halted his springing stride. ''Don't forget now, Eugenia, I can sell this old white elephant for you whenever you say the word. You're not getting any younger, you know, and I don't know just how long I can hope to dig up any kind of buyer for this place.''

After Jack's departure, Greg excused himself for a nap in his airy back bedroom upstairs, and Mrs. Potter retreated to her own room at the front, looking down and east over the lake.

So she wasn't getting any younger, as if that mattered. Neither was Jack, in spite of all his running, and neither was a two-year-old. What did matter, painfully, was that MacKay, who had so ardently savored his days, and Jackie, whose beauty might only have ripened with the years, were not going to get any older.

The late September sun was lower in the west, and was dropping south as well, a reminder that the short days of autumn had begun, when Mrs. Potter came down from her bedroom in bathing suit and towel robe. The day was still warm, and a swim in the bright cold water of Blue Lake might provide refreshment that an hour of fruitless, circular speculation in her room had not given her.

The lake, which ordinarily would have been entirely her own at that time of the day and year, was dotted with boats. She saw canoes, rowboats, two sailboats at the far eastern end, and she detected the muffled roar of an outboard around the hidden bend in the shoreline past the Pink House toward the southwest. This is odd, she thought. The summer people are all gone now, except for occasional weekends, and the local children are in school.

No, come to think of it, today, Friday, was to be a school holiday of some sort, a regional teachers' meeting in Rock Rapids, as she recalled. She had seen the notice in the school hallway last night.

Last night? Could it have been less than twenty-four hours ago that she and Greg had set out for that first cooking class at the high school?

The school holiday explained the number of boats on the lake on a September weekday midafternoon. All of young Harrington was out, just as she and her brother Will, and Julie and Lynette and Paul and Jack had been out in their day, rowing, sailing, paddling, shoving, diving, shouting, laughing, on the beautiful, clear blue waters of their own Blue Lake. The now-superintendent of adult continuing education had certainly been with them—a tall, thin, daring diver and a frequent winner in their constant water-jousting competitions. Ralph DeWitt probably had chores on the family farm then, and she remembered Dottie, then Dottie DeBoos, only vaguely from those days. Dottie and Ralph had not then been part of the gang, although they had become accepted members of the present Harrington establishment. If there is such a thing, she thought.

But of course there is! She corrected herself briskly. Talk of a classless society in small-town middle America is absolutely phony. There is a right and a wrong side of the tracks, even in Harrington, Iowa, population forty-seven hundred and whatever it is now. There are the Haves and the Have Nots, and Mrs. Potter knew very well (and had always known) that Grandpa's money and her father's gentle and generous presence as president of the Harrington bank had ensured that she and Will were permanently enrolled among the former. Lynette was a Have, and so of course was Julie, once Julia of the long golden sausage curls and the big red house behind the evergreens. Paul—naturally all Dorrances were born Haves. The Vanderpools were Haves, and so consequently was Jack, no matter how greatly his youthful peccadilloes might have disturbed the town's watchful mothers.

On the other hand, while the DeWitts and the DeBooses and the Felderkamps, all prosperous farm families, were in no way deprived and might have been markedly well-to-do, they were not the town decision-makers and opinion-formers. Their wives did not belong to the Pioneer Bridge Club.

Much farther down the scale, Mrs. Potter realized, was the family of the original Varlene. And then there were the relics of construction gangs on the railroad, or of early settlers unlucky in their choice of land or in failure of health or will.

It was among these latter that the Walters family might have ranked. Tenant farmers on one of Grandpa's few bad buys, a poor quarter section north of town, they had moved into Harrington after the death of the father. Mrs. Walters had become a reluctant, somewhat sullen cleaning woman in order to support her four children. She had come to Indian Point "to oblige" at special times of the year, like the period of exciting, exhausting general upheaval known as spring housecleaning. Rugs, even heavy carpets, were taken up and hung over sturdy steel clotheslines, there to be whacked with ornate beaters made of twisted metal or rattan. Walls were washed, then recalcimined with a wash of fresh color. Cupboards and closets were turned out (odd mittens found, broken toys discarded), floors were scrubbed and waxed and polished with a heavy weighted brush at the end of a long swiveled handle.

Mother and Grandma and the current hired girl, plus the some-time help of the glowering Mrs. Walters, presided over, reveled in, or slaved away at the important, week-long ritual. Family meals were of the pick-up variety—leftovers, sandwiches, store-bought cold cuts otherwise rarely seen. When the frenzy reached its peak, Grandpa usually decreed a dinner at the Inn—fried chicken, mashed potatoes and yellow gravy, hot rolls and pie—at which Grandma and Mother would look suitably wan, although dressed for (and with appetite for) the festive occasion.

Between times, Mrs. Potter reflected, things were considerably different. What Grandma called "a lick and a promise" was about all that was expected of the hired girl. Actually she was much more what is currently known as an *au pair*. Country families, first- or second-generation arrivals from northern Europe, wanted their daughters to become familiar with the ways of town and of their new country. The hired girl, who ate with the family, whose even-tual acceptance into the country gentry was assumed and even en-couraged, was there as much to learn—from Grandma about American cooking, from Mother about how to set a table and how to give a ladies' luncheon—as to make beds and wash dishes, which was about all she did.

Of the Walters clan, only Alice had gone on to finish high school—a tall, dark, quiet girl whose face she found hard to re-member, even though she saw her occasionally now at the Dor-rances', at whose home she appeared daily to clean, wash and iron, and to clear away after (although not to serve) the excellent meals which Lynette herself usually prepared.

When had Alice begun to call her *Mrs. Potter?* she suddenly wondered. Certainly it would have been 'Genia and Alice (or was it Al?) at Harrington High. Not until after her years away from Harrington and her return visits, as from another world, not as Eu-genia Andrews but as Mrs. B. Lewis Potter.

Elsie, the other sister, had been her brother Will's age. She was now the lady bartender at the Inn. Then there was Louis, who after repeating eighth grade until he was sixteen, had happily graduated to his lifelong ambition of running the Inn's parking lot.

She had scarcely known Bertha then. She remembered a big,

handsome, well-curved teenager (in an age when Lynette's flat, slim-hipped, boyish figure was more fashionable) with the same unshiny black hair, dark skin, and bright blue eyes she still retained. How lucky MacKay had been to keep her as his housekeeper. And he had been a generous employer, she knew, even buying Bertha's small car for the trips back and forth into town. She felt sure he had provided for her in some way in the case of his death.

With the returning thought of MacKay, Mrs. Potter braced herself and dived into the cold, clear water. She swam briskly to the float, the canvas-topped wooden platform moored a hundred feet out from the dock. She returned with a lazier stroke.

On the sun-warmed bleached planks of the dock, next to the small red canoe which was beached there and beyond the mooring posts of the sturdy outboard motorboat, Mrs. Potter stretched out gratefully. She was on the verge of sleep, her head pillowed on her arms, when she was aroused by hallooing voices from the porch of the house, up the gentle grassy bank above the dock.

The DeWitts, Ralph and Dottie, rushed down the slope to embrace her before she had gathered her towel and robe to make her way to them.

"We had to let you know we are *with* you." Ralph spoke into one ear.

"What are friends *for,* if not to be present in time of trouble?" Dottie added, her arm around Mrs. Potter's damp waist on the other side.

Interspersed with words of scriptural comfort, which Mrs. Potter tried to find comforting, the two managed to convey (a) that they had felt sure that ever since her dear husband passed away, Mrs. Potter and MacKay would make a pair, (b) that taking one's own life was the most grievous of sins but that all final judgment is in the hands of a mightier power and we must trust in divine forgiveness, and (c) that such forgiveness was going to be strained to the limit in the case of that Miss Morsback who had gotten herself involved in a nasty murder last night.

Mrs. Potter let the flow of their certainties (how many of both their sentences begin with "*It is my firm belief,*" she thought) slide around and over her head, trusting that she was putting in the right noncommittal responses from time to time.

When they reached the porch steps, she excused herself neatly. "Please let me put on something dry," she said—a statement rather than a request—"and here is Greg who will, I'm sure, get you a glass of sherry or something while I'm changing."

She dressed quickly in a long, bright Mexican housecoat. As she combed and put up her wet hair she paused and slowly set aside a new brassy hairpin, no match to all the others, all worn down from a darker brown to the dull steel beneath. Then, stirring herself, she put on a light flick of gray eye shadow, heartened herself with a generous splash of a new cologne, and returned to the porch.

There she found the DeWitts facing Greg in what seemed an oddly defensive posture. All three were having soft drinks of some sort, and Greg had set out a bowl of her fresh-salted almonds, which were disappearing rapidly.

"Greg, here, doesn't seem to share the same ideas we have about the sinful nature of man, 'Genia," asserted Ralph in almost truculent tones, crunching nutmeats purposefully with his square white teeth.

"And it isn't as if he *knew* that Morsback woman before last night. '*Vengeance is mine; I will repay, saith the Lord.*' Romans 12:19," Dottie told her.

Greg replied with oddly stubborn firmness, "That's really what we're talking about, isn't it? That the Lord is the one to take vengeance, not us? Oh, I'm sorry, Aunt 'Genia. I don't mean to be rude to your friends, and I'm afraid that is just what I've been doing. Please forgive me, Mrs. DeWitt, Mr. DeWitt."

The two nodded stiffly, smiled in a jerky way, and returned to their words of intended solace for Mrs. Potter.

Ralph's blue eyes were shiny marbles in his round red face and the gray of his crew-cut hair seemed to bristle. " '*If thou do that which is evil, be afraid; for he bearest not the sword in vain.*' Romans 13:4."

"But Ralph," Mrs. Potter demurred, "I never knew MacKay to do that which was evil."

"Not MacKay. I'm talking about that girl. '*The wages of sin is death.*' Romans 6:23."

Dottie came in quickly, with a propitiating sweetness. " '*All we like sheep have gone astray.*' Isaiah 53:6." Her puffed pinkish hair, well sprayed, did not quiver in the breeze across the porch.

"Anyway, what we really came to do was to offer condolences," Ralph continued. " '*Pure religion is this, to visit the fatherless and widows in their affliction.*' St. James 1:27."

"Oh, but you mustn't consider me as MacKay's widow," Mrs. Potter interposed hurriedly. "We were good friends, that's all. Besides, I've always thought the important part of that verse was the end bit. You know, how it goes on, '*And to keep himself unspotted from the world*'? That always sounded to me like the hardest part, not just going around visiting widows and the like."

"Ralph just didn't finish the verse, that's all," Dottie explained somewhat stiffly. "Anyway, as he said, we really came to tell you we are *with* you, and to ask you to dinner next week. '*Use hospitality one to another without grudging.*' St. Peter 4:9."

On this note the guests arose, shook Greg's hand with hearty forgiveness, then again warmly embraced their hostess. Exacting her promise to let them know whatever they could do, assuring her of her place in their daily (nightly? hourly?) prayers, Ralph and Dottie returned home to Harrington. There, they insisted, they would expect Mrs. Potter and her nephew for dinner some night very soon.

"Whew. I'm sorry, Aunt 'Genia, but *whew*. Unless you need me, that's one dinner party I'm going to get out of."

"I'm afraid they gave you a rather bad time, love. If you'd known them as long as I have, though, you'd know they're both basically good people. It's just that they've always taken themselves pretty seriously, and it's hard to enjoy people who seem so totally humorless. But just let me tell you a little about them.

"For a while they had a rough time financially and they had a struggle to make a go of it in their little appliance business. Then some way they came into some money—I forget how, if I ever knew. Finally the business flourished and they took up golf and the tennis club and the country club scene, and they were pretty earnest about all that, too.

"Just lately they've gone into this religious thing—no, I shouldn't say that, that's much too cynical. They now seem genuinely dedicated in their new church group, just as they were in the Methodist church in the old days, when Dottie played the organ there."

"New preacher come to town?" Greg queried idly.

"Yes, indeed. 'Madly charismatic' is Julie's description, but needless to say she and Hoddy don't go in for that sort of thing themselves. Reverend Jim-Bill Sanders, or something like that. Very strong on the confessional and what he calls one-to-one relationships with his flock, whatever that means. Other than that I don't know much about him."

Mrs. Potter left the porch then, to check by telephone on Bertha. Alice was at home, it seemed, from her day at the Dorrances', and she answered the phone at the Walters' small house. Bertha was lying down, Alice said, and Doc had given her something to relax her nerves. Anyway, she had been up to watch some of her regular afternoon stories on the TV. She never missed her stories if she could help it, and Alice thought that was a good sign.

No, many thanks, there wasn't anything Bertha needed. She'd let her know you asked. Bertha thought the world of her, of Mrs. Potter.

Greg came out of the center sitting room, the small, cozy square room they all had always preferred to the stiff and uncomfortable front parlor. There the prism-cut light in the bay window glass had been one of the delights of young Eugenia's childhood, spilling its rainbow on her outstretched hands. The slippery yet scratchy black horsehair upholstery, still unworn, had been an affront to her young bottom.

In the parlor the furniture frames were of black mahogany, with carved lions' heads at the ends of the armrests; the feet were carved and clawed, ending in fierce bronze talons, each of these clutching a shiny ball of marble, presumably to protect the now-faded but firm old carpet. An upright piano occupied one wall, flanked by more of the inhospitable carved chairs. On the faded damask wallpaper there hung several of Aunt Hillie's watercolors, prim flower arrangements in gilt frames. One of these, a tight bunch of violets, appeared to be encircled by a giant green caterpillar. It was not until recent years that Mrs. Potter had been relieved to see this instead as a ruff, or a cuff, of gray-green heart-shaped leaves. It still looked like a giant caterpillar unless she thought about it.

Through an open archway, which could be closed with sliding oak doors, the sitting room was the family's favorite gathering place. It was warm with books, with the small corner fireplace that had always burned cannel coal in Mrs. Potter's youthful recollections, the big chunks splitting to reveal magical fissures of spark and flame. I wonder where one could find cannel coal now, she asked herself. We'll be using that fireplace soon.

The room held comfortable rocking chairs, Grandpa's big Morris chair, a comfortable contrivance of oak and brown leather, and, best of all, Grandma's wonderful curved couch in one corner. In early years, Mrs. Potter had imagined herself—delicious thought—playing Madame Récamier on that couch. To what audience, and saying what, her imagination had failed to tell her.

In one hand, Greg now bore the old family Bible, in the other one of Mrs. Potter's lined yellow pads. "Just going to check a few of those quotes of the DeWitts', Aunt 'Genia. I have some friends in a group in Santa Clara County, back home, and I got sort of interested in the religion thing."

I will never cease to be amazed by the young, thought Mrs. Potter. "Well then, love, if you're occupied, I think I'll spend a little while in the garden before dinner," she said.

This time, Mrs. Potter meant not the south lawn and the still beautiful old flower beds of dahlias and chrysanthemums, but the vegetable garden in the open area behind the barn. For the next peaceful hour, her thoughts were a blank except for those connected with the season's end, and how soon (very soon, she thought) she must wrap and put away the many yet unripened green tomatoes before the first frost.

Two of these she selected now, huge firm globes of jade, to make fried green tomatoes for tomorrow's lunch. Greg might like that. There was old-fashioned side pork in the refrigerator—thick slices of unsalted bacon—to be fried brown and crisp. If not, she'd use regular bacon. She would cut the green tomatoes in thick crosswise slices, dust them with cracker crumbs, and sauté them in the pork drippings. Then, setting the tender and almost translucent green-amber slices on one of the old ironstone platters to keep warm in the oven, she would pour off most of the fat, and use the same skillet to make a rich milk gravy. With the garnish of the crisp brown pork strips, this had been one of Grandpa's favorite meals.

She cut tender stalks of late broccoli, enough for the two of them for dinner. Lamb chops from the freezer to broil, she thought, and maybe a baked potato? She pulled up and carried to the compost the last of the lettuce plants, now too far advanced in senility to provide even a few leaves for garnishment.

The garden time had been restorative, and apparently Greg's biblical studies had been absorbing. But when the two of them sat down to dinner in the early September twilight, neither of them felt much like eating.

Saturday morning. Another bright blue September day, golden-rod glowing alongside the old macadam back road, gentians moving in the light breeze on the way to the old bridge, *the* Bridge of Mrs. Potter's youth.

Two twelve-year-olds on bicycles, each balancing a spinning rod over his shoulder with one hand, each with tackle box and lunch in his bicycle basket, headed up the old road from the direction of Harrington.

Their gravel-voiced banter went on as they made their way over the old surface of the road, broken and pitted.

"Pickerel should be running good at the bridge today. Anyways crappies," one proclaimed knowingly.

"How much you bet I get the first one?" countered the other.

They left their bicycles beside the road in their usual spot at the bend just before the approach to the bridge. Poles in hand, they stopped short at the unexpected sight of the little flowered green VW at the side of the road ahead of them.

"Holy Toledo, it's Miss Versteeg's."

"What's *she* doing out here on Saturday morning, anyway? Can't get away from those dumb teachers no matter what you do."

Upstream, above the small hump of the concrete bridge, its stained sides crumbling, its steel supports exposed and rusting, was Little Blue, marshy in its farther reaches, the water of the small lake reflecting the morning sun.

Downstream, beneath the narrow span of the bridge, the current flowed gently on its course to the larger lake below. The boys squatted, discussed the attractions of their several lures, debated the charms of a never-fail wobbler-shiner versus those of a plastic purple worm with a gyrating chromium tail.

They dropped their lines and let the gentle movement of the water carry them downstream.

At the same moment they both saw the body, face down at the edge of the bend below the bridge, the pale blue pants and top billowing out in the slow-moving water. The current pulled gently at the floating feet. One long braid, its gold now tarnished with murky strands of waterweed, had caught on a snag of log at the edge of the stream.

What Miss Versteeg was doing that Saturday morning was resisting, placidly, the downstream pull of Little Blue Inlet.

Mrs. Potter learned of the drowning when she and Greg arrived at the courthouse that early afternoon, as Pete Felderkamp had requested.

The boys, Pete told her, had pedaled back to town at such speed as they could manage, encumbered with poles and gear. One of the Hayenga twins had been on patrol on Main Street (the new parking meters and their consequent violations required extra duty on Saturday, still Harrington's farmers' traditional shopping day) and they had rushed to him with their story, the quiver and break of their changing voices giving it an added measure of horror.

"It's Miss Versteeg," one was repeating. "She teaches family and sex and that dumb stuff at our school. We *know* it's her."

"It's her car all right enough," the other insisted. "We'd know that old VW anywhere, all those nutty flowers she put on it. It's all full of throw-up now, though. We opened the door and it almost made Kenny sick, too."

The twin radioed his chief, who, like all but the very newest residents of Harrington, needed no directions other than the words "old bridge." He and the other twin raced out the old roadway and clambered down the flowery brush embankment to the edge of the inlet, down a path worn smooth by generations of young fishermen retrieving snagged lines.

There they retrieved the drowned body of Varlene Versteeg, age twenty-eight, teacher at Woodrow Wilson Junior High School. Next of kin a great-uncle and aunt, Mr. and Mrs. Walter Versteeg, with whom she resided at 145 East Third Street.

"How sad." Mrs. Potter suddenly felt that this was a last, intolerable blow, but to whom she could not say. "How very, very sad. When did it happen, do you know? Sometime yesterday?"

"Doc seems to be pretty sure on that part of it," Pete told her. "Thursday night, probably late Thursday night."

"Thursday! But hadn't someone missed her?" Mrs. Potter asked. "Surely her aunt and uncle—"

"Well, they *were* worried sick but they were afraid to call anybody, it looks like. From what I can gather Varlene had given them a dressing-down recently about not checking up on her all the time like she was a kid. She was going to start living her own life—stuff like that. So when she didn't come home from the cooking school Thursday night, well, they remembered about the teachers' meeting in Rock Rapids on Friday and they figured she'd gone over there to spend the night with some schoolteacher girlfriend of hers."

"And Friday night?" Mrs. Potter persisted.

"Same thing again. Scared and worried, but telling themselves she'd stayed over a second night just to teach them a lesson. They're a pretty sad old couple today, I can tell you that."

They all agreed it was just too much. All in one night, and in Harrington, of all places. A murder, then what looked like a suicide, and now a drowning.

The legal formalities for which Pete had asked them to appear consisted of reading long typed statements which had been prepared from the twins' notes. Pete had made a later, more thorough search at MacKay's house, a search that had produced the distressing evidence of the missing knife. The twins had taken fingerprints, using their new mail-order kit, and those on the car, the desk, and the kitchen were those they expected to find—MacKay's and Bertha's, of course, Greg's on the garage door and on the ignition key where he had switched off the motor. Mrs. Potter and Greg were asked to give dispositions describing their own observations that morning, as well as statements of their activities following the class on Thursday evening. Any further legal steps would depend on the county attorney's decision after the report of the coroner, Doc Winkelman, was complete.

It was nearly three-thirty when Mrs. Potter and Greg left the pale yellow sandstone fortress that was the county courthouse. Leaving the car in the parking lot there, they headed on foot down the tree-shaded street to the old Ragsdale house a half block away. As they walked Mrs. Potter had an opportunity to notice Greg's freshly washed hair and beard, shining in the autumn sunlight. Still too much hair, she thought, but at least it looks better.

The house was square, white, forthright, and ugly. And *comfortable,* thought Mrs. Potter, remembering happy times and impassioned youthful political discussions there with Charlie's parents. George and Leona Ragsdale, as a team, had been publishers, editors, reporters, advertising salesmen, columnists, everything, for the Harrington *Herald-Gazette.* Whether it was the society pages, the editorials, the local farm news or local politics, they had brought wit and energy to the country weekly newspaper.

In later days Leona had been crippled by multiple sclerosis, and George equally so by the loss of her partnership. They were both dead now, killed by a speeding oil truck as they tried to cross the highway one rainy fall afternoon.

Charlie opened the big oak front door, with its three rectangular inserts of heavy plate glass, before they had time to ring the bell. She was dressed in tight jeans and sandals, but instead of the open-necked, rolled-sleeved boy's short she'd worn to the cooking class, she had on a long-sleeved pink turtleneck pullover, perhaps to observe the formality of their visit. Again she seemed an embodiment of her greeting card character, Debby.

"It's very good of you to make time to come, Mrs. Potter," the husky voice greeted them. "And Greg, you too. Come on in. The kettle's on and I hope you'd like some tea."

As they came through the doweled and latticed golden oak archway separating the square front hall from the larger room, Mrs.

67

Potter had pleasant memories. The room, as it had been in Leona and George's day, was full of cheerful, colorful clutter—books, magazines, plants, flowers. A fire was laid on the well-used brick hearth, ready for the first cool evening. A small table held a tray with three thin cups and saucers, small plates, and fine, old well-washed linen napkins.

Mrs. Potter tried to shake off the depression weighing upon her. "Madeira embroidery, Charlie, think of that. I'm sure that mine, which had been Mother's of course, finally wore out about ten years ago. These must have been your grandmother's! How have you managed to keep them?"

"Only because I save them for special occasions now, Mrs. Potter. I think I'm down to the last half dozen. Would you two excuse me a minute while I fetch the tea?"

This is the last thing I would have expected, mused Mrs. Potter, as Charlie left the room and Greg idled about picking up magazines and looking at book titles. Tea, of all things, from a young woman who looked as if she should be singing protest songs to her own guitar accompaniment. *Tea,* and Grandmother's Madeira napkins, and a roomful of burgeoning, blossoming plants that a professional nurseryman might envy.

When Charlie reappeared, her mild astonishment increased. There was fragrant, hot, smoky Souchong tea, an extra jug of hot water, a plate of thin buttered slices of frosted homemade raisin bread. Nothing else, but this in its way perfection.

Nothing else, that is, except for a small round tray presented in an offhand, almost brusque manner to Greg. "Several friends of mine have gone through the hepatitis bit," Charlie explained. "I thought you'd better have this on the side. Boiled eggs, done the way my father liked them. I'm a vegetarian myself."

Greg's word of thanks was a monosyllable, but he ate the eggs quickly and with obvious enjoyment. They had been scooped, hot and soft, from their shells into a thin Chinese bowl. There were crisp, thin soda crackers on the side, which he crumbled and added. The tray held not only small shakers of salt and pepper, but a tiny round glass dish of curry powder as well, with a miniature ivory spoon.

Charlie watched him closely, then appeared to relax as he seasoned and ate the savory mixture.

To make conversation, and also because she really wanted to know, Mrs. Potter queried her hostess, "Homemade raisin bread, oh my dear, wherever do you find something like this in Harrington?"

"Wish I could oblige you with the name of the little old lady who whips it up for me." Charlie shrugged. "The fact is, the little old lady is me. One of the things Dad insisted that I learn to do was to make bread, and actually now it's the part of cooking that gives me the most pleasure. Whenever things with my work aren't going right, or whenever I need to let off steam, I bake bread."

"Marvelous, marvelous, my dear." Mrs. Potter made a mental note to bring up the subject of French bread at a later time. Now, of course, they were there at Charlie's request because she had some problem to talk about. That first. The bread technique could wait, as it had been waiting for a good many years.

So, instead of bread baking, she led the talk to Charlie's reason for wanting them to come.

"What I needed to talk to you about, Mrs. Potter," explained Charlie in her low, grating voice, "is Jackie. Jackie Morsback. It's puzzling for me, and personal."

"If it will help, please talk," was Mrs. Potter's almost reluctant response. "Whatever it is, I can promise you that it won't be repeated."

"Of course I know that. Mother and Dad both loved you, you know, and trusted you. And so I do, too, and I need some help."

Over second cups of the hot, smoky tea, Charlie talked of Jackie. A few years older than Charlie, she had been a fellow student at a small liberal arts college in the southern part of the state. At that time, more than ten years ago, they had shared similar family tragedies. Charlie's parents had been killed in the seemingly meaningless slaughter on the highway. Jackie's parents had died, within weeks of each other, shortly after her father's release from prison for bank fraud.

The Morsbacks had lived in a small upstate New York town named Rhynesdorp, and Jackie's father had been that respected small-town figure, the president of the local bank. (Mrs. Potter expressed a feeling of kinship.)

There had been an untidy scandal about bank fraud, involving a sum of almost a million dollars, a tremendous amount for that time and for the size of the bank. Something to do with fictitious loans, Charlie thought.

Mr. Morsback had been tried and found guilty despite his protestations of innocence, partly because of incriminating details unearthed by cross-examination of the bank's chief teller. He had been sentenced to fifteen years in federal prison. The money was never recovered.

Mrs. Morsback had not left the house after the time her husband was sentenced, and was not seen again except by a handful of people in the town until the casket was opened at her funeral. Mr. Morsback, paroled from prison, died soon after she did, still insisting that someone else at the bank had been guilty of the theft.

Since she had been only five at the time of his conviction and her mother had been almost as much a recluse from her own daughter as from former friends, Jackie did not, so Charlie thought, miss her parents very much. She was pretty much used to being on her own.

So, Charlie continued, it was probably knowing that they shared a similar orphaning bereavement that first brought them together as college friends, even though their reactions to the parental deaths had differed.

"We were friends," she went on, "but not close friends. Certainly not close in the way people around here talked about. I mean to say, Mrs. Potter, we were not lovers. I hope I haven't shocked you?"

Mrs. Potter, at sixty, was shocked by very few things except cruelty, major or petty. Greg looked totally unmoved. She murmured encouragement for Charlie to continue.

So, it seemed, the two young women had maintained a casual friendship through the years since they left college. Charlie, after art school, tried pottery making , then sculpture, and finally faced the realities of earning a living. The Debbies, as she called them, had been part of her everyday life since she had been a teenager. At the advice of a friend—Mrs. Dorrance, she said, Aunt Lynette— she had submitted a folio of these drawings to a large greeting card company in Cedar Rapids. From the time of their acceptance, Debby and her doings and her pals and her pets had found instant and smashing success in the greeting card world. There were now Debby dolls and Debby blue jeans and even Debby ice cream, all

70

of which provided added royalties. The work kept her busy; it paid well enough for her to live here where she wanted to be and to maintain the big, old, comfortable square house.

"Jackie thought it was a cop-out," she went on. "That's to say I should have been trying to do serious art, and that I had been side-tracked by the money."

Mrs. Potter might have been heard to say, barely, audibly, that she knew what a cop-out was.

"Funny thing about that was that Jackie really wanted money so badly herself. Of course her folks didn't leave her any, because there wasn't any to leave, under the circumstances. She used to joke about it in a way I never thought was very funny. Said she wished her father had only told her before he died where he hid that million dollars.

"Money," Charlie went on, "and besides that, power. Power over people. Those two things were more important to Jackie than anything else in the world."

"Funny thing I hadn't met the girl before last night," Mrs. Potter put in. "I usually know what's going on around town, one way or another, and since she's been here since early summer—"

"You missed meeting her at that party for Mr. Redmond at the start of the summer," Charlie told her. "She and I got there late, and I think you were just leaving as we came in. Anyway, the summer has been a busy season for me, and while Jackie got to know a lot of Harrington people, it really wasn't at all in a way that would have been a part of your life."

"The important thing, I suppose, is what you wanted to talk to Aunt Eugenia about," Greg interposed, somewhat diffidently.

Charlie took a deep breath. "Well, then, about Jackie's murder. Pete Felderkamp has been here twice to ask what I could tell him. So far I'll have to admit all I've told him is just things like what I was doing that night after class, which was being right here alone. What I need advice about is just how much to tell Pete now."

Thought of the quick, brutal stabbing in the parking lot held the three silent for a moment, and then Mrs. Potter spoke. "So far, I can't imagine that any of this would help him, can you, Greg? Except the name of the town in New York State, Rhynesdorp, did you say? You should certainly tell him if you know of anyone there or from your college days, or from wherever Jackie was before she

71

came here this summer, who might have reason to want her out of the way. That, and if Jackie had relatives who should be notified."

"I don't know of anyone like that from her past, and there weren't any relatives. But please wait—I haven't got to the part I don't know whether to tell Pete."

Charlie took another deep breath. "Jackie came here the first part of the summer. She phoned me from Washington. Not Washington, Iowa, Washington, D.C. She said she'd quit her job there and needed a rest. She worked for some big government bureau and I think she had a really high-powered job. She was a smart girl and she was ambitious.

"It was all right to have her here for a while, but after about six weeks I had to ask her to leave. The reason was, Mrs. Potter, I think she was planning to blackmail people. People here in Harrington, friends of my folks, people we all know. Actually, I think her list included most all of the people at that cooking class, and I think that's the only reason she signed up for it."

The story was unpleasant, tawdry. Jackie had hinted, in fact had boasted, to Charlie that she could exert demands on a number of Harrington's first citizens.

There was Jack Vanderpool. The rumors of their being seen together were, Jackie claimed, quite true. These meetings had included more than one noontime rendezvous at the slightly seedy Starlite Motel south of town, several miles beyond the genteel precincts of the Blue Lake Inn. Jackie had been amused by the effect of a soft-voiced hint that she planned to call on Jack's terminally ill wife, Marie.

There was Paul Dorrance. Charlie had been shocked beyond words at the suggestion that dear Uncle Paul might have feet of clay.

Jackie's further, even more ominous pressure point against the

Dorrance family involved Roger Two, and an eventual and profitable marriage. She had been explicit about a possible Dorrance heir, at which Charlie's revulsion had been complete.

If not Roger Two, Jackie had another good prospect in mind, she said, maybe an even better one, since he was old enough that she could be sure of being a rich widow while she was young enough to enjoy it.

Hearing these revelations, Charlie had asked her to leave. Jackie, however, instead of leaving town, had moved to a furnished apartment at the Harrington Arms.

As a parting taunt, the night she left, Jackie had assured Charlie that she could put anyone in Harrington in the palm of her hand if she chose to. She hinted that Hoddy Hofmeyer had a problem he'd die rather than have known. She boasted that her latest conquest was the new preacher, the Reverend Jim-Bill Sanders. From him, she said, she had cozened not money, but information precious to her future scheming, a juicy tidbit gleaned from his exhortations to his new flock to confess and repent.

Whatever it was that the Reverend Jim-Bill had told Jackie, Charlie said it had to do with the DeWitts, Ralph and Dottie. Something about money they had inherited, way back.

Jackie's last jeering warning had been personally painful. "What's more, if you ever tell anyone any part of this, I'll make sure that everyone in town believes what a few of the dirty old gossips have been saying about the two of us, you and me."

There was a pause. Greg, silent throughout the recital, now asked quietly, "And that bothered you? You kept quiet because of that kind of threat?"

Charlie answered with forthright conviction. "Of course not. You miss the point. These people who were being hurt were all people I know, people I've always known. I thought it would just make it worse for them to know Jackie had told me. And then all at once she was dead, and now I don't know what to do, really." Charlie's husky voice raised a perceptible half note and Mrs. Potter rose to put an arm around the girl's shoulders.

"Let's sort this thing out now, Charlie dear," she said comfortingly, "what of any of this you should tell Pete, and what maybe should just be buried with Jackie."

Greg's counsel and Charlie's inclinations followed her own.

With matters in their present state of shock and confusion at the courthouse, where officialdom was coping simultaneously with a murder, an apparent suicide (could MacKay have been the older prospect on Jackie's marriage list? Mrs. Potter wondered sadly.) and now with the sorry Versteeg drowning, Monday should be time enough to decide what information Charlie must give to the police. The implications were serious, in that any of Jackie's possible blackmail victims was marked, at the moment of revelation, as a potential murder suspect.

We may be obstructing the course of justice, Mrs. Potter acknowledged to herself, but surely it can wait for another day while we all think about it.

In hopes of creating a minor diversion to cheer the still slightly shaky Charlie, she spoke gently as she and Greg said good-bye.

"Before we leave, Charlie, two things. First, you always used to call me Aunt 'Genia, and I hope you'll do so again if you feel comfortable with it.

"Next, may I ask what kind of vegetarian you are? Do you eat eggs and cheese?" (The descriptive term "ovo-lacto," which Mrs. Potter had recently come across, had such a bald biologic sound to it that she could not force herself to say it.)

Whether Mrs. Potter liked the word or not, that's what Charlie was. As they left, she presented them with a wrapped loaf of her raisin bread and a package of her own special homemade English muffins.

Before they went back to Indian Point, Mrs. Potter and Greg stopped at the market for a few quick errands, and on the way Mrs. Potter told him about the bill-paying protocol of an earlier Harrington.

"On the first of every month, or no later than the second," she told him, "Mother paid her bills. She left the house all dressed up, just as she would have been to make afternoon calls, which people did in those days. Only instead of her little case of calling cards she took her Harrington Savings checkbook. She was considered quite emancipated that she was allowed to do this herself, instead of having Daddy take care of the accounts.

"Will and I usually went along, as I recall. It was worth getting cleaned up for. First we'd go to the bakery. Mr. Radebaugh, and very polite he was about it, would hand Mother the Andrews bill, which he had all ready for her. While she, being equally formal and very gracious, examined it carefully, then wrote out her check, Mr. Radebaugh gave Will and me a chocolate eclair or a jelly doughnut, either of which was a fairly rare treat for us in those days.

"Broeck's was usually the next stop—the grocery store that used to be on the same corner where the supermarket is now. Broeck's was the best. Mother and Mr. Broeck went into the little back office for the formalities, and Mrs. Broeck, very slowly and carefully, provided the treat. First she took a little pink-and-white striped paper sack and shook it out, very precisely, to make it unfold. Then, with a shiny scoop, she filled it with the biggest chocolates in the candy case, which ran the whole front length of the store. They may not have been the best, but they were certainly the biggest. Ice cream drops were what they were called—haystack-shaped humps of white fondant with almost no taste except that of sugar, covered with thin, hard dark chocolate.

"Will and I were allowed to eat one each, right there in the store. Mother put the striped sack in her handbag then and the rest had to be saved to be passed around after supper."

Mrs. Potter wanted to tell Greg about the dry goods store next, and the wonders of the little money cups with their screw caps that banged and clanged along taut brown cords from the several departments—children's, ladies' ready-to-wear, yard goods, millinery—to the office on the open balcony above. Since he seemed to be absorbed in remote, inner thought, however, she concentrated instead on her grocery list.

Sunday morning, and a nice breeze from the east carried the sound of church bells from town. Nine o'clock, thought Mrs. Potter, and time for Sunday school at the Dutch Reformed. She'd try to get to morning service at eleven at her own church, but first a big breakfast for Greg—sausage and fried apples and hot corn-bread—was already in the making.

As the food finished cooking, she took her own pot of breakfast tea to the back stoop, enjoying the September sun and the crisp, dry air. Still no killing frost, but she must remember to pick and wrap those green tomatoes by tomorrow at the latest. "Remind me, please, Greg," she told her nephew as he joined her.

"Sounds like a lot of work, Aunt 'Genia, and more green tomatoes than you and I'll ever use. Why don't you ask someone to help and then take a share? Maybe Charlotte would like some, and why don't we ask Ed Casaday?"

"Good idea, love. Would you call them for me?"

Mrs. Potter did not know which surprised her more—Greg's unwonted initiative in proposing the plan, or his choice of names for the suggested invitees. *Charlotte?* Charlie Ragsdale, of course, but Greg had hardly said two words to the girl yesterday at her house. *Ed Casaday?* That could only be John Edward, otherwise known as Eddie-boy to his employers and to most of the other shore residents on their side of Blue Lake.

The plan relieved her conscience, well schooled since her childhood in not wasting food. Now the tomatoes will be picked and wrapped and used, she thought. I suppose all my life I'm going to remember those starving children in Armenia who would *love* to have those bread crusts you're hiding under the rim of your plate, four-year-old Eugenia. Or those cooked carrots, or, nastiest of all, those canned Italian plums. Am I really still eating things, she wondered, just to please *Herbert Hoover?*

In spite of the strictures of her youth, Mrs. Potter usually cooked enough for two when she prepared a meal for one. Consequently, when Pete Felderkamp pulled into the back drive, there was plenty for him to share Greg's hearty farm breakfast on the back porch table. He insisted on making his accompanying pot of coffee himself, while Mrs. Potter continued with her tea and Greg drank his usual two glasses of milk.

The purpose of Pete's visit was to outline, for his own review and for any possible help from Greg and Mrs. Potter, the known facts to date of the three separate Harrington tragedies of Thursday night.

"This is what we know for sure so far. Maybe nothing makes

76

sense in connection with anything else, and maybe it never will, but this much I've checked out pretty thoroughly.''

About Jackie, Pete began. After the cooking class, which ended at nine, Jackie made a phone call from the new cut-rate drugstore, right near the high school. This was about nine-fifteen, maybe a little later, according to pharmacist Buddy Engstrem. Buddy had kept the drugstore open a little late that night after Doc had phoned to say that Henry Harjehausen's wife was sick and that he was sending Henry to pick up a prescription.

Buddy said Jackie had a Coke, looked at her watch and then went to the pay phone. He was ashamed to admit it to Pete, but he edged over to hear what she said. Lucky she hadn't closed the booth, because she had sort of a soft voice. He didn't get whom it was she was talking to, but he did hear her say she had broken both dates and she'd meet him—whoever it was—at the Blue Room.

Right after she left, that cooking school fellow, what's-his-name Redmond, came in and bought a roll of Tums. Cooking school, buying *Tums.* Buddy thought this was funny, a real side-splitter, but the Redmond fellow didn't seem to get the joke.

Henry came in then, got his prescription, and Buddy closed up.

About Jackie's apartment, Pete went on. He and the twins had searched the place. Nobody living in the building had heard her come in that night. Miss Ormsby, who's a little deaf, thought she had heard voices outside about ten-thirty and Mrs. Silsby, Babe, that is, thought she had heard a car door slam, she didn't know just when.

Jackie's apartment was the one originally planned for a building superintendent, before Don Davids in 3A bought the place and decided to act as super himself. Hers was on the ground floor rear and you could come in either from the front hall of the building or by its own separate entrance off the parking lot. The back door was unlocked when Pete and the boys made the search. They didn't find anything you would exactly call a clue, except that there did seem to be more cash around the place than you'd have expected, almost eight hundred dollars was what they found. Don said she paid her rent in cash. Norton's said the same thing—cash—for her rental car.

About alibis. Nobody in the class, the people who apparently had been among the last ones to see Jackie alive, seemed to have a

77

very good alibi for the time of the murder. Everybody told Pete they were just home alone or together with each other. Only that teacher, that Mr. Redmond, seemed to have any kind of proof for where he said he was, there at the guest cottage.

Seems he's got a kind of dictating gismo, Pete went on. He calls it a "tank," and it's in his Chicago office. All he has to do, any time of night or day, is to dial the special phone number for this tank and then he can dictate a whole batch of stuff right into the phone. Whatever he dictates gets recorded on some kind of tape there. Then when the secretary comes in next morning, the first thing she's supposed to do is switch it on and see if there's a recording waiting for her to go to work on.

This Redmond said he'd been on the phone dictating a new chapter of his cookbook from about ten-thirty, he thought, until nearly midnight. Pete checked the long-distance phone records on this, and sure enough, there had been a call put in from the cottage phone to that special Chicago number at 10:21 and it had kept on going until 11:46. Pete even checked by calling the secretary herself on the regular office line and she said, yes, she'd come in on Friday morning to find a long recording to transcribe, a whole new chapter in the cookbook.

If it wasn't for the pretty certain-sure evidence that Mr. Moore had killed the girl and then himself, Pete knew he would have to do some more checking. As it was, it looked pretty well wrapped up. There was the farewell note. He didn't need to remind Mrs. Potter what it said after the part where Mr. Moore wondered if she would ever be able to forgive him. Or had she forgotten?

Pete could quote it by heart: "*What I had to do tonight was terrible beyond belief. . . . When it's all over, I hope I can count on you to understand. . . . Always remember that I am yours. . . .*"

"What makes it final, to my thinking," Pete said, "is that post-script. I don't know about that Dalmatian coast business" (Mrs. Potter found her face suddenly hot) "but you can't miss the meaning in '*when I put out the light at last.*' Pretty sad, pretty bleak. Can't have much doubt about a suicide after you read that, can you?"

The other part of it, about Jackie's murder, Pete went on, was beginning to look pretty well tied up, too. The twins, with their new Detective Investigator (all right, it was a mail-order kit, but it worked and the boys knew how to use it) had found MacKay's fingerprints on the left front door of Jackie's rental car. And Bertha had to admit that the knife was in the rack in the kitchen when she did the supper dishes Thursday night, or else she'd have noticed. Not much got past Bertha. In fact, she told Pete, come to think of it, she'd used that very knife cutting up cold roast beef and potatoes and onions to make MacKay's supper salad before he went to the class.

Now all of them knew the knife wasn't there the next morning. So MacKay had the opportunity, the weapon (the book said there were three things to check), and as for the motive, well, Pete had some pretty good theories about that, too.

Anyway, he was mighty glad not to have to go over those alibis a second time. Everybody had been mad as hops when he asked some questions the first round, and his job wouldn't be worth two shakes if Mrs. Dorrance chewed him out again.

"You may not realize what I'm up against," Pete said. "Now you folks, Mrs. Potter—the old Andrews family, the Dorrances the Vermeers, all your crowd—you just aren't too used to being asked where you were when, and why. Anything bothersome for you, any problem, you just get on the phone and get it cleared up in one call. Call the major, call Don Pfingsten at the bank, call whoever's county attorney, call the editor of the paper—all you have to do is tell the right person you have a little problem, and it gets handled."

Mrs. Potter nodded sympathetically. She could see, she told him, that it might be hard for him to check certain alibis, but she hoped he'd go on and tell them what happened at the Blue Room Thursday night.

Pete poured himself another cup of coffee and continued. "You know Elsie Walters, sure you do," he told her. "That's Bertha and Alice's sister, bartender at the Inn is what she is.

"Well, I just got back from going to see her this morning," Pete said. "Met her and all the whole family of them, the girls and old Louie, just as they were leaving the house, and I walked the way to Sunday school with them. They still all go, just the way they always did when old lady Walters was alive."

According to Elsie, MacKay met Jackie there at the Blue Room after the cooking class, and they left together. Separate cars, of course, but Louie said he followed out right after her, just a bit after ten-thirty.

Varlene was there at the Blue Room, too, Elsie and Louie both said, and she left a little later, pretty much spiffed.

Now everybody knew old Louie wasn't quite right, but you could count on his word, always could, anyway. Even old man Norton at the garage always had a good word for him, though he couldn't keep him on there; said the other fellows were always teasing him and nobody got any work done. Anyway, it's a good job for old Louie there running the parking lot at the Inn, and there's not much gets past him, even if he is a little loony.

"And that's about all of it," Pete finished, "except for what Doc had to say. I'll read you the notes the twins took on that."

Jacquelyn Morsback's death had been caused by the severing of the right jugular, one of the trunk veins of the neck. A sharp, narrow blade had been plunged into the hollow of the throat, then jerked forcibly to the right. Death had been certain, bloody, quiet, but probably not instantaneous. There was no sign of drugs or alcohol beyond the two drinks she had at the Inn. There was no sign of other blows or further violence. Miss Morsback was, however, about six weeks pregnant.

MacKay Moore had died from carbon monoxide poisoning from the exhaust of his automobile in a closed garage. There was no apparent other cause, except for a slight bruise on his forehead where he had fallen to the concrete floor, possibly in a last-minute change of mind and an attempt to open the garage doors.

Varlene Versteeg had died, quite simply, of drowning. The alcohol level in her blood could not be accurately determined after two days in the water, but a count of her unaccustomed drinks at the Inn, as attested by barlady Elsie Walters, suggested that intoxication had been the probable reason for her to blunder out on the old road to the Bridge, slip down the old childhood path to the inlet, and lose her footing there. There was no sign of any blow or other injury.

Mrs. Potter had a sudden, sharp recollection, a picture of eight-year-old Varlene, red-cheeked, square and sturdy, white-blond pigtails bouncing as she splashed in the shallow water, joining a hilarious Andrews family safari for frogs in the marshy upper waters of Little Blue. Who else was there she could not remember, only the sunny day, the reeds and clear, shallow blue water, people in bare feet with rolled-up pants' legs, Grandma with her skirts tucked high, people laughing, frogs elusive, and eventually a memorable feast of fried frogs' legs.

She could not recall why Varlene should have been with them that day, except that all Harrington children knew the old bridge and fished there. Probably they had simply gathered her into the family party. Her memory was of a solemn, earnest little girl, gradually drawn into the laughter and excitement of the chase.

"So that's about it," Pete repeated, bringing her back to the present. "We think the county attorney is going to put the lid on it. MacKay stabbed Jackie for reasons of his own and then he took the easy way out. Varlene got drunk, is what she did, slipped her foot by the edge of the inlet, and got herself drowned.

The three sat silent, but Mrs. Potter's mind was screaming. *No. No matter how it looks, there is no way MacKay could have stabbed that girl.*

Another set of church bells sounded from the direction of town, and Mrs. Potter rose. "I really need to be in church this morning," she told them. "I've got to stop thinking about all this for a bit, and then ask a little help for us all."

Most of all for those three who are dead.

Pete and Greg, in an effort to relieve the serious concerns of the morning, offered to police-up the kitchen, and they both professed to find this term very funny.

So Mrs. Potter went upstairs to collect a hat, a floppy-brimmed straw of a soft, faded red. It was not and had never been fashionable, but without a head covering of some kind, in spite of present-day customs, Mrs. Potter would have been uncomfortable in church.

A murder, a suicide, an accident. As always when she was puzzled, Mrs. Potter's first impulse was to reach for a lined yellow legal pad—the same kind she used for grocery lists, party plans, family correspondence—to try to bring her thoughts into some kind of order.

Jotting down notes from Pete's earlier report, she briefly listed (1) what they know, and (2) what they think they know; then she halted.

I can't believe what I'm thinking, she told herself. All of my conjectures are about people I know, *have* known, most of them for years, some since my earliest childhood. One's old friends simply do not get involved in matters of violent death, either as victims or assailants.

Yet there was the incontrovertible fact of Jackie's murder. The force and precision of the knife across that beautiful creamy throat could not have been an accident.

Charlie's story had named people Jackie might be pressuring: the three Dorrances, parents and son; the Hofmeyers; the DeWitts; Jack Vanderpool. These comprised almost the entire enrollment of the cooking class.

However, in Harrington or elsewhere, there could be others equally (or even more) suspect. It would be easier to think that the murder had been the work of a vicious and unknown outsider. Maybe it was a jealous lover from wherever Jackie had lived previously. Maybe it had been a mindless attack by a drug-crazed vagrant.

If so, Mrs. Potter decided, such matters were for the police. Pete and the twins would do the best they could.

Reluctantly formed opinion told her, however, that if one of the members of the class, one of the friends of her youth, was involved, then perhaps she—with her years of acquaintance and the added objectivity of her years away—could understand who had been driven to this violence. Perhaps she, from this special viewpoint, could put herself into the killer's tormented mind.

Mrs. Potter decided she must think and remember more about these people whom she knew so well. This important question was what these old friends might, or might not, be able to do, and what they might be able to take in the way of provocation.

Of one thing she was certain. MacKay's note to her was not that of a murderer or a suicide. In his own richly overblown style, he was, she knew, simply apologizing to her for what did indeed seem to him terrible and beyond belief—that he had joined Jackie at the Blue Room instead of taking her, 'Genia, there after the class, and that he felt guilty because he had not been completely truthful about it. In this part of the letter, Pete had mistaken the perfervid apology of a gallant old Don Juan for the last words of an anguished murderer.

The postscript that Pete had found a depressing confirmation of MacKay's intent to kill himself—what had been Pete's words? *sad, bleak?*—had seemed quite different to her. Mrs. Potter recognized this only as a continuing gambit in the mutually enjoyable game of flirtation they had been playing for years. MacKay was, by this mention of the Dalmatian coast, simply reassuring her that he still thought of her as a desirable woman. And as for "putting out the light" he had meant just that, she thought, and no more.

She realized the contradictions in her interpretations. First, in the body of the letter, she believed that MacKay was employing his usual hyperbole. Second, in the postscript, she was insisting that he was making a simple statement.

However contradictory, all of this connected with "what he had to do now." Mrs. Potter thought of the open phone book at hand, the stack of memo pads, the pencils at the ready, the still-glowing lamp on the polished desk. Whatever MacKay was about to do then, she felt sure, it was not going to lead to his self-destruction. She suddenly felt sure that it related to Jackie's phone call to him from the drugstore. MacKay would never have been able to resist a woman's plea for help, any woman's, most especially an appeal from a woman as devastatingly beautiful as Jackie Morsback.

In addition to MacKay's note, there were a number of troubling questions that apparently she alone knew enough to wonder about.

What had Varlene been doing at MacKay's house after the cooking class? Bertha was too good a housekeeper to have left a stray hairpin on the garage steps. The brassy gold one Mrs. Potter had, by chance, poked into her own hair the morning of MacKay's death could only be a counterpart to those that anchored the crown of heavy yellow braids circling Varlene's round head.

For that matter, why should Varlene have chosen that night after the class to go out and get drunk, something that apparently she had not been known to do before?

What was Jack Vanderpool signaling to Jackie when he held up two fingers and she nodded yes?

Why did Edward make puppylike advances to Roger Two, only to be rebuffed?

What was John Edward Casaday doing in Harrington, anyway? One might have thought New York, perhaps San Francisco? A young man who appeared to be what Mrs. Potter would call "a little light on his feet" seemed unlikely to feel at home in this small town. (She refused to use the term *gay*, thinking it in this context a meaningless waste of a lovely, lighthearted word.)

Why was Ralph sheltering Dottie, just as he had done when she came in from country school to Harrington High? Mrs. Potter remembered her then, shy, young Dottie DeBoos, along with the Walters' children and Harold DeFreese and Kenneth Oberholzer, all of them timid in their first encounter with "town kids"—those urban sophisticates, the privileged ones, the city dwellers.

With the kind of irrepressible and irresponsible twists of mind that occasionally beset her, Mrs. Potter stopped to wonder about Dottie's initials. How would you monogram a pocket flap for someone named Dottie DeBoos DeWitt?

Shaking her head at her own mental vagaries, she returned to the yellow pad.

Who was the father of Jackie's baby? Pete had appeared unconcerned about her pregnancy.

Why was Lynette so defensive, and what was shaking her usual aplomb? How were things going with Paul, and at the Dorrance plant? Was Julie drinking more than usual?

What, she asked herself, was going on in Harrington?

If the answers were not being sought through official channels,

Mrs. Potter decided that she'd do what she could. There were too many loose ends to be ignored.

Starting with that late September Sunday evening, Mrs. Potter began her not-entirely-social rounds.

Lynette had suggested their coming to supper, and when the invitation was repeated on the red sandstone steps of the church after morning services, Mrs. Potter accepted for both herself and her nephew. Monday it was to be dinner at the Hofmeyers. Greg had chosen Tuesday morning to invite Charlotte (formerly Charlie) Ragsdale and Ed (formerly Eddie-boy) Casaday to help pick green tomatoes. For Tuesday night Mrs. Potter had accepted the dinner invitation of the DeWitts, expressing Greg's regrets, with Jack Vanderpool to be their one other guest.

Each night before she went to sleep Mrs. Potter found herself with more questions, and each day before lunch she went over her yellow lined pads with more notes and additions and changes.

Today, staring out across the blue of the lake, she jotted a reminder of the two-wheeled hand truck in MacKay's garage; a cart upon which anyone might have been able to move an unconscious man. Like the others, this was a point to ponder briefly, but it led nowhere.

The slow Sunday afternoon came to an end and she put aside her papers to shower and dress. Whatever she had (or had not) accomplished, this evening she and Greg were to go to the Dorrances', to their big near-replica of a southern mansion on the beautiful but now unfashionable southeast side of the lake. With the long Dorrance lake frontage, it actually mattered very little that their nearest neighbor on the north, a half mile away, was the Starlite Motel, and that on the south shore, even farther away, was the nearest of the small, somewhat tacky summer cottages, now interspersed with an occasional modern slant-roofed condominium.

As they drove south out of town, on a sudden impulse Mrs. Potter asked Greg to pull in at the motel. Even though it was still full daylight, the rusting neon sign was dimly glowing, and a few uncertain lights flashed around the word *Vacancy* below.

"Please wait here for me a minute?" she asked him. "An old friend of mine runs this place, and as long as we're a few minutes early for the Dorrances, I'd like to stop in and say hello. No, please don't bother to come. I'll only be a minute."

Well, it might be true at that, she assured herself as she went in through the grimy blond wood door which marked the office. My old friends do show up everywhere around here.

It was a strange face, however, that greeted her at the desk, a bald froglike face surfacing out of a Des Moines *Sunday Register*, a face centered with a wet-looking unlighted cigar.

"Naw, don't know anybody by name of Vanderpool." The cigar came out long enough for him to answer. "Nobody that name on the register, far's I recall." The cigar went back into the soft mouth and the face went behind the newspaper.

"Perhaps if I described him? Tall man, about my age, reddish hair, very high forehead?"

"Naw. Never saw him."

With more determination than she would have given herself credit for, Mrs. Potter held her ground. In that moment she saw a woman's face, vaguely familiar, in a doorway just beyond and behind the figure at the desk. Without speaking, the woman pointed toward an arrow and the words *Rest Rooms,* then disappeared down the dingy corridor.

"Excuse me, I'm going to find your ladies' room," she said resolutely. It was worth a try.

As she turned quickly down the hallway she had to sprint to follow the scurrying figure, whom she suddenly recognized.

"Orma! Orma Kalmers! We sat next to each other in Miss Mattoon's Latin class!"

The woman motioned toward the door marked *Dolls.* Once inside she spoke hurriedly, her voice low.

"He'd kill me if I let on the name of any of our day trade," she said, "but who cares? This dump is about to fold up anyway."

The voice became a whisper. "I heard you ask about Jack Vanderpool, and I sure *do* remember him, 'Genia. Probably a whole

86

lot better than you do from the old days, all things considered. What counts now is, Marie was a real good friend of mine and it makes me pretty sore to see how he's carrying on.''

Orma opened the door slightly and took a quick look down the hall. ''You bet old Jack comes here, couple times a week all this summer. Takes Number Fourteen, where you can park in back and not come in through the lobby. Shows up about two in the afternoon, most times.''

Orma's whisper became a hiss. ''Of course *she* gets here first and gets the key, fills the ice bucket from the machine in the hall to have everything ready for him. Fine goings-on for a man whose wife is dying, and her an absolute saint to boot.''

The *she* of the clandestine meetings appeared to answer Mrs. Potter's quick description.

''Yeah, dark, young, knockout.'' Orma slid down the hall as she spoke.

Mrs. Potter left the small room quickly, eager to get away from the whispering echo, from the faded plastic flowers and the overpowering floral scent that bespoke public toilet. She rushed past the equally dingy door marked *Guys* and past the frog face at the desk.

''Sorry, Greg,'' she managed almost cheerily as she got into the little car beside him, ''new people here now, it seems, but I wanted to ask about the couple who used to run the place. Now we can go to the Dorrances' and be right on time.''

Paul, Lynette's husband, welcomed them as they parked in the circle of the crushed-stone driveway. His ritual kiss of greeting was delivered with his customary apologetic stiff bow, almost a parody of a curtsy. Pudgy, diffident, sheltered by thick gray hair and eyebrows, Paul appeared an unlikely progenitor for Roger Two, who had remained on the open porch, holding his Greek sculpture pose beside one of the tall columns there until they were well on their way in his direction. Paul limped along briskly to keep up with Greg's long strides as they followed Mrs. Potter to the door.

Lynette took immediate charge as they entered. They'd go straight on through and out to the lakeside for cocktails on the dock, she said. Paul was to light the charcoal right now in the outside grill for the steaks later. Roger was to put on a light sweater under his blazer, please darling, because the lake breeze would be cool and he had sounded sniffly earlier in the day. 'Genia had a wrap? Fine. They would proceed to the gazebo.

The small screened summerhouse at the end of the long dock was delightful in the warm September early evening. Lynette, with her usual attention to detail, had provided fruit juices on the drinks tray for Greg. Paul poured Wild Turkey on ice for Mrs. Potter, his wife and himself, with a generous hand.

Roger Two said he'd stay with white wine on the rocks, thanks, to save calories. Lynette said wasn't it marvelous that he had never put on an ounce over his high school football weight? Roger Two flattened his stomach muscles and gazed out at the western sunset over the lake. Paul slumped in his canvas chair and ate another handful of salted nuts. Mrs. Potter sipped her bourbon and savored a large, garlicky black olive.

Then, hoping to postpone any mention of the triple tragedies of the week, in spite of earlier resolves to pursue the subject, Mrs. Potter attempted the diversion of food talk. "Have you or Roger Two any bright ideas for using poached chicken breasts?" she inquired. "You missed this, Paul, but that was the assignment at the cooking class the other evening. I'm sure that Lynette thought of something wonderful on the spot."

"Only that my recipe is going to be something served on or with wild rice," Lynette declared. "I've found a great new place in Wisconsin where I can get it, and it's awfully good. Clean, dark and husky, long grain, just the way we always loved it."

"Only fifty times as expensive," Paul said mildly. "Do you know that we three are probably of the last generation ever to think of wild rice as anything but a luxury?"

"All I've ever had was the kind that's mixed with white rice,"

Greg confessed. "I think it's terrific, but I've never had it straight."

"We all grew up on it," Lynette told him. "Whenever Daddy went hunting or fishing in Minnesota he'd buy it directly from the Indians there, and come home with bags of it."

"Mother's brothers used to send it to us, the same way," Mrs. Potter added. "We always had it with game—duck or pheasant, venison or elk of course, and with rabbit or quail—and all of those were on the menu quite often at Indian Point."

"With currant jelly in little dots on the top in the serving dish," Lynette recalled gleefully. "And then what was left over we had next morning for breakfast, heated up again, hot like oatmeal, with cream and sugar."

"You had wild rice for breakfast?" Greg was incredulous.

"That's right, love. Your father and I did, too. You must give me the address of your Wisconsin place, Lynette—I suppose it's under the name of Chief Something or Other? He can call himself Sitting Bull for all I care, as long as he has the real stuff, for less than the price of an arm and a leg, that is."

"I didn't say it was cheap," Lynette said firmly, then changed the subject. "Another quick drink, everybody, and by then the charcoal should be ready."

Glasses in hand, they moved back to the brick-paved terrace on the lake side of the house. Paul broiled, to Lynette's carefully timed directions, an enormous thick and tender steak, which she then carved and served in thick pink slices topped with her own special garlic-herb butter. There was a bowl of green salad, skill-fully mixed by Roger Two (my own dressing, he said, something I invented myself, using Poupon mustard) as his mother directed operations at the grill. There was a loaf of hot sliced and buttered sourdough bread. For dessert, along with big cups of rum-laced coffee, there was a plate of Lynette's famous double-chocolate malt brownies.

"And what do you make of the antics of our young chief of police and his deputies?" Lynette inquired, as she set out the coffee-pot and the rum bottle, and nodded to Paul to pour.

"Antics? I thought he was handling things pretty well, consider-ing what's been dumped in his lap these last few days," Mrs. Potter answered, "and when you think of what's happened in town. A newcomer gets murdered, and a pretty glamorous newcomer at that. A good friend—of yours and Paul's and all of us—dies in what has to be a terrible accident—or else he kills himself, which to me is impossible to believe. And a nice, respectable junior high teacher, whose family we've known all our lives, is drowned in what apparently was a drunken fall. I think Pete junior has his hands full and is doing pretty well."

"Well, of course the circumstances are trying, 'Genia, and I'm as sorry as you are about MacKay's death, however it happened. I was just wondering how you felt about young Felderkamp asking questions about how and where *you* spent last Thursday evening?"

Mrs. Potter passed the question along. "Paul, do you really feel Pete isn't up to the situation? And you, Roger Two?"

Paul made vague noises. "Too, too bad to have this sort of thing happen in Harrington," he said. "Young Felderkamp may be in over his head—"

Roger Two shook his golden mane in a disparaging way and held out his cup for more coffee.

Lynette answered for them both. "Don't be so wishy-washy," she told them. "I for one am not going to tolerate any more of Pete's hardheaded Dutch impertinence and that is that."

"We've probably had the last of his questions," her husband said soothingly. "After all, he did not have to ask you about the evening, since you were at the class. And possibly it made sense for him to question Roger. You tell me that he escorted the girl there that night."

"Not really escorted, Dad," Roger Two put in. "We met outside and went in together. She had her car, you know."

"Pete still had his job to do in asking you and all of us what we were doing that night." This was, for Paul, the equivalent of taking a strong stand. Mrs. Potter remembered when he and Lynette had been married. There were those who insisted she had chosen him, a several-times-removed cousin, for two reasons. One was that she would not have to change her name from Dorrance, which in Harrington was like being named Rockefeller-Roosevelt-Astor. The other was that there would be no question about who was running the show.

"Had you heard that the Morsback girl was pregnant?" Mrs. Potter asked, and waited for shock waves.

The question had less effect than she had expected. Lynette said lightly that she'd always thought that girl was something of a tramp.

Paul's earlier vague murmurings were repeated, his mouth tightening, as he remarked that it was not only too, too bad, but also a shame and a blot on the good name of the town.

Roger Two sipped his coffee and stretched his legs, then sneezed. Lynette said she had *told* him he was coming down with something and perhaps he should have a bit of rum in his coffee, along with the rest of them. Greg defied his diet, unexpectedly, by saying that *he'd* have a drop, if he might.

As she considered the matter later that evening, Mrs. Potter told herself that any one of the three Dorrances might resent Pete's questionings, however tactful, and might possibly have had some (enough? she wondered) cause to want Jackie removed from the scene. Any one of them, also, depended on the corroboration of the other two that they had all been at home the evening of the murder. Not necessarily an ironclad alibi, for she knew that all three would have considered any lie quite justified if the good name of Dorrance was threatened by any association, however, remote, with an ugly and sordid slaughter in a parking lot.

The evening provided a tremendous side benefit, however, for Greg, of whose mechanical and automotive interests Mrs. Potter had had only an inkling until his after-dinner conversation with Paul and Lynette.

"I hadn't any idea you were so knowledgeable about this moped business of ours," Lynette told him, "even to knowing just how and when Daddy decided to make the changeover from power lawnmowers. You must come and visit the factory."

Then, in her positive way, she added an aside for her husband. "Paul, I'm sure we can find Greg a job at the plant." She turned to her guests. "It would be good for you, Greg, to have something to do. You look a lot better than when you got here and it's high time you got out of the house for a bit, for 'Genia's sake as much as your own."

As the moped conversation went on, Roger Two, at his mother's urging, offered to show Mrs. Potter the new hobby shop he and his father shared, just off the terrace.

Both of them were presently engaged in making carved replicas of old wooden decoys, he said, and the smell of wood, the gleam and precision of their sharp carving tools and knives filled the shop. The names of the carving tools were unfamiliar to Mrs. Potter, as Roger opened drawer after drawer of carefully labeled instruments. Some knives resembled long, sharp needles, others, stilettos, and there was a fantastic range of those in scimitar shapes, evoking thoughts of Arabian Nights intrigue, of gauzy veils and dancing girls and fierce eunuchs guarding the sultan's harem.

Marveling at their number and variety, Mrs. Potter turned from the tools as Roger led her to several wood carvings in progress. "This mallard is mine," he told her. "Nearly finished now. I think it's rather good, actually."

Admiring Roger's craftsmanship, Mrs. Potter had a generous impulse. "My father had a handsome old Canadian goose decoy," she said, "and maybe you'd like to see it."

Then her attention was drawn to a small and malodorous wire cage at the far end of the room. Within the meshed enclosure was a drooping mallard drake, his tail feathers dragging nearly to the newspaper-covered floor.

"Why, he's starving!" Mrs. Potter exclaimed. "Look, he's been tearing up the paper for food, and his water dish is completely dry! How long has he been here like this?"

"Norm Swanson brought him in—oh, last week, I guess it was," Roger Two said indifferently. "I was using him as a model, but this has been a busy week with one thing and another. I'll try to get Norm to pick him up tomorrow. Not much use as a model now, dragging around that way."

Mrs. Potter had left the shop as he was speaking, returning with a glass of water and a half loaf of the garlic bread from the patio sideboard.

"There you are, old fellow," she told him, as she filled the drake's cup with water and put water-soaked bits of bread beneath his yellow bill. "Oh, my, I hope we've got to you in time."

Roger Two did not look up from the decoy on the workbench as she spoke. He took a few deft cuts in the wood with first one, then another sharp carving tool. "No matter," he remarked idly. "I think I'm getting it now pretty well. And thanks again for the offer of the goose decoy. That's one I'd really like to have."

With unwonted stiffness, Mrs. Potter reminded him that the old wooden goose could only be on loan, and that she would mention the offer to his father later in the season when perhaps they would have more time for carving.

When they left the house later and were driving back around the north shore of the lake to Indian Point, Greg told Mrs. Potter many things about mopeds that it had never occurred to her to want to know. She refrained from telling him about Roger Two and the dying mallard.

That same September Sunday night before she went to sleep, Mrs. Potter stared at her lined yellow pad, thinking of new questions.

Taking up her pen, she wrote hastily, as her mind contrived possible explanations—outrageous scenarios, she told herself—for Jackie's murder.

The first of these dealt with Lynette. Lynette was always first, as she had been since they were children. She would imagine a scenario for Lynette, suggesting how Jackie was killed, and why:

LYNETTE

"You probably think I want to hang on to Roger Two," Lynette tells Jackie scornfully, "or you think I actually care that you're pregnant." The two women are speaking at Jackie's apartment, where Lynette has gone to confront her after the cooking class. Paul and Roger Two were asleep or watching television and they did not hear her leave.

Jackie begins well-rehearsed lines about public disgrace to the Dorrance name. Lynette interrupts.

"You think the Dorrances need to worry about a thing like that? A pregnant bride or a bastard baby? I thought you were smarter than that."

93

Jackie responds with equal scorn. "Smart enough to marry your darling Roger, anyway. Smart enough to run things around here—the plant *and* the town—even better than you do. I'm just as tough as you are and a lot younger and more attractive. I've had a government job for the last few years that taught me all there is to know about committee infighting and how to run a meeting so people will do what I want them to do."

Jackie looks at Lynette with an air of calm challenge, and continues. "You, madam queen, are going to retire," she tells her. "Roger is going to develop the east end of the lake with all that waterfront you're so proud of, and make more money than the Dorrances ever saw before, and I'll show him how to do it. And I'm going to run Harrington, just the way you do, but with a lot more style."

Lynette feigns a strategic retreat. She asks Jackie to accompany her to her car, perhaps suggesting that she has brought a large sum of cash with her.

In the parking lot Lynette takes from her car the sharp boning knife she has brought from her own kitchen—an idea inspired by the demonstration at the class.

Using knowledge gained in biology classes and in her nurse's training, plus the drive of her strong, well-disciplined small body, Lynette plunges the knife into Jackie's throat in precisely the right spot. She then removes it calmly and wraps it in Kleenex (she is always organized) and quietly drives back home before she is missed.

The tissue is flushed away, the knife carefully cleaned and put back in place. (In Harrington, there will be no laboratory examination of kitchen knives, at least not of those in the kitchen of the town's first family.)

Lynette notes that the kitchen curtains look a little limp. She leaves a note for Alice, who comes in each morning at eight, reminding her that these should be washed and freshly starched.

How would you like it, Mrs. Potter asked herself as she finished writing, if an old friend of *yours* found it this easy to imagine *you* in the role of killer? She felt uncomfortable. Lynette had always ruled the roost in Harrington, granted, but she had worked hard and won the title fairly (except maybe for that one small rival company in bankruptcy court).

No one will ever see these, she told herself apologetically. Forgive me, Lynette, and anybody else I write about. I don't really think you did it. Certainly not that Paul did, although she made up a story about him next.

Paul Dorrance

Mrs. Potter's announcement of Jackie's pregnancy at dinner that night actually has come as no surprise to any of the Dorrances. Paul's consternation arises because it is now to be a published fact in the community.

Jackie and Paul have been conducting what was for him a first, tentative, and highly guilt-ridden affair. Jackie shrewdly plays on Paul's need for praise and reassurance. They have had a discreet weekend together in Minneapolis and after that he decides to end the liaison.

Jackie uses unerring aim in finding his most vulnerable and painful spot. She tells him that their Minneapolis weekend was a great bore for her.

She then tells him he is going to become her doting father-in-law, and why.

Paul's revulsion at this announcement is complete. His own sense of guilt and the possibility that the child may be his own, rather than his son's, is more than he can bear.

He goes to Jackie's apartment sometime during the cooking school class and awaits her return, armed with a sharp, deadly knife from his wood-carving tools. When she arrives, after leaving MacKay at the Inn, she again taunts and enrages him, tells him he is too fat and lame to catch her. Then, surprised by his strength and violent intent, she tries to escape.

Jackie runs out of the apartment, but is too late in reaching her car to get away. Paul returns home to Lynette with a report of a Chamber of Commerce meeting, to which she does not listen.

Writing about Roger Two will be easier, Mrs. Potter thought, still upset by the scene in the hobby room at the Dorrances earlier in the evening.

ROGER TWO

"No problem," is Roger Two's response to the news that Jackie is pregnant. "I have the name of a good place in Sioux City. Will five hundred be enough?"

As he casually peels off the bills, Jackie amazes him with her insistence that he marry her. He suggests that the baby may not be his. She is virtuously indignant and threatens to go to his mother.

Roger Two stubbornly refuses to face either alternative—responsibility for the pregnancy or disgrace to the Dorrance name. He (as was Lynette) has been made aware of the murderous appeal of knives by the cooking class demonstration.

When Jackie insists on going home alone after the class, he follows her car and sees MacKay meet her at the Inn. Returning home, he enters the wood-working shop quietly from the patio entrance, selects a lethal tool (or perhaps goes to the kitchen for a knife) and waits for Jackie in the parking lot behind her apartment.

She tries to escape him, but he easily restrains and stabs her, then returns home, uses a new conditioner on his hair, watches the late movie on TV.

That last was horrid, Mrs. Potter told herself. You shouldn't be enjoying this.

Next morning, Monday, Julie Hofmeyer had telephoned. Dying to see her, 'Genia dear, and that *darling* Greg. They still could come to dinner tonight? Absolute *heaven* to have someone in the kitchen again, and Eddie was a treasure. At seven? *Perfect.* So much to talk about.

Before evening there were several things to be done, and the first would be a condolence call to Varlene's great-aunt and uncle. Although Mrs. Potter had never known them well, Walter and Carrie Versteeg and the Andrews family had been good friends in Grandpa's time, and the recollection of a laughing, red-cheeked child, blond braids dancing the sun, and of Grandma's obvious delight in her company on the frog-catching day, again brought a lump to her throat.

Instead of ordering florist's flowers—Harrington Pots and Posies maintained an uncertain supply of these and its facilities would be overtaxed at the moment—Mrs. Potter looked to her own garden. The smaller dahlias were beautiful now, in a rainbow of colors from dusky blackberry to palest apricot and deep rose. When she had cut enough for several large bouquets and put them in the deep cutting pail to harden in cool water, she looked in the old pantry for suitable containers.

One bouquet she'd take to Bertha later, and there was a big green pottery jug which appeared to be right for this. For the Versteegs, however, she found on the top shelf exactly what she wanted—Grandma's old cut glass basket. It had probably been a wedding present to Grandma and Grandpa, and perhaps it would be something of a prize for a present-day collector.

How perfect, she thought. The Versteegs will treasure the vase as a gift, and it is completely right that Grandma's glass basket and the flowers from her much-loved old garden should carry her message of sympathy and sorrow at Varlene's lonely drowning.

Aunt Carrie was resting, a bustling neighbor told her when she brought her offering to the door of the neat white square house on East Third Street. However, she was told, Uncle Walter would receive her in the front parlor.

There in the gloom, heavy plush curtains drawn against the late morning September sun, she found Walter Versteeg. His back was ramrod-stiff, his eyes fixed straight ahead, as he sat in a carved mahogany armchair that was almost a twin of those in the front parlor at Indian Point.

As Mrs. Potter spoke her name and offered her words of sympathy, Carrie entered the room and motioned Mrs. Potter to a matching stiff mahogany settee, where she seated herself primly beside her.

"Poor Varlene," she said, shaking her head, its thin gray braids wound tightly in a stiff double circle, a reminder of Varlene's thick golden crown. A tear dripped down the long thin cheek and was quickly wiped away by a neatly folded white handkerchief held in a spotted, arthritic old hand. "We were always afraid she'd go bad, the way her mother did, but we never thought it would take her this way."

Her husband spoke for the first time. "Drinking, that's what did it. Drinking, driving, who knows what kind of carrying on she'd come to?"

He seemed to forget that Mrs. Potter was sitting beside his wife on the hard slippery settee. "Just like her mother. I always told her she'd have to guard her ways or she'd come to a bad end."

Mrs. Potter recalled long-forgotten details of an old Harrington scandal.

Varlene's grandfather, Peter Versteeg, an upright man, a strict father, had known that the wages of sin were eternal hellfire. When he learned (only by chance after prayer meeting, Mrs. Potter thought) that his unmarried daughter Bernice was "in a family way" he knew it was his duty to mete out righteous punishment.

Bernice's young lover came to the house to ask permission for their marriage. It was denied. The boy was a migrant harvester, in a day in which traveling teams came in with harvesters and reapers, since few farmers could afford their own large equipment. He was Polish, he was Catholic, he was itinerant. All three of these were unforgivable sins to Peter Versteeg.

When the two insisted that they must marry, the old man asked them to wait while he left to think on it.

When he returned, it was with his loaded squirrel gun. At close range he shot and killed the young man, then turned the gun on his daughter. His shot was low and hit her knee.

From that time on, Peter Versteeg never again spoke to Bernice, although he did not turn her out of his house and apparently she had no place else to go. He went on trial for the young man's death but was acquitted by a jury who agreed that he had only been doing his duty. Bernice, alone and unattended in her dotted-swiss bedroom, died in childbirth. Her father, remorseful at last, shot himself the next day.

Peter's childless younger brother Walter and his wife Carrie took the baby and named her Varlene. Nearly as righteous and unyielding as Peter himself, they had raised the child, Mrs. Potter felt sure, in an atmosphere of repression and reproach. It seemed likely that she was often reminded of her sinful mother's misdeed and of her own role in the tragedy, simply by being born: the cause of her mother's death and of her grandfather's.

Could it be that the day of the frog-catching was one of the few joyful moments in a solemn, guilt-ridden childhood?

Walter's querulous voice brought her back to the present. "All started this summer, didn't it, Carrie? She began getting those outlandish ideas?"

"What happened this summer?" Mrs. Potter asked gently.

"Don't know, something about thinking she was ugly and fat, wishing she had black hair, nearly killed herself trying to stick to some kind of crazy diet. I think she wanted to look like that new girl, you know, the one that got herself stabbed the other day? A fine lot *she* was, I may say." Aunt Carrie sniffed loudly, now perhaps as much in scorn as in sorrow.

"I didn't know she knew the Morsback girl before the cooking school class," Mrs. Potter said. "Did they see each other often?"

"Don't think they exchanged two words, far as I know," Carrie Versteeg said loudly, more to her husband than to Mrs. Potter. "Way I figured it, Varlene just saw the Jezebel and made up her mind she wanted to look like her."

"Like her mother, just like her mother." Walter's square shoulders rocked back and forth in the stiff, uncomfortable chair. "Just like when Peter had to shoot that young no-good Polack. You remember that well, don't you, Louisa? You knew my brother Peter?"

The old man was calling her by her grandmother's name, but Mrs. Potter answered quietly. "Right after prayer meeting, wasn't it, Walter? Yes, of course. And after the baby was born and her mother died, I think Varlene came to live with you?"

"So she did, so she did. And we tried to give her a good Christian upbringing. Now see what it's all come to." Walter retreated into silence.

"We've had such a time of tragedy here in town," Mrs. Potter continued cautiously. "Now, MacKay Moore was a good friend of mine—"

"Yes, we *knew*." Carrie looked at her closely. "Heard you two were sweet on each other, although if you don't mind my saying so, we thought you were a little past that sort of thing."

"Be that as it may," Mrs. Potter went on hurriedly, "and there wasn't really anything to it, I was wondering if Varlene knew Mr. Moore at all?"

Walter's hearing suddenly became sharper. "Why, that philandering young whippersnapper!" (Mrs. Potter's eyebrows arched. *Whippersnapper?* MacKay, a man nearly seventy?)

"I recall a few years back when that Moore fellow came here to Harrington. Wasn't a woman in town he didn't take a shine to. Of course, our Varlene didn't know him. If she had of, I'd have taken a horsewhip to both of them, and don't think I couldn't do it either." Walter sat up even straighter in the hard-backed chair.

"Now, Walter," Carrie said soothingly, "don't you get yourself worked up. She didn't know him at all. And whatever the man was, let's hope he repented at the end, just before the gas got him."

Somewhat shaken and newly aware of the way that both news and gossip travel in a small town, Mrs. Potter rose to say goodbye. As she left, she had Carrie's repeated assurance that the Versteegs would treasure Louisa's cut glass basket. Indeed, they had its exact twin in their own china closet, Carrie said, and now they could put out a matching pair on the parlor table.

Mrs. Potter walked to her car reflecting sadly on Varlene's short life. How dreadful to grow up with constant reminders that you were likely to turn out bad, just like your mother. It would not have taken much to stir up a rage that might have included the whole world. Jealousy of Jackie's lissome beauty could have been the trigger. Varlene's first angry response, it seemed, had been her rebellious and unhappy drinking bout. Her growing rage, combined with the strength and legendary violent temper inherited from old Grandfather Peter, might have led to something much worse.

Mrs. Potter resolved to find out more about Varlene's stop at the Blue Room the night of the cooking class. It was just short of noon, a little early for lunch business at the Inn, and maybe a good time to catch Elsie with time to talk.

Elsie Walters was on duty when Mrs. Potter came in, but except for a rumpled-looking man in one corner, sample case beside him, papers and an overflowing ashtray crowding a coffee cup on his small table, the Blue Room was empty.

Not heading for her usual table in the corner by the window, where she and Julie occasionally met for lunch and where she and MacKay had often lingered over a cocktail or a nightcap, she went directly to the bar.

"You going to sit up here, all by yourself?" Elsie greeted her. "Never saw you in here alone before, 'Genia."

Interesting. She said 'Genia and both her sisters say *Mrs. Potter*. No reason why they all shouldn't use her first name, after all the years they had known each other, but perhaps being a bartender encouraged more self-assurance than Bertha's job as housekeeper for MacKay, or Alice's for the Dorrance household.

"Thought I'd just stop in for a minute, Elsie. Actually I'm about done in, with all the awful things that have been happening since last Thursday, and if I ever needed a drink it's right now."

"A martin, then? The way you and Mr. Moore used to like them?"

Again interesting. It's 'Genia, but Mr. Moore. Anyway, a martini (MacKay always called it a *martin*) would be welcome at the moment, after the cold, dark righteousness of the Versteeg parlor.

The icy drink appeared at her elbow. "Double twist of lemon, Bombay gin, and just a whiff from the vermouth bottle," Elsie assured her. "It'll do you good."

"I hope Bertha's all right. I've been concerned about her, the strain of MacKay's death, then being questioned by Pete and the twins." That should be a safe starting point.

Yes, Bertha was doing okay. Doc had given her some more sleeping pills, and today when she left the house Bertha was up and watching her soaps, which was a good sign. Oh, and Bertha wanted to say thanks again for her phone calls.

"I know MacKay was here with Jackie Morsback the night before they both died." Mrs. Potter thought she'd better get that said quickly, then get on to her primary questioning, which was to be about Varlene.

There was no need to continue with leading questions. Elsie had a bartender's easy ability as a raconteur.

Well, the first thing that night, Elsie said, was that Varlene Versteeg—teacher at the junior high, you know, 'Genia—who to Elsie's absolute knowledge never set foot in the Blue Room before—showed up. Waltzed in by herself, not very long after nine o'clock.

Varlene sat up at the bar, right where you are now, 'Genia, and she ordered, of all things, a dry martini. Said she wanted it very dry, four to one. Elsie couldn't get over that. *Four to one.* Whoever wants any kind of a martini these days don't want more than waving the cork of the vermouth bottle over the glass, same as you do. Four to one was something Elsie only even *knew* from reading old-time bar guides, and she wasn't any chicken herself.

"Neither one of us is any spring chicken, 'Genia," she said jovially, "though I'd say you and I seem to be holding up better than most. Ready for another martin?"

Not yet? Well, anyway, Elsie figured Varlene was just trying to show off a little and act sort of smart stuff, so she gave it to her, and then another one when she asked for it. Varlene drank them down like medicine and she kept looking around to see who was coming in. Crossing her legs like, and looking at herself in the bar mirror.

Mrs. Potter looked down at her own crossed knees on the barstool and grimaced slightly at her own reflection in the mirror behind Elsie. "Yes, I think I will have another, but no hurry," she said.

Well, soon, Elsie continued, say maybe about nine-thirty, that girl Jackie Morsback came in, and she was by herself, too. Now Jackie hadn't been in town but the summer, maybe, but she was already a regular in the place. A couple of salesmen at the end of the bar pricked up their ears like, and started to sniff around, which

102

they hadn't done any of for Varlene. Jackie went back to the dark end of the room, said she'd order later.

Elsie's story went on, with obvious relish at having an attentive audience and no interruptions. Just a minute after that, she said, Mr. Moore came in.

Now Elsie was always glad to see Mr. Moore, would have been even if Bertha hadn't been working for him all these years. He was a regular. Good tips, always asking how are you, always saying you look great, Elsie. Never out of line, except he was always making a play for somebody, if you know what I mean.

At this point Elsie had the grace to pause. "Of course with you, 'Genia, it was a different story. We know you didn't take him all that serious. But you may as well know that he was, well, what you might call a ladies' man."

How is she so sure I didn't take him all that serious? Mrs. Potter asked silently of her fresh glass on the bar. She thought about Bertha, ignored and invisible in the background, but perhaps listening, as she and MacKay had drinks in front of the big kitchen fireplace.

Well, to go on. Elsie wanted her to know Varlene was so flustered when Mr. Moore came in that she spilled her drink. Went on talking to him about how *exciting* to share an interest in gormay cooking, stuff like that.

Now, Mr. Moore treated her nice, but he gave her only about ten quick seconds before he said you'll excuse me won't you, and went to join Jackie at the table in the back.

When Elsie went back to get their drink order they were talking very low and quiet. Sitting mighty close, too, and it came to Elsie maybe this was something serious with Mr. Moore, after all those years of his being a bachelor. Only he sounded more mad than lovey-dovey, if you catch my meaning.

Well, after Mr. Moore said hello and good-bye to her so fast, Varlene got all red in the face and said she'd have another drink, this time bourbon and ginger ale. In fact, she had a second one of these, and then if you can believe it, a third one. Elsie made those last two drinks pretty light. Figured Varlene wasn't used to all that hard stuff.

All the time she just sat there, right on that very barstool, and she stared up at that big old stuffed walleyed pike up there on the

103

wall, and every so often Elsie would look at her and she'd be red as a beet. No, *purple* red, *darker*.

"I wonder if Varlene knew Jackie?" Mrs. Potter inquired with seeming idleness. "Or if *she* was ever one of MacKay's girlfriends?"

Not a chance of it, neither one, Elsie assured her. She'd have been the first to know. Not much got past Elsie in Harrington, here at the bar where she was. Not past Louie, neither, out at the parking lot. Was 'Genia staying for lunch, by the way? She'd keep that corner table for her if she was. Meantime, what about another martin?

Hastily, Mrs. Potter said no, no thanks. As she swung down from the barstool, she decided to make her questions direct. "You don't know any reason, Elsie, why Varlene might have disliked Jackie—might have been jealous of her?"

Well, naturally, she must have hated her guts. Elsie could be direct, too. But you could bet your bottom dollar they hadn't ever said two words to each other. That Jackie was too busy—Elsie drew out the words slowly, *tooooo busy*—around town to have time for any little old girl schoolteacher.

No, 'Genia, no connection any way possible between Jackie and our little Dutch friend, Elsie assured her. Varlene was just plain drunk that night, in spite of all Elsie could do to keep her from it. She wasn't used to the booze and what she had really hit her. Once she got in that car of hers she must've just kept on wandering around until she finally ended up at the old bridge. Probably got out to *go* after all that ginger ale. No way you can tie that in with what happened to Jackie.

Mrs. Potter lingered at the bar. "What does Bertha think about all this?" she asked. "Does she think MacKay might have stabbed that girl? Who do *you* think did it?"

For the first time Elsie paused.

"Never mind, I'll see Bertha later," Mrs. Potter assured her. "I just wondered if Pete had been around to ask her again about what happened that night. Not that she could have known much, of course."

"No, no, I don't mind answering," Elsie replied hastily. "It's just that I hate to have to say it, 'Genia. We think he did, stab that girl I mean. Nice as the man was to me and to Bertha there at his

104

house, we think he did it, went off his rocker. He looked grim as death when they went out of here that night. And then what Louie heard him say—well, when you leave, you can ask Lou himself about that.''

Elsie looked at Mrs. Potter quizzically. ''Hon, sure you don't want to grab a quick sandwich or something while you're here?'' she asked. ''A cup of coffee, anyway?''

Mrs. Potter looked at her watch. It was short of noon and the room was still empty, but she knew that soon it would be full and that she would have to talk to too many people she knew. ''Thanks, Elsie,'' she said, ''I think I'll head for home before everybody and his uncle shows up. I'll powder my nose first, and then I'll see Louie in the parking lot before I leave.''

The powder room on the second floor of the Inn was deserted and Mrs. Potter seated herself at a small wicker desk in a corner of the fuchsia-flowered ''ladies' parlor'' that was its anteroom.

Rummaging in her large purse for pen and notebook, she knew she must write down at once her thoughts about Varlene.

The obvious scenario, of course, was simply that Varlene had drunk too much, had become confused after leaving ' e bar, and had blundered out the lakeshore drive and onto the old road. She had stopped at the familiar landmark of the old bridge and decided to ease her whirling head with a splash of cool water. She had slipped on the grassy path leading down to the inlet and had drowned.

That seemed to have the simple ring of truth.

However, writing furiously on the small looseleaf pages, Mrs. Potter created another scenario. As she wrote, she realized that her stories were taking on a distinctly soap-opera quality. The style seemed to be addictive, like Bertha's attachment to her daytime stories of passion and revenge, betrayal and greed. She scribbled on.

Drunk, embarrassed, Varlene feels rejected by the world as she leaves the parking lot of the Inn. Driving slowly to allow for the giddy whirl inside her head, she knows she cannot return to her uncle's house. She fears that most dreaded reproach, "You're turning out just like your mother."

Only one person, all evening, has said a nice word to her. She'd go out to Mr. Moore's house, that's what she'd do. She'd thank him for being so nice to her.

Driving slowly, Varlene reaches MacKay's house. He leaves his desk, where he is writing a note of apology to Mrs. Potter.

MacKay decides that the best thing to do is to make Varlene some coffee and then send or take her home. Varlene follows him to the kitchen, but before he can make the coffee, she shows signs of becoming actively ill. Trying to get her into the fresh night air as quickly as possible, he propels her, retching and stumbling, through the door into the garage.

Varlene is a heavy girl and she is sodden with drink. She lurches against MacKay, awkwardly knocks him off balance. He falls heavily, losing consciousness as he strikes his head on the concrete floor.

Dazed, sick, unable to think clearly, Varlene begins to leave the house with MacKay still unconscious on the floor. She decides he needs medical attention, considers trying to get him outside to her own little car in front in order to take him to the hospital.

He is too heavy to lift. She loses a hairpin, unnoticed, in an effort to move his body.

At this point Mrs. Potter realized that one of the two, either MacKay or Varlene, would have had to start MacKay's car before he lost consciousness. All right, she told herself, MacKay did. He got Varlene in the car, started the motor, then went back to open the garage doors. The girl made a surprising slide from the car seat, and then the lurching encounter Mrs. Potter had imagined took place behind the car, where MacKay's body was found.

In any case Varlene's scenario had to be played out.

106

Unthinking, scarcely aware of what she is doing, Varlene stumbles out through the kitchen to her little flower-painted car in front of the house.

She heads for the old road, the familiar old bridge, the refuge of her childhood.

Perhaps she then remembers that she left MacKay lying on the floor of his own garage. Perhaps she is only aware of her own misery and drunkenness, of her newly rebellious nature.

"God forgive me," she prays. "Just like my mother. Just like my mother."

She knows what she must do. Varlene commits suicide by jumping from the old, crumbling concrete railing, plunging to her death with her blue eyes wide open, her blond braids flying free at last.

The car was pleasantly cool, the motor running, when Mrs. Potter emerged from the Inn, Varlene's scribbled scenario in her handbag. "Had it in one of the sheds for you," Louis told her proudly. "Just got it out when they said you was coming."

They said? Mrs. Potter had met several friends as she left the Inn, and the parking lot was already well filled with Harrington's more affluent lunchers. She had seen Lynette briefly (moving briskly toward a Planned Parenthood luncheon); Paul Dorrance had apparently arrived separately and was with a group including the president of the bank and Jack Vanderpool; even Roger Two had been coming up the wide stairs of the side portico as she left.

No matter who told him (and Louie really *was* sort of loony, just as the kids used to say in school), at least he was smart enough to know what kept him in tips.

As he handed her into her small station wagon, Louie's wide

grin remained fixed across his flat face. Like the others of the family, Louie's eyes were bright blue, but he lacked Bertha's sharp focus and Elsie's direct and questioning gaze. Unlike the others, who, like Alice, were dark of skin, truly dusky in coloring, Louie's skin and hair were fair, almost totally white.

"Pretty nice little wagon you got here, is it?" he asked, beaming, his white face close to the open window, his breath strong with stale tobacco, "pretty good mileage all right?"

Pretty fair, she assured him. Maybe not as good as a little old VW, say, but better than a Mercedes. Did he remember Varlene Versteeg's little car, or the big old car Mr. Moore used to drive?

Louie stopped to concentrate and Mrs. Potter sat back in the car seat to give him plenty of time.

His answer, once he had got it together, was surprisingly detailed, and it included most of the things she wanted to know about the parking lot part of the story of the previous, tragically final Thursday evening for those three people leaving the Blue Room.

Did she want to know when he last saw Mr. Moore's car? Louie told her it was last week, on a Thursday night. A Mercedes 250SE was what Mr. Moore drove, and he left at 10:31 P.M. Louie always checked his watch for times (he proudly exhibited a large gold wristwatch) and he could remember every car, in and out, even though they didn't charge for parking there at the Inn.

Mr. Moore came out from the Blue Room with that dark-haired girl, the new, pretty one who used to be visiting at the Ragsdale place. Rental Monza from Norton's was what she had.

That left only two cars in the lot that night, both overnighters, one Missouri license, one Illinois, beside the Versteeg girl's old painted-up VW. Green, decals all over it. That one left at 10:38.

"What a wonderful memory you have," Mrs. Potter told him earnestly. "How was Varlene doing, by the way, when she drove out of here?"

Louie stared at the gravel beside the front wheel. "That was Walter and Carrie Versteeg's girl," he finally said. "Great-niece she was, mother died right after she was born, old Peter Versteeg shot the father." He had it all straight.

Now, last week was the first time, far as he knew, she'd ever been to the Blue Room, Louie continued carefully. Came alone, went out alone. When she left she was walking slow and a little

108

wobbly and he was hoping Elsie hadn't let her have too many drinks. He knew Elsie was good about things like that, but still and all, a nice young girl by herself, you couldn't be too careful.

Still, he said, Varlene managed to get out of the lot okay, and since she was driving as slow as she walked, he'd sure thought she would have made it home all right to Third Street. Never figured she'd get all the way out to Little Blue and then fall in and drowned herself.

"Louie, your memory is wonderful." Mrs. Potter hoped she wasn't laying it on too thick. "Tell me about Mr. Moore and that Morsback girl that night. *They* weren't drunk, were they?" She knew they had not been, but any question would serve.

There was another long pause.

Mr. Moore never took too much, Bertha said so too, even out at his own place. He was okay, but he was *mad*. Just slapped a dollar into Louie's hand any old way, didn't ask how he was or say good-night or anything.

"Now what do you suppose made him act like that?" Mrs. Potter's question this time was honestly curious.

Louie's pause became so long that she began to wonder if he had heard her. He stared at the ground, and then she watched his lips begin to move, silently.

Finally, as if he had been bringing words and whole sentences out of deep recesses in his memory, Louie spoke.

"*Nearly one million dollars.*" That's what *she* said.

"*But you were only five years old!*" That's what *he* said.

"*Baby, I'm going to get tough.*" That's what she said.

"*Don't be in a rush. I'll take care of things. I promise you.*" That's what he said.

And then I couldn't hear any more, Louie told her. She got in the Monza from Norton's and drove off, and then Mr. Moore *he* roared out of there after her in the Mercedes.

"Are you sure he followed her?" Mrs. Potter asked, very quietly. "Wouldn't he have turned right, instead, heading for home on the lakeshore road?"

This time Louie's answer was unhesitating. Nope, *we know* he turned left toward the Arms. *We know* he turned left right behind her. And he looked mad as hops.

Mrs. Potter's good-bye handshake held a folded bill. As Louie shuffled away to his shed, where a loudly ringing phone bell was sounding, he turned back and spoke again. "That's a real nice little machine," he said.

And a nice little machine it was, she thought, as she paused, then turned out of the lot to the right, heading at last for the lakeshore road, for home and for some kind of late pick-up lunch.

Two martinis, while more than she would think of having before lunch except on most special occasions, did not give her any thought or concern. A car pulled out abruptly from the curb ahead of her, and she braked neatly to let it precede her.

At the one stop sign she had to pass before reaching the shore road, she was suddenly chagrined to realize that she had been slow in halting. She had managed to come to a stop, but not until she was well out into the intersection. It was a tremendous relief to see that there was no cross-traffic at the moment, but obviously the car behind her (she did not let herself look back to see if she recognized the driver) must have seen, and she wished there had not been that witness to her embarrassing breach of traffic safety.

Shameful, she told herself. Tipsy at noon, and not even realizing it. It's a good thing you aren't driving on Main Street, or this would be all over town before suppertime.

Her thoughts returned to Elsie and Louie and what she had learned from them. As she slowly followed the winding road westward along the lake, she forgot her brief, red-faced embarrassment, and her speed increased to a normal pace.

A million dollars? Five years old? What was the name of that town in New York State where Jackie had grown up? Her mind was busy and she drove with automatic skill and ease.

As she came over the one long hill on the lake road, just before the place where the old macadam road branched off to Blue Lake Inlet, a child on a wobbling bicycle appeared suddenly on the road before her.

Quickly, firmly, Mrs. Potter pressed the brake. There was no response, no slowing of the small car, even as she repeatedly, finally frantically, pumped the brake pedal. Out of control beneath her demanding foot, the car swerved wildly as she was forced to turn sharply across the narrow road to miss the child.

Summoning all the calm she could manage, she tried to control the car with the steering alone. Driving as her father had taught her years ago, on Iowa winter snow and ice, her feet left the accelerator and the useless brake, and she concentrated on turning, ever turning, as far as possible, into the direction of the skid.

At last the child was safely behind her, standing beside a fallen bicycle. But at the foot of the hill, just before the curve, the small car again swerved, righted itself, twisted, and plunged on. A giant maple tree loomed ahead and Mrs. Potter felt herself aimed inexorably at meeting it head-on.

A final desperate wrench spun the car into a shallow culvert on the wrong side of the road, slowing its momentum to a head-spinning jolt.

Incredibly, both Mrs. Potter and her little car were unharmed . . . heart pounding, motor running. For some time there were no other sounds.

Mrs. Potter was suddenly aware of a smooth and pleasant face at the car window, a cap of neatly combed black hair, a voice precise, pedantic.

"My dear Mrs. Potter, may I help you? Have you had an accident?" It was James Redmond, and the car that had materialized beside her as she sat motionless in the ditch was pointed, as she was now, in the direction of town.

It was a tremendous relief to let a competent man take charge. The cooking school instructor would drive her home to Indian Point, then would return with Greg to do whatever was necessary to the little brown station wagon. Mrs. Potter was ready for a cup of tea and a nap, and maybe even the cup of tea would be too much trouble.

"Of course I'm all right," she told Greg when she came downstairs later in the afternoon. "I've been terribly lucky, that's all. The child wasn't hurt and neither was I."

No, Greg, assured her, and it didn't even seem that the car was much damaged. He'd have been able to drive it in to the garage himself except that the brakes were completely gone, and it seemed safer to have Norton's come out with the tow truck. He had stayed right with the mechanic when they went over it, and the answer was simple enough. The brake fluid was gone, that's all. Some way the bleed valve (whatever that was, Mrs. Potter thought) had come loose, so that every time she hit the brakes, a bit more of the fluid pumped out. Apparently by the time she reached the hill on the lakeshore road, it was gone and so was any control of the car.

Had she had any trouble with it earlier in the day?

"Not that I remember, love. I'm sure it was all right when I took it out of the barn this morning and drove to the Versteegs', and it certainly was when I left the Inn. I remember having to pull up sharp when a car swung out from the curb, and the brake worked fine then."

They'd do that, work all right for a time or two, Greg explained. Let's see, could she tell him how many times she'd have had reason to use the brake pedal after she left home?

First, one time at the Versteegs', right? And then, he added, you stopped when you came to the Inn and again when you left the parking lot later, just as you drove out into the street?

"I expect so," she said. "Then I had to slow down quickly for that car pulling out. And finally there was the stop sign."

It must have been leaking quite badly by then, Greg thought, in order for the usual automatic response—red octagon, foot on the brake pedal—to have stopped the car, not at the corner where it belonged, but well out into the intersection.

It was something of a relief to know it had not been the drinks, after all. And it was good therapy now to prepare a hearty tea, with scrambled eggs and ground cherry preserves. "I missed lunch and we won't be eating until late at the Hofmeyers'," she reminded him.

"Now Aunt 'Genia, are you sure you feel up to going out tonight?" Greg was incredulous.

Mrs. Potter did not tell him so, but her thoughts were on questions for her yellow pad. Of course they'd be going to have dinner with Julie and Hoddy. She had a most particular question in mind.

112

From experience Mrs. Potter elected to arrive at the Hofmeyers' nearer to seven-thirty than the hour of seven Julie had named. In their case she knew that what she might consider a half hour late would be just about right for them.

As she and Greg approached the recessed front door of the Pink House, the large formal house beyond Indian Point on the western end of the lake, even beyond James Redmond's cabin and the now-shuttered house of his hosts, they were greeted smartly by the new addition to the Hofmeyer household.

"Good evening, Edward." Mrs. Potter smiled at him as one would greet a pretty child.

Greg's "Hi, Ed," was less formal.

They followed the graceful small figure, surprisingly broad of shoulder, tapering to trim and narrow hips. His white shirt fitted smoothly into high-waisted black trousers, and he walked gracefully, his legs swinging from the hips like those of a dancer, his body motionless above the waist.

In the garden room overlooking the privet-edged path to the quiet lake, Julie and Hoddy were awaiting them, each with a tall stemmed goblet of iced vodka in hand.

" 'Genia darling, you look marvelous! And Greg, do come right here and sit beside me and tell me everything scandalous about Stanford!"

As Greg tried to cope with his hostess's questions and with the bare arm tucked warmly through his own, Hoddy asked Mrs. Potter what she would have to drink.

"I know you make the world's best martinis, Hoddy," she told him, just as, not too truthfully, Mrs. Potter had told a number of men. Actually, no one made a martini to match those Lew used to make for her, although he never drank them himself. "But tonight

I feel like something long and light. Maybe a tall Scotch and water—lots of ice and lots of water, please?''

Mrs. Potter knew that the cocktail hour at the Hofmeyers' would be just that, an hour at the very least. Theirs was not a house for a martini, of which one was never enough, but of which three—always and inevitably—were one too many.

How little changed Hoddy appeared after all these years, she thought. Although he was nearly ten years younger than Julie, a fact Julie preferred unmentioned, that still put him now at—let's see, it must be fifty-two? He kept the unquenchable boyish smile in the square face, the sturdy neck and shoulders of a wrestler above his still-trim and erect carriage. The crest of dark hair was ungrayed. Hoddy looked much as he had when, not yet thirty, he had first come to Harrington.

Mrs. Potter also reflected on another facet of small-town life. We all know each other's ages, she thought, many of them with exactitude based on birthday party memories or on who was first to get a driver's license. There are very few small secrets in a small town, even though certain large mysteries may remain quietly buried for years.

This seemed the right time to pry at one of these, long-undisturbed. ''You know, Hoddy,'' she began, as they stood with their drinks at the tall window overlooking the lake where the Hofmeyers' big outboard, the *Blue Bird*, was moored at the dock, ''I've never heard you talk about your life as a little boy. I know you love to hunt and fish and I'm told you're very good at both. Did your father teach you those things, or did you grow up in a sports-minded community, or what?''

''Oh, sure.'' That's what she got for asking devious questions and too many at once. What had she learned from *''Oh, sure''*? She must be more direct.

''Was it here in the Middlewest, or back east in the Adirondacks, or out west, or where? I don't ever remember your talking about it.'' Mrs. Potter groaned inwardly, realizing that again she had asked several questions.

''We lived in a lot of places,'' Hoddy replied easily. ''My father's work kept us pretty much on the move. I don't think I ever spent more than two years at any one school. You don't know how

114

lucky you and Julie and the rest of the gang here were to have had such a nice, stable, *rooted* growing up.''

"Of course we were lucky in many ways, but we missed a lot, too. You must have grown up knowing so much that we didn't, particularly in learning tolerance and in being at ease with different kinds of people. But didn't you have a favorite place—a place you really wished you could have stayed?''

Hoddy's laugh was infectious, and Mrs. Potter realized anew how his easy charm had captured the hearts of both Julie and old Grandmother Vermeer. " 'Genia, you're a wizard! I've just been thinking about a girl named Francesca Kaltenmeyer—that was her name, I promise you—and let me tell you, there was a time I thought I was going to die if I couldn't see Francesca again. It was like this . . .''

The explosions of laughter that punctuated Hoddy's story were contagious. As he finished, he removed the glass from her hand and motioned toward the array of bottles and shining crystal on the bar across the room. "I'll just freshen these and be right back," he assured her, departing on a fresh burst of reminiscent laughter.

So much for that line of questioning, Mrs. Potter thought. I'm terrible at this.

Edward returned to the room, gliding with his dancer's thrust of leg, his torso motionless, bearing a silver tray of hors d'oeuvres. Canapés bearing caviar and anchovies, some with flutings of cheese, were among the varied offerings, and the tray was bordered with a wreath of carved vegetable flower shapes that would have challenged any of the Redmond creations at the cooking class.

Greg concentrated on the more substantial offerings. Mrs. Potter was content to admire, after a first sampling, having long ago learned discretion at this stage of dinner.

As always, Julie touched and moved several items about delicately, but did not eat. It would be the same at dinner, Mrs. Potter knew. Julie honestly did not enjoy food very much, but she made gestures of appearing to do so, perhaps so that no one would notice how much she was drinking.

Hoddy, Mrs. Potter then noticed, and with near unbelief, was watching not the appetizers, not his guests (he had again just replenished glasses all around) but—could she be imagining?—he seemed instead to be looking with an air of bemused appraisal at the slim, swinging hips in the tight, high-waisted black trousers.

'Genia, my dear, she rebuked herself, you are really going too far. All these modern novels have you looking for complications that do not exist.

It came as a relief when Edward announced dinner.

There in the dining room, old mahogany glowing, heavy silver reflecting the light of many candles, conversation followed a predictable pattern. They covered all those topics that generally occupy people who see each other often: weather, gardens, local affairs, local gossip. The recurring theme, of course, was the shock of the three tragic deaths of the preceding week. Every known fact, every commonly held conjecture, was aired, and then repeated.

"Well, I can say it again, it's perfectly terrible about MacKay, but I still say I can see how it might have happened." Julie had said this before, in various ways, several times. "He wasn't getting any younger, you know, and he's always been a great success with women. Now you *know* he was, 'Genia. So if that Morsback person—you wouldn't call her a *girl*, would you?—if she wouldn't fall for him, maybe even made fun of him for trying his old line on her, well, all I can say is—it's perfectly awful to think about, but it could have happened. And then he got frightened afterward, felt terrible about what he'd done, and he took the easy way out."

A new question had entered her mind during dinner. The soup plates were being removed. When her hostess said the name Morsback, Mrs. Potter distinctly heard a muffled "*Bitch!*" as the white-shirted figure passed behind her chair.

Hoddy contributed little to the discussion, but when the subject of Jackie's pregnancy was mentioned, Mrs. Potter thought she had not only imagined he looked pale. Later, with a change of topic—at this point welcome to them all—he spoke with increased animation and heightened color.

As always, his first attention was for Julie. He made a complimentary reference to her good looks, her acumen as a collector of art. After dinner, he said, he was eager to show them Julie's most recent acquisitions of antique Florentine silver. There was one beautiful sixteenth-century dagger that was a real find.

Hoddy was as generous with praise as Grandmother Vermeer

116

had been with money. Not that he did not have plenty of the latter as well, it seemed. Hoddy had arrived in Harrington "well provided," as the saying went, and as owner of the local grain storage facility he had earned a good living. More recently, his new concern, Harrington Beef, was flourishing. The Hofmeyers had progressed beyond what Harrington called "comfortable" and had even gone beyond the state termed "well-to-do." There were, however, no acceptable words for this. It was not possible to say "rich" or "wealthy," not in polite society in Harrington.

Dinner had followed the pattern of the canapés—elegant and expensive. It was also very good. There had been clear turtle soup with sherry. To follow, Edward had displayed his skill with puff pastry with a new dish that he called Chicken Wellington.

"Your idea for a way to use poached chicken breasts!" Mrs. Potter exclaimed, and Edward smiled modestly. "It's delicious! Mr. Redmond will be ecstatic!"

It would not be right, she knew, to hope that Edward would want to share his exact recipe. He was, after all, a professional, whose value in the marketplace was in part dependent on the mystique of his cooking secrets.

She could, however, guess pretty well how he had made it. A square of puff paste large enough to envelop the wine-poached chicken breast, dotted with butter and enhanced with a slice of good pâté before sealing and baking, she thought. The sauce was light and delicious—white wine, mushrooms, shallots?

" 'Genia, you're woolgathering again," Julie said from her end of the table. "Now listen to me. You have got to admit I'm right about MacKay. I know you were crazy about him—"

"No such thing," Mrs. Potter protested. "He was great fun to be with, we all knew that. But you're really exaggerating, Julie, when you suggest there was anything serious between us."

"Well, the whole town thought you had some kind of thing going," Julie went on, "but that shouldn't keep you from seeing this clearly. The man simply went off the deep end about the new girl in town, and when she ticked him off, which she apparently did from the story you hear from the Blue Room that night, MacKay went off his rocker."

It was a reprieve to find Edward now passing a platter of nicely cooked garden vegetables, arranged with artistry, a good French wine. For dessert, *mousse au chocolat*, then demitasse and liqueurs in the living room with its pale mushroom velvet furniture, its muted Chinese rugs.

As they drove back to Indian Point, Greg now comfortably established as nighttime chauffeur, Mrs. Potter thought again about Edward's Chicken Wellington, and then about fashions in food.

A few years ago, everybody was knocking himself out trying to make Beef Wellington. Then there had been the rage for fondues (and the rage at burned tongues, from those too forgetful to change forks after plunging their bits of steak or whatever into the communal pot of boiling oil). Next, was it quiches? And then there had been crêpes, crêpe-makers, crêperies, until it seemed that nothing new could possibly be rolled into a pancake.

Recently there had been a great rush for the food of the Middle East, and the parsley-bulgur salad called *tabbouleh* had turned up with certainty at every third summer party for a while.

On a more homey, less sophisticated plane, thought Mrs. Potter, there was carrot cake. One day you'd never heard of it, and the next, everyone you knew was making one, and every restaurant in town (this was in Tucson when she'd come in to town from the ranch) was featuring it. *Carrot* cake. Food fads are like jokes, she thought. You don't understand how they get around, but all at once everyone in the country is repeating the same one.

The yellow pad and pen were on the bed table, and, in spite of her long and exhausting day, Mrs. Potter was wakeful after the Hofmeyers' dinner and the coffee and cordials that followed. The next two scenarios flowed effortlessly.

JULIE

I've grown up with everything but love, Julie tells herself. Grandmother did what she thought was her duty, but she never really loved me. And Hoddy—I've never been sure. Maybe I'm too old for him.

Julie swallows another untasted gulp of vodka. Even if this is all we've got, I'm not going to lose it.

Julie leaves the Pink House about ten-thirty the night of the cooking class, hearing Hoddy's healthy snores coming from his separate bedroom. She remembers the purported deadly history of the newly acquired Florentine dagger. She takes it with her as she drives carefully to the Harrington Arms.

Seeing a lighted ground-floor rear window, in which Jackie's provocative silhouette is unmistakable, Julie speaks in the strong, low tones she has practiced in reading male roles, as she sometimes does when attendance is skimpy at the playreading evenings of the Drama Society. She calls enticingly from the shadows below the window.

"Guess who's here, Jackie. Come on out. I've got a surprise for you—something you'll like."

Jackie, sensing adventure, gain, or merely the challenge of mystery (and secure in her own sense of power), comes to the parking lot outside her door.

Julie stabs her, returns home, remembers to wash the dagger and finishes the bottle of vodka.

Pretty farfetched, Mrs. Potter thought, and again I am being madly disloyal to an old childhood friend by considering such a possibility. The whole situation is crazy.

HODDY

The girl's voice is strident, jeering. "You know what I think, Mr. *Harold* Hofmeyer? I think you really aren't much interested in women, in spite of all that macho stuff. All that hunting and fishing business, poker with the boys, wearing cowboy boots to the office—you can't fool me. I saw your eyes light up when little old Eddie-boy came into the drugstore the other day, twitching his hips and batting his eyes."

The unthinkable has been thought. The unspeakable has been spoken.

Hoddy's long-bladed folding hunting knife, which he car-

119

ries as religiously as his pipe and his stockman's cane, silences these heresies.

These scripts are getting murkier by the minute. Mrs. Potter shuddered. But could it have happened, the ultimate and unforgivable insult of truth—if that's what it was?

Next day just before ten, Mrs. Potter telephoned Julie with her thanks for a nice evening and Edward's splendid dinner, just as on the previous morning she had telephoned her thanks to Lynette.

I'm always disappointed, she told herself, when I don't hear from people, one way or another, after I have them to dinner. A note is nice—she thought of MacKay and his extravagant praise, his distinctive scrawl, always in her mailbox the morning after a dinner party at Indian Point.

Flowers, well, it has been years since anyone did that.

Anyway, it was her own established practice to express her thanks personally and promptly on the morning after almost any social event. At the risk of disturbing an exhausted hostess, resting comfortably on her laurels, she telephoned, admitting at the same time that it often provided her with a wonderful opportunity to discuss the party food, who said what about whom, what in general was going around in town at the moment, all viewed in light of the previous evening's sociability.

This morning she remembered to ask Julie about Miss Bee's possible advice in having her hair done over. Nature's frosting might be doing the job, she had told herself last night at the Hofmeyers', but Julie's smoothly curled silver-beige head had looked a lot better, she thought, than her own long, pulled-back hair and the great, heavy gray-blond bun, constantly sprouting hairpins.

"I'll call her and say I want you fitted in when I go next week,"

Julie had promised. "You can watch what she does to mine, the monthly touch-up. And then let's have lunch at the Blue Room?"

That same September morning was bright and nippy, and Mrs. Potter was relieved to learn that Greg had scheduled the green tomato picking. The forecast predicted that the first killing frost of the year was on its way.

Edward and Charlotte (how nice to be able to call them by those good names, thought Mrs. Potter, if I can just remember) arrived promptly at ten. Edward, in matching green shorts and striped T-shirt, looked slightly blue in the cool breeze. Charlotte wore a long-sleeved, high-necked sweater against the chill of the morning, but she too was in shorts, cut-off blue jeans.

Between the four of them, they soon had five big baskets filled with carefully newspaper-wrapped tomatoes. One basket was for Charlotte to take home. She thought she might try a recipe in an old cookbook of her mother's for green tomato chowchow. One was for Edward to take back to the Hofmeyers. They'd be divine, he said, just to ripen as they would for salads and garnishes. One basket, of course, was for Indian Point, for the same kind of delayed ripening.

Here, the ripening chamber would be the old cyclone cellar, a detached underground shelter that had always done double duty as a root cellar for the old house. Outside the back door of the kitchen, this appeared as a grassy mound, about twelve feet across, not enough higher than the surrounding lawn to present any problems to a lawnmower. On the side facing the kitchen was a short flight of concrete steps leading down to a heavy wooden door set into the ground. This, like the doors of the house, was never locked and presumably keyless. Whoever had mowed the lawn— young Eugenia or Will or the hired man—was supposed to trim around the edges of this opening with grass clippers.

Opened, the door exposed a round, stone-faced cisternlike chamber with a dirt floor, a room perhaps eight feet in diameter.

Mrs. Potter had clear recollections of how the cellar was used. "Better safe than sorry" was not considered a cliché in the Andrews family. That was what Grandpa said each time he roused the family in the night or interrupted family supper to lead them all, with military precision and unquestioning obedience, to the shelter. Wind would scream overhead, trees and crops might lie desolate later, but the family had always emerged lucky and thankful to find themselves (and the house above them, fortunately) unhurt when the cyclone had passed.

The last baskets of tomatoes were to be delivered as presents to persons deemed worthy. The first would go to Bertha, now living with her family in town. Charlotte would take these to the Walters' house later. The other was to go to the DeWitts, at whose house Mrs. Potter was expected that evening to dinner.

"And there are just about enough left for an old-fashioned green tomato pie," she said. "Grandma's green tomato pies were famous in these parts. Shall we see if we can find a recipe?"

Edward made pastry with professional ease and speed. Mrs. Potter crumbled brown sugar, flour, and butter to layer with the thin tomato slices Charlotte's quick knife was producing, along with paper-thin shreds of whole lemon to be interspersed among them. Greg amused himself cutting and twisting Edward's velvety pastry dough into lattice strips to crisscross the top of the pie.

In fifteen minutes the pie, prepared according to Grandma's carefully handwritten recipe, was in the oven.

Charlotte excused herself to go upstairs for a minute. Greg left to check a magazine article on mopeds he wanted to show her when she came down. Mrs. Potter asked Edward if he'd sit with her for a moment on the front porch and look at the lake while they rested from their labors.

"Beautiful out there this morning, isn't it?" she asked.

Edward's answer was wistful. "I simply adore Blue Lake," he told her. "I can't get enough of it. This is the most gorgeous place I ever saw and I never want to live anywhere else."

It proved easier to question Edward this morning than it had been for her to extract information from Hoddy the night before.

He had grown up in a small country town south of Des Moines.

He hadn't been a very good student in school but he'd always liked to help his mother cook, and both he and his sister loved to make costumes for all the school plays.

(And now, wasn't it simply marvelous, Mrs. Hofmeyer was going to let him join her playreading group and maybe they'd even do a fantastic little theater production this fall? He'd simply adore to do the costumes and the lighting.)

It had been easy for Mrs. Potter to steer him to the subject of his arrival in Harrington. From his hometown he'd gone to Des Moines to try to find a job. The only thing he could find at first was yard work, but eventually he was able to persuade one family among his employers to try him out as extra help in the kitchen when they were having a party. Before he knew it he had a full-time job with them.

The incredibly wonderful thing was that they, the Rummels, decided to buy a new vacation house on Blue Lake and to bring him with them for the summer. The minute he saw the lake he knew he had to stay forever.

Had he met any Harrington people since he arrived? Any friends beside the people he worked for?

Edward's face became a rosy suffusion of love and joy. "You know Roger Two?" he asked her earnestly, "Roger Dorrance? You remember, he was at your cooking school class?"

Of course, she assured him, she'd known Roger Two since he was a baby.

Well, the Rummels knew the Dorrances, and almost every day all summer Roger Two came over for lunch with them, to swim or play tennis, or (Edward spoke now with palpable yearning) to water-ski behind his big boat, the *Blue Lightning*. Now, in his position, Edward couldn't presume, of course, and besides, the Rummels kept him terribly busy all summer, with more guests than you would believe. But he was still hoping, still *dreaming,* that maybe someday Roger Two would come over and ask him to go out in the *Blue Lightning* and show him how to water-ski.

"Well, that's something you ought to start to do right now. Anybody who loves Blue Lake as much as you seem to should be out on it this minute, on this beautiful morning," Mrs. Potter told him. "Greg can find some trunks for you—there are all sizes up there someplace—and you two and Charlotte can go out right now in the *Blue Fish*. See it down there at the dock? I'll just sit here and read while the pie bakes.''

"Maybe, as you say, that pie would be even better cold, Aunt 'Genia,'' was Greg's verdict later as the four ate lunch on the porch, ''but I don't see how.''

Afterward, as Mrs. Potter again took up her lined yellow pads in her own quiet upstairs bedroom, she searched back over the morning for possible added notes.

Edward—unstable character? Certainly not well defined in the masculine role, to put it mildly. (And certainly wearing eye shadow, this time green, she noticed, to match his outfit.) What kind of threat might Jackie have posed for Eddie? Particularly if he saw her as competition in his hoped-for friendship with Roger Two?

And Charlotte. What kind of terrible anger might flare up as a result of betrayal by someone you had sheltered and trusted as a friend?

CHARLOTTE RAGSDALE

"You're not going to tell any of these Harrington clods what I've got in mind for them,'' Jackie tells Charlie, the night she boasts of her blackmailing plans. "Just remember what I've got on *you*, kid.''

Charlie winces.

Mrs. Potter has searched for a motive for Charlie to want Jackie out of the way. Gossip about their relationship did not appear to bother her deeply. She took a wild guess.

"You promised you would never tell anyone about Mother and Dad, Jackie. I don't know why I ever told you, except

124

that I was so shaken up, and I thought you were too, when our parents all died at the same time.''

"Harrington is just the place I'd tell it, old dear," Jackie tells her. "Think what the headlines in the *Herald-Gazette* would be! '*Respected former editor and wife die in bizarre suicide pact. County political scandal exposed.*' ''

She went on. "Or how would you like this one, from one of those weekly papers you can buy at the supermarket? '*Did George and Leona Ragsdale have a right to appoint an unknown truck driver as their executioner?*' The whole country would lap that up.

"And so, old thing, you'd better stay out of my business now. One peep out of you and that cornball weekly of yours—the paper that still bleats about dedication to the Ragsdale standards—is going to know the whole story. The town is going to find out how their revered editor and his wife really died, and why."

Charlie first agrees to be silent, then realizes she will never be free of this blackmail. Later, fascinated, almost hypnotized by the flashing blades at the cooking class, she decides to silence Jackie's threat with her own threat of force.

She appears at Jackie's door later that evening, after walking around the block watching for her apartment lights for more than an hour. She tells Jackie that unless she leaves town immediately she intends to kill her, producing the knife to prove her intent.

Jackie feigns indifference, then unexpectedly trips Charlie and seizes the knife, laughing, chasing her with it to the parking lot.

Charlie turns, they scuffle, fall, and Jackie loses her grip on the knife. Charlie manages to grasp it, and she plunges it into the throat of her attacker, by chance hitting a vulnerable spot and killing Jackie immediately.

She escapes with the knife, returns home to clean it and herself. The only visible marks of the struggle are a bruised throat and forearm, requiring her to forgo her usual open-throat rolled-sleeve shirts for the next week, in favor of cover-up pullovers.

It begins at the start of the summer, when Roger Two is a frequent guest at the summer cottage where John Edward Casaday is employed.

For Eddie it is love at first sight. He eagerly watches for Roger Two as he careens past the dock with a fine spray behind his water skis, for Roger Two as he arrives for tennis and lunch, his tanned skin aglow with health and a bracing cologne, for Roger Two as he appears on the evening scene, wearing a yellow shirt, sleeves rolled back, a silk ascot at the open neck, tight white trousers outlining his muscular skier's legs.

Eddie admires and adores Roger Two from afar. He does not presume to offer any advances. There is only his silent devotion as he goes about his duties at the cottage.

After Labor Day, however, when his Des Moines employers have left the cottage and Eddie remains as caretaker, Roger Two makes his first (and perhaps entirely casual) visit there not as a guest of the owners.

Whatever is said, it is possible that Eddie misconstrues indifferent amiability as active encouragement. He rejoices, magnifies in his imagination the meaning of the visit and each word of the conversation. He signs up for the cooking class when he learns that Roger Two plans to do so.

When the object of his adoration arrives at that first class with Jackie clinging to his hand, Eddie is stricken to the heart.

It is a quick matter for him to return to his quarters for a sharp boning knife after the class, and to go with it to the parking lot of her apartment building to await her return.

"Bitch!" he whispers (the same word, same inflection Mrs. Potter overhears later at the Hofmeyers' dinner table) as he darts out of the shrubbery.

This sounds frighteningly real, thought Mrs. Potter. The only thing is, Edward is the person on the list I know least about.

As she considered these scenarios for Charlie and Edward, neither totally implausible, Mrs. Potter realized that her possible suspects so far, with the exception of Charlie, were all people Jackie had met since her arrival in Harrington in early summer. The next

126

candidate, and fairness insisted that she must include him, must have known her before then, and somewhere else.

With reluctance almost amounting to dread, she forced herself to write.

GREGORY ANDREWS

Marijuana and hard drugs, as well, are part of the California scene.

Jackie Morsback, newly out of her perhaps scarcely more sheltered Iowa college, gravitates westward and takes up residence near the University of California campus at Berkeley. Through mutual friends she meets Greg Andrews, a graduate student at Stanford.

Greg has rejected what he considers the alcohol-aspirin-caffeine-tobacco addictions of his parents' generation, but he considers his own occasional use of marijuana to be harmless.

Rashly, he experiments with heroin, and it is from an unsterile injection of this drug that he contracts hepatitis. He is drawn into a deadly trap by which he is used as a minor seller, as well as purchaser, of the drug.

Fortunately, he voluntarily seeks the treatment he needs to free himself from his brief addiction and from the claims and threats of his former suppliers.

When Greg sees Jackie at the cooking class, he cannot be sure she is in Harrington by chance. He sits silent and unhearing throughout the lecture, aghast to think she may be following him, perhaps as an agent of this dreaded group.

After the class, as he awaits Mrs. Potter in the school parking lot, he manages a moment's conversation with Jackie before she drives away, and obtains her apartment address. She makes a reference to past associations, and he construes this as a possible threat to tell Mrs. Potter and his father of his so-far successfully concealed and shameful secret.

Following his after-class snack at Indian Point, and after Mrs. Potter has gone to bed, Greg slips out of the house and quietly backs the Subaru out of the barn.

He goes to Jackie's apartment, arriving after she gets back

127

from her meeting with MacKay. She receives him warmly, and they talk (warily, on his part) of mutual acquaintances.

Jackie sees no reason in this case to delay blackmail procedure, and she makes a direct and substantial demand for money to ensure her silence. Greg, terrified, is roused to a frenzy of strength. He seizes a long-bladed paring knife from the apartment kitchen, or perhaps a letter opener from the living room desk.

He advances wildly. Jackie flees out of doors, hoping to call for help, yet knowing how little can be heard (ordinarily an advantage) from her apartment by the tenants above.

Before she can summon aid, Greg, half-crazed, stabs and kills her.

He disposes of the weapon, whatever it has been, by throwing it into the mouth of Little Blue Inlet as he returns home over the new bridge. His next morning's questions to Pete Felderkamp are all attempts to learn what clues, if any, the police may have found.

Greg later appears easily and promptly convinced that MacKay has killed Jackie and has then committed suicide. It is to his advantage to have the mystery thus settled.

For that matter, Mrs. Potter thought wearily, the last point would apply to every one of the suspects. If any one of them was guilty, he would go scot-free if MacKay was adjudged Jackie's killer.

Putting the lined yellow sheets aside at last, Mrs. Potter found there was time for a swim in the lake, a quick and invigorating dip before she dressed for her third dinner engagement of the week.

Three nights in a row, she thought. I don't see how I can be holding up so well, especially when instead of napping after lunch I am writing these awful scenarios. The chief debilitating effect seems to be the threat to the waistline. Cottage cheese for you tomorrow, my dear.

Mrs. Potter no longer felt self-conscious about talking to herself. Most of her frients admitted to the same habit. Occasionally she was surprised and amused to realize that she even addressed herself as "my dear," in a rather superior and patronizing way.

It was even more amusing when she found it necessary to speak to herself firmly. Then she would preface her advice with, "If I were you, Eugenia Potter, I would certainly . . ."

"I feel rather badly about not wanting to go to the DeWitts' with you, Aunt 'Genia," Greg remarked as he put the basket of green tomatoes in the back of the little station wagon. "Tell you what, I'm not busy or anything. I'll drive you in, maybe stop and see a friend in town, pick you up whenever you say."

Mrs. Potter accepted without questions, although privately wondering what friends Greg might have acquired in Harrington. He and Roger Two were about of an age, but they hadn't seemed to hit it off particularly well Sunday evening. Greg's only signs of interest and enthusiasm then had been in after-dinner conversation with Roger Two's parents about mopeds and the Dorrance company. Who else then? Surely not Charlie, not Charlotte Ragsdale? After all, he had been with her most of the morning and through lunch. Anyway, she was grateful to be driven to the DeWitts' and to be called for, and she noticed with mild interest and satisfaction that Greg now seemed to be shampooing his fair hair and beard every day.

Jack Vanderpool's big Cadillac was already in the driveway when she arrived, and the three—he, Ralph and Dottie—were outside the new split-level house. They were discussing a path worn across a corner of the velvety green lawn, and two breaks in the neatly trimmed hedge that defined the corner lot.

"They started it with their snowmobiles last winter," Dottie was saying emphatically.

"Now every bicycle, moped, and tricycle in town considers it a public thoroughfare," Ralph complained.

"I've gone to see every mother in the neighborhood," Dottie went on, "and not a one of them will admit that her little darling would do such a thing. From the house we can't see when they're cutting the corner, let alone who's doing it.''

"What about watching from this garage window here, then letting loose with a little salt and buckshot?" Jack Vanderpool suggested, his long face creased with a smile. "Sting a few little backsides, teach them a lesson? I'd be glad to spell you at the window off and on for a few days and we'll have a little fun.''

Mrs. Potter winced at the thought of young Harrington backsides being punctured with salt and buckshot, which sounded painful and possibly dangerous. What kind of people would talk about shooting at a child on a tricycle? Of course they're all joking, she knew, although she felt uncomfortable looking at the vein throbbing at Ralph's broad temple, just below the bristling crew cut.

As they stood there Greg rushed back from halfway down the street to deliver the overlooked basket of green tomatoes. The party moved indoors and the subject was forgotten.

Both Dottie and Ralph were good cooks of the country school, both coming from local Harrington farm families where good food was served generously, enjoyed mightily, and then talked about enthusiastically. Mrs. Potter knew that the garden gift would please them, and she also knew that another excellent dinner was coming.

Yes, I promise, she told herself, cottage cheese and nothing else for the rest of the week.

The four descended three steps to the living room, ornamental white and gilt railings flanking the wide treads of the stairway.

Ralph continued fretting about the child-invaded corner of lawn. "*If thine eye offend thee, pluck it out*," he began, his own round, bright marble eyes looking around at the others accusingly.

Dottie interrupted. "Now remember, Ralph, we aren't going to do any more quoting of scripture in public," she admonished. "We went back to our old church last Sunday, 'Genia, and it's our firm belief that we're back now where we belong. Ralph is going to teach his adult Bible study class again, and I'll be back at the organ." She patted her firmly fluffed pink hair.

Both guests expressed approval at this announcement, and Ralph said something Mrs. Potter did not quite hear, something about false prophets leaving for greener pastures. She thought this

130

probably referred to the Reverend Jim-Bill Sanders and to the possibility, of which she had already heard rumors, of his leaving Harrington.

Their host brought up the subject of drinks. "Now I know you like to take a little something, 'Genia," he said, squeezing her arm affectionately, "and maybe Jack here will be a sport and join you."

With hearty raillery he added a comment that made Mrs. Potter uncomfortably aware that her tardy stop at the traffic sign was already common gossip in Harrington. "You won't be driving tonight, 'Genia, so you won't be getting into trouble again."

Mrs. Potter, pink-faced, wanted to explain about the brake fluid, about her near-miraculous deliverance from hitting the child on the bicycle and from her own expected end in a head-on collision of auto and maple tree, but at that moment admonitory warmup sounds from the organ filled the room.

An elaborate electric organ, mounted on a green baize platform, dominated one end of the turquoise and white living room.

"I'll just put the finishing touches on supper while you two are imbibing," Ralph told them, "and if you twist her arm I think Dottie will give you a little cocktail music."

He returned with thimble-size cut glass tumblers, carefully filled with cream sherry, from which the two sipped decorously as the organ recital began. Brief and cheering, it started with "Roll Out the Barrel," as the tiny glasses of sweet wine were drunk. "Valencia" followed, and then "Stardust."

Jack leaned forward during the recital. "You know, you're a blamed good-looking woman, Eugenia." He patted her hand on the arm of her chair, his own hand crisp with red hairs at the wrist and at the base of the fingers. "Don't you ever get lonely out there at the Point?"

Mrs. Potter, with a small smile, removed her hand in order to take up her small glass again, trusting he would not notice that it was already long empty.

There was a sprightly encore from the organ in response to their applause, and at that moment Ralph returned with "Supper's ready."

Now the four ascended to the dining room level, separated from the living room only by its elevation and a white and gold ornamental divider like the railings flanking the stairs in the front hall.

The dining area was also turquoise and white, Dottie's favorite colors, except that its walls were white; those of the living area were bright turquoise. The wall-to-wall carpet here was a geometric turquoise and white pattern, while that of the living room was all white in a sculptured design.

The table was set with embroidered turquoise organdy placemats and centered with a silver epergne. This held four unlighted turquoise candles surrounding a central arrangement of jewel-like plastic grapes, each fat bunch in a different shade of blue, green, or violet.

Menus, almost as much as houses, are a reflection of personality, or so Mrs. Potter had long felt. To her thinking, the DeWitts' house rather predictably mirrored Ralph and Dottie's ideas of good taste and good living.

She had confidently expected that tonight's dinner would provide good food. To her surprise, the actual menu bore little discernible relation to the decor of the house.

Slightly humbled, Mrs. Potter realized that she might not know her old friends as well as she had thought.

Following Ralph's mercifully brief blessing there was a leg of lamb, crisply browned on the outside, rosily pink within, faintly redolent of garlic, which he carved with expertise and speed. There was a hot dish resembling scalloped potatoes, except that the raw potatoes had been grated, not sliced, then baked in a covering of cream and seasonings until tender within, brown and crusty on top. As salad and vegetable in one, there was a chilled casserole of *ratatouille*—sliced eggplant with tomato, onions, sweet red and green peppers, and zucchini—its faint garlic fragrance echoing that of the roast lamb, the whole bathed and baked with a mellow glaze of olive oil.

"Now really, Ralph, how did you learn to cook like this? I know that both your family and Dottie's were always known for good food, but honestly, this is *not* Iowa home cooking. If it were, you'd have given us stuffed baked pork chops, maybe, and creamed corn, and you know it."

Not giving them time to reply, she went on. "Besides, it's hard even to *buy* lamb in Harrington."

132

"Remember old Mr. Amundsen?" Jack spoke as he buttered a second hot roll. "Striped apron, straw hat? Sort of a white-faced fellow, remember?"

"What I remember," Mrs. Potter said, "is Mother telephoning her morning order and having it delivered in time to have the meat cooked for dinner at noon, when my father came home from the bank."

"I remember the sawdust on the floor," Ralph added, "and all those cats."

"Our family picnics were usually steak fries," Mrs. Potter continued happily. "We still have the old stone grill out behind the barn. I remember Mother saying she'd need eight of his best twenty-five-cent porterhouse steaks, and Mr. Amundsen told her she was pretty extravagant, ordering a whole steak apiece for the children. Porterhouse tails were considered good enough for kids, and actually that was the part we liked best, broiled until the meat was brown through and the fat all crisp."

"We butchered our own," Dottie said, "so I really don't remember Mr. Amundsen at all. But I certainly remember our picnics. Cold fried chicken, ours were. Pa didn't take to cooking out-of-doors but he did love picnics."

The discussion continued with a litany of Iowa picnic food and outdoor eating, with a side excursion into the related realm of Fourth of July oratory, and then summer evening band concerts in the park, occasions commonly prefaced by family picnics.

"Jack here was always trying to get me off into the bushes on band concert nights," Dottie said with mock reproach. "You were a caution, do you know it, Jack?"

"Good thing Mrs. DeBoos never let Dottie out of her sight, or she might have gone with you." Ralph spoke with proud, possessive fondness.

"You're awful." Dottie giggled, and suddenly Mrs. Potter remembered a dimpled face and short curly hair of the color known as strawberry blond.

After a second helping of *ratatouille,* Mrs. Potter spoke again of the dinner before them. "You know, none of us grew up knowing much about garlic and herbs and things like this heavenly eggplant dish."

Dottie was the one to answer. "It was all Ralph's doing, 'Genia,

133

and it started when he was in France, World War II. He was a flyer, remember (Mrs. Potter had forgotten, and now looked at her host in a new light), and he had to parachute down behind the lines.''

Ralph continued, ''The French family who hid me taught me a whole new way of cooking, little food as they had then. And so I got interested, and when I came home Dottie and I both just took it up from there.''

''It's a superb dinner, and we thank you.'' Mrs. Potter spoke for herself and her fellow guest, who possibly did not share her secret wish that Ralph had learned to enjoy wine as well as French food during his enforced stay abroad. A glass or two of a good Beaujolais would have been this dinner's crowning touch.

As if in answer to her thought, Ralph said, ''They taught me to cook quite a lot with wine, you know. Since all the alcohol evaporates with heat, we've decided that there's nothing in it against the way we were both brought up.'' Mrs. Potter resisted the demeaning urge to ask what was on hand in the way of cooking wine at the moment, and only nodded politely.

''I know you're used to a lot of fancy cooking, Eugenia, all the places you've lived,'' Jack said, almost shyly, ''and I certainly take to this French stuff of Ralph's myself, even though I certainly believe in the health food Marie and I eat most of the time now. But you know, if you want to know my true name, give me good old plain country food. No offense intended now, Dottie, no offense.''

''I'm with you,'' Ralph added unexpectedly. ''We had the lamb tonight—a little rare for our regular tastes, I might as well admit—and the *ratatouille* just to put on the dog for 'Genia here, if you must know.''

Mrs. Potter was slightly embarrassed. ''Whatever you two had cooked would have been perfect, and you know I'm really a very plain country cook myself. Incidentally, you both probably read magazine menus and recipes, and maybe Jack and Marie do, too. What do you think ever happened to mashed potatoes and gravy?''

Totally out of style, all four agreed. Rice was in. Pasta was in, in all shapes and sizes. Gnocchi and spaetzle and grits were in. But mountains of dear, lovable, delicious mashed potatoes, their generous craters filled with the liquid gold of melting butter or overflowing with the rich lava of good brown gravy, had disappeared from the printed page without a trace.

Even if any kind of gravy was admitted, they went on, you were supposed to put it on your meat, not on your potatoes, for heaven's sake.

"When I was about fourteen," Jack confided, "remember, before they had school lunches and we all went home for dinner at noon? Well, I used to ride my bike home *dreaming* about mashed potatoes and gravy. I used to think I could eat a wagonful of mashed potatoes and gravy."

"And so did I," Mrs. Potter confessed.

"Wasn't it lovely to have been that thin?" Dottie sighed, but not very convincingly. She patted her firm middle, still creditably trim in the snug turquoise pants.

"Dessert is going to be Iowa farm cooking, not French," she continued. "I made a fresh peach pie this morning, and we're going to have it the old-fashioned Dutch way. You remember, 'Genia? With a spoonful of good cottage cheese on the side? Only at our house we always called it Dutch cheese—did you? I'll bet Jack's Grandma Vanderpool always served pie that way."

It seemed that yes, indeed, all the Vanderpools had been very keen on cottage cheese with fruit pies of all kinds, especially peach and rhubarb, as Jack recalled. However, his Grandpa Jake didn't call it either cottage cheese or Dutch. He called it *schmierkase*.

Over dessert, with large cups of coffee, talk progressed from food, gardens and weather to the eventual and inevitable topic of overriding interest for them all, and for most Harrington residents that September week—the shock of the three surprising deaths the previous Thursday night.

Naturally, the other three already knew that Jackie Morsback had been pregnant at the time of her death. All knew of MacKay's farewell note and its exact wording. All knew the story of Varlene's visit to the Blue Room and of her unsuccessful attempt to make a play for MacKay.

Jack, as insurance broker, was expecting a verdict of suicide from the coroner's office, with the undisguised hope that any claim on MacKay's life insurance policy could be declared invalid. "Not that I'd have to pay it myself, of course," he told them, "but I always think the less the company pays out the better my record looks in the main office.''

Ralph and Dottie now spoke with small compassion, but at least more than they had shown earlier, about that poor girl Jackie. Still, all in all, they were of a mind that maybe she got what she deserved, and it was their firm belief that the whole thing should be settled as quickly as possible and forgotten about, for the good of the whole community.

Recalling that Dottie's uncle, from down near Spencer, was a district court judge, Mrs. Potter felt quite sure that this might be an expression of official opinion.

Varlene's drowning was held to be a sad object lesson in the evils of drink. Both the DeWitts and Jack had been to call upon the sorrowing Versteeg aunt and uncle, as Mrs. Potter had done, with their condolences.

There were the customary inquiries for the health of Jack's dying wife, and it seemed to Mrs. Potter that he reacted with an oddly inquisitive rise of his thin red eyebrows. Why should he look surprised? she wondered. She always asked about Marie, everyone did. And the answer was always the same, and everyone was terribly sorry, and that was that.

Greg's ring of the door chimes signaled the end of the evening for Mrs. Potter. In response to hospitable invitations for him to come in for a cup of coffee (good heavens, Mrs. Potter thought, Greg would quiver all day if he even drank a cup at breakfast, let alone at this hour), he was quick with his thanks and his apologies, which Mrs. Potter amplified with explanation of his convalescence and his need for an early bedtime.

They drove home in companionable silence. He did not volunteer, nor did she ask, his whereabouts during her evening at the DeWitts'.

After the pie and cheese, Mrs. Potter was too full and sleepy to consider a late last dip in the lake before bed, even though she knew there would be few more warm nights when it would be possible. She was certainly in no shape to start a new page on the yellow pad.

Mrs. Potter smiled as she slid off into sleep. How utterly right that the DeWitts' dinner should have been what it was, considering their unquestionably sincere, if slightly variable, Christian belief.

The Feast of the Lamb, she murmured to herself, remembering

136

an amusing, inspiring, and eminently usable cookbook of a few years back. No, it was *The Supper of the Lamb*. The author had been an Episcopalian divine, someone named Capon, a man she had always wished she might have known in any of three roles—as host, guest, or priest.

Just as Mrs. Potter was drifting off to sleep, she suddenly sat bolt upright in the moonlight. Without turning on the light she reached for the yellow pad on the bed table beside her, and filled the page with a large scribbled question, trusting that she could read it in the morning.

She could.

"How paratrooper silence enemy?"

Before dawn the next morning Mrs. Potter began rather painfully, on her scenarios, trying to believe that each one could be true as she wrote it down.

She reminded herself, however, that it was easy to magnify small matters. Because people spoke with relish about peppering young Harrington backsides with buckshot didn't prove a streak of vicious cruelty. They were just talking. It was not possible to preface any of her stories with the DeWitts' favorite phrase. Dottie had repeated it at last evening's parting. "It is my firm belief it will turn cold soon," she had pronounced.

What Mrs. Potter was about to write was not her own firm belief, although she could find parts of it credible.

THE DeWITTS

"How did I know about your Aunt Ada Marie?" Jackie repeats their question briskly. "You don't think the Reverend Jim-Bill would tell a fib about a thing like that, do you?"

Dottie's face is white, her magenta lipstick and pink hair

the only color above her white blouse. Ralph's round face, in contrast, seems like a great radish, the red veins on his nose and cheeks disappearing in the general flush of high color. "Just what are you saying about a respected preacher of the Word?"

"Exactly what I told you," Jackie says in a businesslike way. "Twenty-five years ago you two didn't have a cent and were way in debt with your little two-bit radio shop. Then Dottie's rich aunt got sick and Dottie went to stay with her. She died of pneumonia, poor old girl. Maybe she would have anyway, but that open window when it was ten below, and that thin damp blanket didn't help her much, you can say that about it."

"She *wanted* to die." Dottie is almost crying. "She was praying for God to take her. How could I know we'd inherit all that money?"

"When you were her very loving niece? Don't be silly. Everyone who hears about it will know exactly why you did it, so cut out all that religious stuff."

Jackie goes on relentlessly. "You may think DeWitt is a respectable name around here—big appliance dealer, big church people, friends of the Dorrances and Hofmeyers and all that, but you'll see where you stand when this gets out.

"Unless," she continues, "unless you want to contribute to a good local charity I can recommend to you."

Ralph and Dottie may or may not pay blackmail to Jackie, but they come to an early realization that her threat must be permanently silenced.

Either of the DeWitts may do the actual stabbing. Dottie has helped with the butchering of hogs and steers on the family farm since her childhood. Ralph, at one time part of the French underground, is deadly in his proficiency with a silent, single knife blow.

Mrs. Potter pondered now another ending for this particular scenario, although she did not know the principal character, the Reverend Mr. Sanders. Reminding herself guiltily that she was writing pure fiction, she gave it a fresh heading:

THE DEWITTS (alternate finish)
138

After making their first blackmail payment, Ralph and Dottie muster their courage to confront the traveling preacher, the Reverend Jim-Bill Sanders. They approach him. How could he have betrayed their heartfelt, repentant confession?

The Reverend Jim-Bill realizes he is caught in a situation endangering the successful future he envisions, his future radio and television triumphs. He borrows a sharp, narrow knife from the kitchen of his boardinghouse. He goes to Jackie's apartment and stabs her fatally.

He returns the well-cleaned knife and heads for Texas. The DeWitts leave his congregation and return to their old home-town church.

JACK VANDERPOOL

Marie is never going to know about this, Jack vows to himself. He's made a bad choice in this girl Jackie. He should have stayed with the little waitress from Ashville, who was glad to get her twenty-five dollars for an occasional noonday meeting at the Starlite on her days off.

This Jackie is a different dish, and you can say that again. He'd thought she'd be insulted if he offered her money, so instead he'd been buying her a bracelet, a gold chain, something like that, thirty-forty dollars say, as a little present each time they got together. And heck, he thought she'd been enjoying those little get-togethers as much as he did.

It's all right for a man to still have the old go in him. That's the kind of guy who makes the 500 Club, isn't it?

But Marie is not going to know about this.

At first, surprise, then shock and consternation—these are Jack's reactions when Jackie first approaches him for money and hints about visiting Marie.

After the first cooking class he returns home, tells Marie who was there, reports on the demonstration. He gives her the nightly pain pills and sedative.

Then, armed with a sharp kitchen knife, he goes to Jackie's apartment and awaits her return to the parking area.

"Look, let's talk this thing over," he tells her. "But this is a bad place for it. How about a walk?"

Jackie agrees, knowing she holds the power hand.

Meantime Jack's fear and fury are mounting. Instead of taking her to the dark and quiet of the town park to kill her, as he had planned, he stabs her at once, there beside the car.

As Mrs. Potter wrote these lines on her growing stack of lined yellow pages, another, possibly more plausible story occurred to her.

JACK VANDERPOOL (second version)

"Then, as the next step, you persuade that Mrs. Potter of yours to sell you Indian Point," Jackie is saying, as she and Jack share a sandwich lunch at the Starlite Motel. "The condominiums go up there, according to my plan, as you see."

Jack bends over the drawings spread out on the motel room dressing table. "I see," he says, "I see. You're sure you've got that undeveloped Vermeer piece, out beyond the Hofmeyers', all sewed up? The land around the cove?"

Jackie smiles. "Relax," she tells him, "I can guarantee it. But it's going to cost you, and you might as well know it. If you can raise the cash, we're partners and we'll clean up on the new Blue Lake Land and Recreational Development Corporation."

She pauses. "If not—"

"You wouldn't let that pipsqueak Roger Two into this thing?" A vein in Jack's narrow forehead throbs a warning. His white hands, bristling with red hairs, lie flat on the papers before him.

Jackie gathers her maps, leaves with a shrug of her beautiful shoulders.

That night, after the cooking class where Jackie has arrived so possessively with Roger Two, Jack tells himself he is not going to be the loser in the real estate bonanza.

After this, an utterly outrageous story suggests itself.

JACK VANDERPOOL (impossible scenario)

What if Marie, acknowledging that Jack's attraction to Jackie

140

was the result, in a way, of her own long and lingering illness, has accepted these meetings not as unforgivable adultery or personal betrayal, but simply as a physical fact of life?

Was it possible, then, that in a tremendous burst of strength and determination, Marie herself might have stabbed Jackie? Her motive might not then be simple jealousy. Rather, she might want to protect Jack's good name, his standing as Harrington's leading insurance broker, his treasured membership in the 500 Club.

Mrs. Potter pondered visiting Marie to ascertain if she might muster physical strength for such a confrontal, then rejected the idea as monstrous. Besides, Jack had said Marie was not allowed visitors these days.

As she telephoned Dottie later that morning with her thanks for the excellent dinner, Mrs. Potter found herself asking a devious question, and again she felt she must inwardly apologize for her constant suspicion of old friends.

"Just when did you and Ralph begin to expand the appliance business from your first little radio shop?" she asked.

"Why do I want to know? Well, it occurred to a few of us" (she blushed at her mendacity and at the same time vowed to herself to make good on this impromptu idea) "that we might have some kind of anniversary celebration. But don't you dare even hint about it to Ralph!"

Securing the date, and burbling about what a tremendous achievement to have built the county-wide business of DeWitt Sales and Service, Mrs. Potter left the phone table hurriedly.

Even if you do arrange the party, she told herself, and of course you will do so now, this is absolutely unforgivable. You spy on your friends. You ask prying questions. Now you're poking into some old buried scandal, possibly unfounded, certainly better forgotten.

To ease her sense of guilt at the betrayal of old friendships, she still felt that she alone was right about MacKay. She was sure he could not have killed the girl Jackie. Even more, she was sure he had not killed himself.

Yet every person she had talked with seemed to believe this to be true, just as every one of them had appeared to find Varlene's death merely an unfortunate drunken accident.

I don't have any answers, she had to tell herself quite humbly. I just feel there's something that the rest of them are missing, and that I ought to find out what it is. If I can. Nobody else even seems to be trying.

For the next few days, Mrs. Potter elected to remain quietly at Indian Point, except for one necessary excursion to market and to accomplish a major household errand. The expected sharp frost arrived, just a week and a day after the first cooking class. The calendar page turned to October. Mrs. Potter spent several hours each day walking along the lakeshore or out to the old bridge, trying not to look at MacKay's empty house when her walks took her eastward toward town, working off her inner tensions as best she could. She tramped westward along the road past the Redmond guest cottage, past the Hofmeyer Pink House, from there along narrow paths and trails circling the far western cove of the lake.

The cooking school series had already been canceled. James Redmond had telephoned, which had given her an opportunity to thank him again for his rescue from the culvert where she and her careening car had come to a miraculously safe stop.

According to notification from the adult education director, Redmond told her, the school had decided to terminate the class.

Mrs. Potter did not tell him that she had gently pointed her old friend the director toward this decision. With three class members all meeting unnatural deaths in one night after the first class, she had felt that none of the rest could possibly face a continuation.

"The school thinks," Redmond went on, "that it would be fair to refund part of the class fees. You think so too? But do you realize that I have rearranged my own fall schedule to include this assignment, and at your special request?"

Politely, he spoke of "certain expenses." The foodstuffs and supplies. The recorder and cassettes he had needed to buy to be able to continue his daily Chicago newspaper column, while still remaining in Harrington for the class.

"Under the circumstances," he said, "do you not agree that the school's share of the fee might well be refunded, but not that portion that has been paid to me?"

In younger days, Mrs. Potter would not have deigned to haggle. Now, with increasing years and self-assurance, she was no longer quick to give in to any demand she considered unreasonable. They discussed the matter, each speaker courteous but firm.

"Very well," he said at last, very stiffly, "I will bow to your judgment."

And, he said, since he would soon be leaving for Chicago instead of remaining for the autumn in the borrowed guest cottage as he had originally planned, he would, if he might, stop by before leaving, with his check for the amount of the refund.

Would Mrs. Potter (who was now tiring of the discussion) be so kind as to arrange dividing the sum among the remaining members of the class?

It was not until later, walking past his cottage entrance lane and noting that he was still in residence, smoke rising from the fireplace chimney and car parked by the gate, that Mrs. Potter thought out just how he had figured the refund. Instead of basing the sum on the thirteen original payments, he had secured her agreement to accept a return based on ten tuition fees. He was, it seemed, going to take a full profit on the fees paid by Jackie, MacKay, and Varlene.

As she scuffed through fallen leaves on the lakeshore path, Mrs. Potter decided not to worry about this minor matter. It would make little difference to any estate of Jackie's, and none to MacKay's. She would herself make up a full rebate of the fee to the elderly

143

Versteegs and then forget at least this one small, sordid sequel to the whole miserable business.

Nevertheless, as she continued her walk, Mrs. Potter realized that she had invented a scenario for each person in the classroom the night of the murder except for the instructor.

She began to think of what she knew of Redmond other than his reputation as a food writer. She counted: that he had been painfully shy and awkward, at least in the beginning, at speaking before the group; that he was careful of both food and money; that he had withdrawn into a hermitlike life in his guest cottage by the lake after his brief, single introduction to Harrington society; that she had originally found him oddly attractive, but certainly less likable after the business of the tuition refunds.

Now, as she walked along the silent, deserted lakeshore path, the words for a Redmond scenario formed in her mind. She was not sure what number it made in her completed (and undoubtedly useless) series. The whole thing had been an exercise in vanity and in futility, she reflected. Still, this additional story could explain several of the unanswered questions on her yellow lists.

JAMES REDMOND

Mr. Redmond's Chicago hostess, eager to display her distinguished guest, arranges a cocktail party to show him off (and perhaps to establish herself with the local gentry) at the start of the summer.

Once the party has been scheduled she learns of her guest's neurotic shyness, although he insists he will go through with the event. The day afterward he is extremely upset, possibly actively ill.

Conscience forces his hostess to try to protect him from further distress. She telephones all her guests of the preceding day, telling them that Mr. Redmond will not be available for the normal sequence of invitations that would have followed this introductory gathering.

James Redmond spends the rest of the summer in seclusion, working on his book.

He vows, as he has before, that he will overcome his basic shyness, and therefore when Mrs. Potter approaches him to suggest the cooking school idea, he forces himself to accede. Perhaps he thinks this modest beginning—a small group in a small-town high school—will be a first step in mastering his fears. He is aware of the vastly increased potential sales of his cookbooks if only he can someday in the future conduct a successful television cooking series.

The first class begins stiffly, but fairly well, he thinks. Then two incidents threaten his self-control.

The first is the appearance of the most beautiful young woman this shy middle-aged bachelor has ever seen. She looks at him directly, with what seems to him both challenge and invitation.

The second upset comes when his attempt at humor—his pretense that all of them are little children and must be reminded to wash their hands before cooking—is obviously a dismal failure in spite of his previous rehearsals before the mirror. He cringes with embarrassment and hurt pride as he retires to the back of the room to wash, and it requires a tremendous act of will to return to his lecture.

He does, however, go on. It reassures him to handle familiar objects and to talk of commonsense facts.

His composure vanishes after the class, when Jackie returns to the classroom through the inner courtyard of the school. (This was the flash of white Mrs. Potter had seen and later dismissed as the result of her own poor eyesight.)

Jackie has returned to suggest a bite of late supper at her apartment. She already has a date until about ten-thirty, she tells him, but she has some good cheese and imported beer and she'd love to have him come by for a little chat about the class and an idea of hers for a future session.

Redmond is excited yet terrified, and his delicate stomach reacts. He drives to the drugstore for antacid pills.

He is waiting when Jackie returns. They decide to take a brief walk before going to her apartment for beer and cheese.

After a few blocks they return, talking meanwhile of the class and of his plans for the following series.

"One thing I hope you won't try again," Jackie tells him with a soft laugh, "is the lisping bit. If you do, I'm going to do my own piece about the Plean Plate Plub—the way they used to get me to finish my vegetables when I was little.''

The remark is intended as a gentle gibe. Jackie does not willfully alienate a good prospect. She mistakenly thinks that Redmond will relax, lose some of his stiff shyness, through a bit of playful teasing.

Instead he is engulfed in a flame of rage, shame, and self-hatred. His self-possession has already been shaken by the advances of this beautiful and desirable woman. He cannot bear what appears to be a disparaging allusion to his attempt at classroom humor.

Scarcely knowing what he is doing, he opens his car door, snatches a knife from the satchel on the seat, and downs Jackie with a single, maddened blow.

Not until he has driven back to his lakeside cottage does the enormity of his deed register in his conscious mind. He throws the bloody knife far into the waters of the lake, then lights a small fire on the hearth and burns the stained square of flannel to a small pile of crumbling ash. His mind now clear, he plans an alibi.

The maple trees provided healthy diversion from such unpleasant thoughts. The frost had lighted the lakeshore road and each softly padded pathway with great arches of color—soft greens and every possible gradation and combination of yellow, red and orange.

As she did every autumn, Mrs. Potter concentrated on looking for the one perfect leaf—for her favorite, its hues that of a Peace rose, lemon yellow, with blushings of pink and apricot.

She had a clear memory of coloring such a leaf on a white page in kindergarten days. Each child had been given a sheet, she remembered, on which four identical maple leaf outlines were imprinted, and each had been told to crayon carefully inside the lines. She even remembered the gummy dark blue pad over which each white sheet had been pressed to reproduce the pattern the teacher had drawn.

It was a far cry from today's free, uninhibited finger painting, but she could still remember that one special leaf and her own excitement at creating such beauty. The same thrill of pleasure came back to her each fall when she thought about that leaf, and she was still looking for one to match its pure perfection.

It was Monday of the next week, on her long daily walk in the bright sunshine, when her thoughts came back to (had they ever really left?) the three deaths.

Whatever the true story proved to be, or whether it ever would be revealed, there had to be someone who did not want it known, Mrs. Potter thought wearily, as she had so many times before.

Clearly, her continuing concern over the matter had been apparent to her friends. Over the past few days she had been receiving some hints, or so they seemed, and even a few bits of pointed advice.

Among these, she wondered, was there a threat, an admonition less than friendly?

It seemed a little chilly now, with a cooler wind off the lake, and she buttoned her sweater.

There had been Paul Dorrance, after church the previous day, pulling her toward him a little stiffly and speaking in a low voice. "The boys at the luncheon club say all that business about the deaths is now officially settled, 'Genia. Lynette and I agree it's better left that way."

When had she received Jack Vanderpool's advice? Oh, yes, she had parked her car at the Walters' before going on her Saturday grocery errand, to see how Bertha and Alice were getting along. Jack had come by in his striped running shoes and in what looked like a replica of his old track suit from Harrington High. His thighs, like his wrists, bristled with red hairs. Breaking his stride to speak to her, he had advised, "Some things are better left alone, Eugenia, better left alone. You ought to clear out and let me sell that old place of yours now while I can still get something out of it for you."

There had been Lynette, stopping by on her way to a town

planning survey of lakeshore development, saying crisply, "Now, 'Genia, snap out of it. You've gone far enough."

There had been a clear message in one of Julie's daily phone calls that some things were better forgotten. If 'Genia knew what was good for her—to keep from going off the deep end, that is—she'd give up all those useless questions about Jackie's death and MacKay's suicide.

"Eddie is absolutely crazy," she had then confided. "Last night he went out wearing blue *earrings* to match his eye shadow, can you believe it?"

However, Julie could not face going into that kitchen again herself. She needed Eddie most especially now, because they were closing the Pink House and moving back into town. Bertha was at MacKay's this week, she continued, and Alice was out there part-time as well, helping her. Probably closing up there, too.

After Julie, who else?

Let's see, on that same day she had gone to town for groceries and she received yet another admonition, this time at DeWitt Sales and Service.

First she had passed the old Sweet Shoppe, she remembered, now modernized for pizza and frozen yogurt. As she passed the open doors, the same cold, damp milky smell was evident that had been the magnet for her teenage appetite, and of Julie's. I can remember, she thought, when she and Lynette and I agreed that the best possible meal in the whole world was this: a BLT on toast and a chocolate malt. Salivating slightly, she thought it still sounded good.

Next door at DeWitt's, she looked at a new refrigerator, a possible replacement for the old monitor-top at Indian Point.

Ralph, as always, had plenty of words to express himself. " 'Genia, are you still stewing about the tragedies last month? The untimely departure of our late loved ones? Dottie wants me to tell you she has talked to her uncle Judge John about this. He says he has complete confidence in our local authorities and that the case is being settled to his total satisfaction."

Mrs. Potter peered into the new refrigerator and looked in disbelief at the price tag. Ralph went on. "It is our firm belief, Dottie's and mine, that we should accept Judge John's thinking on this, and so should you."

Then there had been Roger Two, coming over very politely to ask for the loan of the treasured goose decoy, assuring her he would return it in a week at the latest. "Aunt 'Genia, if you don't mind my saying so, I think you're going a big far on this murder stuff. . . . Incidentally, why don't we set up a joint venture and turn Indian Point into a good real estate development for you? You can put up the land as your half and I'll provide the management expertise. Of course, you'd have to move out right away so the demolition could be done before bad weather."

There even had been Greg and Charlie, whom he had proposed as a dinner guest, on a recent evening in front of the little green marble fireplace. "It must be beautiful at your ranch right now." Which of them had made that suggestion of her leaving?

Giving advice is a prerogative of family and of old friendship. Among these bits of unsought counsel, could there be the warning of a murderer again pressed to believe that safety lay only in further violence?

As she returned from her walk, she decided to take out the *Blue Fish* in what might be one of the last turns of the season. The motor was a bit reluctant, but it finally took off with its usual competence. She made a brief unproductive tour of the quiet west end of the lake, trolling for bass with the line and lures that were always aboard.

As she came back to the mooring at her own dock, Hoddy came by in the *Blue Bird*.

"Last spin of the year," he said. "Hey, 'Genia, I think you ought to know Julie's worried about you, and you know she has a real feel for these things. Says she hopes you're not going to open up any old wounds. No point in hurting people, is there?"

Edward was aboard with Hoddy, obviously happy and busy polishing brightwork.

His advice seemed to be contained in a final question as they cast off.

"When are you leaving for Arizona, Mrs. Potter?"

On the Tuesday morning following Mrs. Potter's reflective (and possibly restorative) weekend, Julie's phone call had come early.

"This is our day for Miss Bee," Julie reminded her. "She'll be expecting you this morning at eleven, and she's just as glad as I am that you're going to do something about yourself at last, 'Genia. Natural is fine, but at *our age?*"

Mrs. Potter had already begun to regret her momentary enthusiasm for "doing something" to her long, thick graying hair. The idea no longer seemed important, with all the other things she had to think about. She had also undergone some middle-of-the-night misgivings about future hairdressing maintenance she could foresee ahead.

Still, she felt herself bound to keep the appointment. Julie had reminded her that after the beauty shop, the two of them would be meeting Lynette for lunch at the Blue Room, and the magic words "just like old times" were, as always, effective.

Quickly out of the shower and into town clothes (the violet Ultrasuede as usual, a soft scarf at the throat, well-polished old calfskin pumps), Mrs. Potter took off for Harrington.

The brakes were working fine as she checked them on leaving her own driveway and again several times on the shore road heading east. She knew that Norton's had done their job and that Greg had rechecked their work carefully. However, she had always taken responsibility for her own car, with Lew traveling so much of the time, and in this case she felt that she must have been remiss about something or other in the owner's manual to have caused the brake fluid to disappear. She tensed slightly, thinking of those nearly disastrous effects.

Once assured that she could stop with her small car's usual obedient response, she continued her progress toward town, enjoying the tapestry of maple leaves overhead.

She was timing this nicely. There would be time for at least one errand, possibly two, before she was to meet Julie at Miss Bee's.

With some amusement, she thought that no one who saw her—respectably clad, respectable and as-yet unfrosted gray hair neatly in place—could possibly guess her errand. She was on the way to the bank of which her father had once been president. She was about to find out, if she could, how to accomplish a simple, foolproof bank swindle.

As Mrs. Potter parked her car, remembering to put her coins into one of the new meter boxes, she found herself face to face with Dottie DeWitt's uncle, her father's old friend and the revered district court judge, John DeBoos.

"Just up from Spencer for the day," he told her. "Hadn't expected to run into you here in town, Eugenia, but I must say it's a pleasant surprise. You look more like your mother every day. Sight for sore eyes, I may say."

Mrs. Potter was enfolded in a huge and surprisingly firm embrace, scented nicely with a mixture of cigar smoke, bourbon and cologne.

"Judge John," she finally managed, "you're exactly the person I need to see. We're all upset here in town about the murder, as you must know, and about MacKay's death. What's the truth of it all? Is there anything official we should know—anything you could tell me, that is?"

"Now you know better than to ask a question like that, child," the judge admonished her, his great bulk filling the sidewalk between her and the bank. "Your mother would never have asked that."

It had been some years since Mrs. Potter had been addressed as "child." She listened obediently.

The judge cleared his throat lengthily and again put a great bear-like arm around her shoulders. "Whatever you may be hearing, my dear, don't fret your pretty little blond head about it anymore."

Mrs. Potter felt her eyes going wide and hated herself for the simper she felt crossing her face.

"Much as I liked your friend MacKay," the judge went on, "and we went duck hunting together more than once—we all have to accept that a man has his breaking point."

"You believe, then, Judge John, that he killed the Morsback girl?" Mrs. Potter found it difficult to speak with her head pinned against the great judicial shoulder.

"I told you, young lady, that your mother would have known better than to ask. Remarkable woman, your mother. Can't think why I ever lost out there, except that I went off to law school and your father stayed home at the bank."

The judge's bear hug relaxed. "Suffice it to say, Eugenia, and you are not to quote me on this, we have gone over the case. Our conferences have been informal, understand, but the prosecutor has discretion to consider the matter closed and I agree with his decision to do so. Better all around this way."

The judge made his ponderous way down the street, and Mrs. Potter stood unmoving for a moment beside her car.

Rousing herself to her intended mission, she looked at the building before her and thought of the bank as she remembered it in the days of her father's tenure.

The building then had been a forthright red brick. When, and by whom, had it been decided that painted, partly exposed, "antiqued" white brick conveyed an appearance of greater worth and dependability?

Once inside, she looked at the paneled surfaces of walnut veneer, the lavish trimmings of dull-finished chrome, as richly heavy as silver. She counted with surprise the number of gated enclosures, each with its executive desk and its second comfortable chair of supple brown leather awaiting its suppliant customer, each with its alert, neatly barbered young man behind the desk.

The golden oak and stained glass of the former interior were gone, as were the high bronze gratings that separated those on the outside from those splendid few within—the tellers who took in Christmas Club payments and dispensed or received carefully counted cash and bills.

Her father's office had been at the front, where it occupied all of the front window space of the building. There had been a smaller, less public cubicle behind it where, presumably, he conducted any private affairs of the bank. His desk had held a big bowl of arrowheads and Indian artifacts collected for him by local farmers who knew of his interest, and it often displayed a prize ear of corn or a giant pumpkin brought in for public admiration.

Mrs. Potter stood for a moment looking at the silvery facade of the present vault, deciding that it did not look nearly as impressive or secure as the old brass door with the big brass wheel, the dial of the sanctum within. Even though she had been allowed to do numbers on the adding machine after school and to play secretary with the typewriter, she and Will were never permitted to touch the wheel of the safe.

"Donnie," she began a few minutes later as she sat in the office of the bank's president, "Donnie, I need to know about something that happened a long time ago."

The sleekly rotund man behind the desk smiled at her benignly. As the daughter of his predecessor in office, he well remembered her after-school visits. Mrs. Potter had special privileges now, as she always had, within these (albeit new and considerably fancied-up) banking walls.

In turn, Mrs. Potter remembered the man she called Donnie as a skinny young beginner in the bank under her father's tutelage. *Trainee* would be the present word for it, she thought. Donald Pfingsten was an old acquaintance, whether she thought of him as a thin young farm boy learning his trade behind a teller's window or as the dignified and portly gentleman who now faced her.

"I've been wondering recently about an old bank scandal my father once told me about," she said. "Maybe you'll remember it, too—something that happened in New York State a number of years ago, a bank swindle that caused quite a lot of stir in country banking circles at the time. Does this strike any chord in your memory?"

"No, not as I can say." The plump hands were clasped comfortably together on the bare expanse of polished desk.

The important thing, she told him, after he had disclaimed any recollection of the names of Morsback and Rhynesdorp, was that she'd been wondering—oh, just idle curiosity, but the sort of thing

153

one couldn't get off one's mind—just how easy would it be for a bank employee to make it appear that someone else in the bank, say even the president, had stolen a lot of money? Could it be done?

"Pretty doggone hard to do that sort of thing nowadays," he assured her, "but you say this was twenty-five years ago? Well, let me see."

Yes, here's one way, he told her after a moment's thought. Before most small banks had loan committees, it was usually only the bank president's signature, even just his initials, that was needed as approval of a bank loan. If there was some way a larcenous junior officer in the bank might have—well, bamboozled was the word, 'Genia—the president into signing some fictitious applications for loans, the scheme would have worked. The junior, whoever it was, could have taken the money for himself in place of the fictional applicant (and in those days it was easy to squirrel money away in Swiss banks, he reminded her) and then as long as he paid the interest on the loan on time, out of his own pocket, nobody would have questioned the transaction.

If the fellow really wanted to frame the president for the job, all he'd have to do would be to make out cash withdrawals from the president's own personal account, and see that these appeared to tally, in both time and amount, with the interest payments. How he'd manage these withdrawals would be up to the fellow's ingenuity, of course. He might even persuade the boss to lend him cash in this way, if they were good friends and the big guy trusted him. He could say he was sending it to refugee relatives in Europe or some such cock and bull story.

Then when the loans came due, the young guy would be completely in the clear. His dough, the money he got from the phony loans, would be stashed away in Switzerland. The boss's okay would be on the loan applications, and it would seem pretty clear to any bank examiner that the interest payments had been made with the cash withdrawals from the boss's own account.

"Nothing to it, really, 'Genia. Just wish I'd thought of it myself, and I'd be lying on a beach on Maui right now instead of being chained here to this darned old desk."

That desk looked pretty slick to her, and Donald Pfingsten was the obvious picture of self-satisfaction. He was joking, naturally, but she felt a momentary flash of anger thinking how vengeful she and Will would have been if someone—skinny young Donnie, for instance—had performed that kind of financial hocus-pocus at the bank in their father's day.

As she came out into the October morning sunshine, still seething with indignation over something that had not, after all, happened in Harrington (and may not have happened in Rhynesdorp, New York, either, she reminded herself), she checked her watch. There was time to cross the street to the small offices of the Harrington *Herald-Gazette*.

Yes, the gum-chewing young woman behind the desk told her, yes, there was a file of old obituary notices, somewhere out back. As long ago as that? Probably pretty yellow by now, in spite of all they could do to keep them, but no way they could put everything on microfilm in this burg. She was busy with want ads at the moment, as anybody could see, but just what was it she wanted?

By offering to do the search herself, and by promising to do it most carefully, Mrs. Potter gained access to the files marked OBIT in the crowded back office, and she turned hurriedly to the year preceding that in which Dottie had said she and Ralph opened the new store. It would have taken awhile for a probate, Mrs. Potter thought, and at least this would be a starting place.

Finally she found it. *Ada-Marie DeBoos, age 92, spinster.*

She scanned rapidly for essential facts. *Pneumonia following a long illness. Relatives: a younger brother, Emil, and his son, John, of Spencer; a great-niece, her devoted companion Mrs. Ralph DeWitt of Harrington, née Dorothy Jane DeBoos. Contributions to the Methodist Ladies Missionary Society requested in lieu of flowers.*

With these items of research accomplished (for whatever they were worth) Mrs. Potter then recrossed Main Street to go upstairs over the hardware store, to the scheduled meeting with Julie for the hair-frosting session at Miss Bee's.

Catching sight of herself in the glass storefront Mrs. Potter thought that maybe she didn't look so bad after all. At least, the violet-clad figure she saw seemed to swing along rather lightly, and whatever the hair looked like, the head appeared to be held up high. Maybe she'd just watch while Julie's was done. After all, at least to Judge DeBoos, she was just a slip of a girl with a pretty little blond head.

"Stop smirking at yourself in storefronts," she said, and a passing stranger stared.

All beauty parlors smell alike. Perfume, ammonia, hot air, female musk, general overlay of warm soapiness. Julie was already in the shampoo chair when Mrs. Potter entered Miss Bee's establishment, and, squinting, Julie waved her a greeting before subsiding into a mild froth of shampoo and water spray.

Miss Bee's shop seemed unchanged through the years. Undoubtedly the new his-and-hers shop down the street, the successor to the old barbershop of her childhood, would be a bit flossier. One would probably find there the ubiquitous walnut, chrome, and overpowering green plants (live or plastic) that were the hallmarks of modernization in much of Harrington. Possibly not all that mushroom-colored velvet as well, she thought, but one could not be too sure.

This single room, floored with blue linoleum, a light sprinkling of frosty beige attesting to Julie's preshampoo trim littering the base of the revolving chair, was obviously an extension of the owner's living quarters. From an open door at the back there came a noisy burst of applause and the unmistakable hysterical screams of the contestants in a morning game show.

Deep vertical lines puckered above and below Miss Bee's rosy lipstick. Her hair was arranged as she had worn it for years, in richly hennaed curls pinned high in a chignon of massed ringlets at the back of her head. From this, one long artful curl was permitted to escape. Its carefully controlled cascade fell between her shoulder blades, those narrow shoulders now gently rounded into a dowager's hump, the soft, curved back of age.

Bee looks old, Mrs. Potter thought. Older than Julie does, than

156

Lynette does, than I feel. She straightened her own shoulders, reflecting as she did so that Bee hadn't grown up with the good food, the good care, that most of the rest of them had.

Bee's life had not been easy since those school days, either. On her feet all day, answering the demands of a crotchety, old invalid parent between customers, most certainly worrying about bills and rent and the cost of a new hair dryer, and perhaps about losing new, younger customers to the unisex shop across the street. It seemed a triumph of indomitable will, not vanity, that kept those auburn curls so rich and luxuriant, as much a gallant assertion of self as an advertisement of her art.

At the moment Miss Bee was busily at work, and she sounded happy. Mrs. Potter recognized the air she was humming. "*Ramona, when day is done I hear you call. . . . Ramona, I wait beside the waterfall. . . .*"

"Hi, Julie, remember that one? Bet you can't take it from there!" she called.

To her surprise, the aproned and towel-swathed figure reclining with head in the shampoo tray answered promptly, singing the next lines in a clear, true soprano: "*I press you, caress you, and bless the day you taught me to care . . .*"

Miss Bee's quaver continued without missing a bar. "*I'll always remember, the rambling rose you wore in your hair. . . .*"

The Harrington High School Sextet! Julie and Miss Bee (then Beatrice Jennings) were the sopranos; Lynette and Marie strong on the middle part; Dottie DeBoos confident and sure as an alto, so that 'Genia Andrews could follow along with her without adding much, either good or bad, to the music.

Suddenly weak with laughter, Mrs. Potter started another. "*Shine, little glow-worm, glimmer, glimmer . . .*"

It had been tremendously dramatic, the six of them had agreed, to render that number in a darkened auditorium, and to dazzle the audience with tiny darting flashlights which they flicked on and off at random as they sang. Meantime, dipping their knees, in unison, first to right and then to left. Left, right, left, right, they flashed and warbled.

"*I can't bear it.*" Miss Bee fell into the other shampoo chair and clutched her thin bosom. "*Weren't we terrible?*"

She could not, however, long neglect the serious business at

157

hand. Intent as a temple priestess following a sacred ceremony, Miss Bee gasped, recovered and returned to the recumbent figure before her.

Mrs. Potter watched now with some horror the steps of the monthly touch-up for Julie's beautiful frosted beige hair. Julie was used to suffering for beauty, she thought, remembering how Grandmother Vermeer had wound those golden sausage curls nightly in excruciating rag curlers. She had tolerated no complaints as she brushed young Julie's ringlets around her long bony fingers the next morning. She had permitted no rebellion against the torture of the canvas "bust bodice" that she insisted Julia must wear under her handmade white batiste slip to keep her posture erect and ladylike.

Mrs. Potter's disclaimers were firm, after Julie had been finished and was placed under the dryer. No, Bee dear, I'm sorry, but that's not for me. No, I really don't want it cut short either, with just a touch of body permanent. Yes, I expect it would be amusing and a change, although I'm not sure I really want to look *piquant*. You think you'd like to see a darling cap of curls, just a little bit lighter and brighter? No. *No.* No, thanks.

Their discussion continued as Julie sat under the hair dryer, oblivious to what they were saying under the hum of the blower and immersed in the latest copy of *Town and Country*.

Miss Bee looked at her quickly, and then, head turned away from the row of dryers, she whispered, " 'Genia, notice how *out of it* Julie looks most of the time these days? The singing seemed to wake her up, but honestly she doesn't seem to know what's going on half the time when I see her here."

Miss Bee leaned closer as she began the shampoo that was all Mrs. Potter had finally decided to let her do. "It's Hoddy, of course," she said. "I really don't know whether or not he was carrying on with that Morsback girl, the one who got killed, but it's my opinion that he wasn't, in spite of what some people say. I don't think Hoddy can cut the mustard—you know what I mean, 'Genia? Not with the girl, not with anybody. If you want my opinion, I think Julie's just sliding away into being an unhappy old maid, just what we always thought she'd be."

It had been agreed that Julie would go on ahead to the Inn to meet Lynette and that Eugenia would join them there as soon as her long hair was dry enough to pin back into its accustomed bun. Feeling frazzled—even a short session under a hair dryer left Mrs. Potter feeling cross, mottled, and unbecomingly red of face—she came into the Blue Room to find the two of them already seated at their favorite corner table.

"I ordered us all Bloody Marys," Lynette greeted her. "Yours is here; Julie and I have each had a sip or two while we were waiting."

"You missed Hoddy," Julie said. "He stopped by for a minute, said to tell you hello, so did Roger Two. My, that boy is handsome, Lynette! And such a lamb!"

"In fact," Lynette continued, "everybody you know seems to have come and gone before you got here. Jack, Ralph DeWitt, Donnie Pfingsten, even our onetime cooking school teacher. You missed the whole lot of them, but they all sat down a minute and said to be sure to tell you hello."

"Oh, and you missed the excitement," Julie added. "One of the Harjehausen kids is working here today as a new busboy and he dropped a whole trayful of dishes right in the middle of the room. They've cleaned it all up now, but what a crash!"

The first taste of the well-iced tomato juice and vodka promised to be restorative, and Mrs. Potter stirred the spicy drink gently with the long straw, and sipped again. It seemed an enormous drink, in a heavy glass as big as a brandy snifter, and it had an odd yet not unappealing taste. Perhaps it wasn't really a Bloody Mary, after all.

"This tastes like Mexican sangria," she said. "Not quite as fiery, but a bit of a citrus taste more than tomato. Was that what you ordered, Lynette?"

Lynette said with her usual air of certainty that the order had been Bloody Marys and that was what she and they were drinking. She also said that 'Genia looked flushed, and did she feel all right? Mrs. Potter retorted defensively that she always looked flushed and felt terrible for a couple of hours after being under a hair dryer. Julie said that, well, since the Bloody Mary was such a big drink before lunch, she'd just have another small one, just vodka on the rocks this time. And as long as you're here, Elsie, might as well make it a double.

Lynette continued sipping her first drink, with carefully measured enjoyment. Mrs. Potter found herself watching with quiet absorption as the red drink in her own glass receded in the large round bowl, slowly exposing the red-washed cubes of ice. It was fascinating. She couldn't take her eyes away from it.

" 'Genia, watch out!"

She heard Lynette's voice dimly. Someone's fingers—her own? —reached uncertainly for a handhold on the drapery at the window beside her chair. A trickle of tomato juice stained the front of someone's violet suede lap. Mrs. Potter quietly slid off her chair onto the carpeted floor of the Blue Room.

Three little girls were playing house in a barn loft. Morning sunlight slanted through unwashed window panes. A faint smell of long-ago stables below hung in the air. Ancient dust between the wide floor boards continued to resist their weekly assaults with a lopsided broom.

One little girl had a dark square Dutch bob and another had yellow sausage curls and the third was momentarily invisible.

The three compared the envelopes and packages of "free samples" each had received through the mail since the previous Saturday morning. There were small boxes and tins of powders— talcum powder, baking powder, flea powder, dusting powder.

There were creams both in tiny tubes and in coin-sized tins—cold cream, cleansing cream, vanishing cream, freckle cream, bust-developer cream. There were tiny sliverlike bars of soap—white soap, green soap, translucent Vaseline-colored soap, tarry dark soap that smelled like horse medicine.

"*And now we'll name the club,*" the girl with the Dutch bob said. "We'll call it our favorite flower and our favorite colors."

A club is more fun if you keep people out, said the invisible member of the trio. Let's not let anybody else in, ever, and let's promise never to tell our secret name.

"Did I tell? Did I give it away?" Mrs. Potter woke up in her own bed, to find her nephew, Greg, inexplicably at her side. Her head ached and she felt guilty and depressed. "Did I tell what PPABC means?"

"It's all right, Aunt 'Genia. Everything's all right." Greg paused delicately. "Mrs. Dorrance brought you home, do you remember? She said—Aunt Lynette is what I'm supposed to call her now—that your drinks at lunch seemed to hit you pretty hard, and she helped me get you to bed. Are you okay now?"

Pansy, Pink and Blue Club. After all these years, I told the secret words, Mrs. Potter thought disconsolately. I'll have to admit it to both of them, Julie and Lynette, and they'll never forgive me.

Anyway, I didn't break the rule about letting anybody else in. Not that new girl, Dorothy Jane, not Bee Jennings, not Marie, not any of those Walters kids.

If you were going to belong to the PPABC you had to have access to a lot of magazines—that's where the free sample coupons were—and to a lot of stamps and envelopes. You also had to have the patience and writing ability to print your name clearly and painstakingly, many, many times. "Miss Eugenia Louise Andrews, Harrington, Iowa."

"Just have a sip of this, Aunt 'Genia," she heard Greg say. "Careful, it's hot, but it'll make you feel better."

Strong hot coffee, in the middle of the afternoon? Mrs. Potter noticed that the windows of her room were all opened wide, that the clean old lace curtains were blowing in the wind, a bright, brisk October breeze off the lake.

Mrs. Potter drank more of the coffee at Greg's urging, and slipped down again under the light blanket. "Something's wrong,

161

Greg," she told her nephew, "and you might as well tell me what it is."

Greg was gentle but he was also direct. "People said you passed out at lunch in the Blue Room," he said. "And you might as well hear it from me. There's talk, Aunt Lynette said, that this isn't the first time."

Mrs. Potter's head ached, and she longed to go back to the playroom in the barn to count the week's treasure trove of new samples.

Instead she struggled back to the breezy bedroom and the strange, bearded young man in the chair beside her bed.

Forcing herself to sit up again, she reached out for more of the strong coffee.

Passed out? She certainly had done just that. *Not the first time?* Whatever Lynette had implied, this was puzzling. She was glad to recognize Will's son beside her to talk this over with.

"Help me get this straight, will you, Greg? Please listen. See if you can help me sort it out."

There was the overshot stop sign, two days ago. The sudden plunge into unconsciousness at the lunch table today. She remembered that as she had slid from her chair she had observed, with perfect clarity, the small black reptile pocketbook with the gold chain handle resting lightly on Lynette's well-tailored lap, and the small matching reptile pumps below Lynette's neatly crossed, tidy ankles.

Greg listened intently, insisting that she begin with the whole story of her morning in town, from the visits to the bank and the newspaper office to the shampoo at Miss Bee's and from there to the single lunchtime Bloody Mary. Mrs. Potter, her head clearing, found that she could answer with full recall of detail.

"Now, to start with, no matter what Mr. DeWitt hinted about your drinking the day your brakes failed," he said at last, "you and I know, and so does the guy at the garage, what happened." (Mrs. Potter began to interrupt with the admission that she had had, after all, two drinks that noon, but stopped herself with this reminder of the incontrovertible evidence of the leaking brake fluid.)

"And about today, Aunt 'Genia," he continued, "from what

162

you've told me, if I didn't know that the Blue Room was a highly respectable place, I'd say somebody slipped you a Mickey.''

''*Chloral hydrate*,'' Mrs. Potter read from Grandma's old medical dictionary, which Greg had brought to her bedside. ''Effective sedative and hypnotic agent . . . prompt drowsiness and sedation . . . concomitant use with alcohol may significantly potentiate sedative action . . . tasteless or orange-flavored . . . usual hypnotic dose five hundred milligrams to one gram taken fifteen to twenty minutes before surgery . . . aftereffect including 'hangover' or depressant symptoms, rare . . . possible slight impairment of liver function.''

Mrs. Potter pressed on the area below her rib cage on the right, where she was pretty sure her liver must be. She poked harder. No pain. She saw no reason to involve Doc in all this. There was bound to be enough gossip making its rounds at the moment anyway, without a headline of *Former Resident Claims She Was Drugged* in the *Herald-Gazette*.

As she finished reading, Greg came back to her bedside. ''Now that you've read it,'' he said, ''what do you think? I've just been out in the barn, underneath the station wagon, Aunt 'Genia. You know it's perfectly possible that someone could have loosened that bleed valve on purpose? Hard to tell now, since the man at Norton's replaced it—hard to see now what would have been marks on it. But, I hate to say it, anybody with a crescent wrench could have loosened that valve in just a very few minutes if he knew what he was doing.''

They both were silent for a moment, staring out over the blue of the lake.

''I know it's a crazy idea, Aunt 'Genia, but do you know anybody who might have it in for you? The brake thing could have killed you, you must know that. This knockout stuff in your drink wouldn't likely have been fatal, of course, unless it caused some other kind of accident. But it sure enough could have been intended to make you look like a lady lush—like someone who wasn't to be taken seriously because she'd been drinking.

"And whether you realize it or not," Greg continued, "any one of several people could have slipped that Mickey in your Bloody Mary before you got there. Julie and Lynette were already working on theirs, and everybody knew you were expected to join them. They told you that everyone they knew stopped by to say hello, and they also mentioned a commotion of dropped dishes in the dining room. It would have been easy for someone to put the dose of chloral hydrate in your glass."

Mrs. Potter sat upright in bed and squared her shoulders. "I've been putting off telling Pete everything I know about Jackie's murder," she began, when Greg interrupted.

"Charlotte and I decided early last week that she'd have to tell him what *she* knew," he said. "I know you advised her to wait, but both of us thought she should make a clean breast of it. The blackmailing, all of it."

"That's something of a relief," she assured him, "and I think Charlie was quite right. Still, there may be a few things I myself should tell him, although I still cannot believe that either the brake business or this stuff in my Bloody Mary, if that's what it was, was anything but pure accident. For all we know, love, it simply was the drink itself that hit me, like a ton of lead, after that morning of rushing around town and then sitting under that hot, noisy dryer at Miss Bee's."

"Really, Aunt 'Genia, don't give me that. The day you pass out cold on one Bloody Mary—come on, now."

"Be that as it may," Mrs. Potter said somewhat severely, "I expect there may be a few things I should tell Pete now, even if it is clearly too late for them to be any help to him."

"Why don't you just send him that stack of notes you keep making?" Greg asked. "I can deliver them to him when I go to work in the morning and you won't have to wear yourself out putting it all down in a letter."

After he left, Mrs. Potter looked at her several yellow pads—notes, questions, the wildly improbable scenarios. She was certainly not going to send these to Pete Felderkamp.

Selecting a fresh yellow pad, she wrote "Dear Pete," and that was as far as she got. Her head ached, she put down the pen and pulled up the blanket against the chill of the late afternoon lake breeze.

When she awoke, it was to the clear realization that she could never, would never, share her scenarios, her murky little suspicions, with Pete.

"I'm sure you have looked into any possible consequences of Jackie's alleged blackmail threats," she wrote, "and there is no need for me to pursue those ideas."

She did think, however, she must tell him of two things he might not have been expected to know or to learn on his own.

"I think Varlene may have been at MacKay's house the night of the murder," she continued. "Here's the hairpin I found there, and I don't think it could be anyone's but hers.

"Also, while it may be a shot in the dark," Mrs. Potter's letter went on, "have you looked into the old bank scandal involving Jackie Morsback's father, in Rhynesdorp, New York? Could there be any connection between that and her death here in Harrington?"

Discarded on the floor beside her was a brief and painfully written scenario. It could have implicated either of two young men. Both of them had been well-off, both had been reticent about their previous lives when they first had come to live in Harrington, a little more than twenty years ago. This story was about MacKay, but with a few changes in detail it would have worked equally well for Hoddy.

MACKAY MOORE

Shortly after the bank president is sentenced to the peniten-

165

tiary, the guilty bank teller leaves Rhynesdorp. A few years later he appears as MacKay Moore in Harrington, Iowa.

He buys the old Taylor place. His investments prosper. He is accepted as a peer and a friend by the gentry of the town, who see in him no failing greater than his weakness for harmless flirtation.

Mrs. Potter quickly dropped that page with the others. *Exit MacKay,* she said to herself sadly.

With this she had written everything to Pete that she intended to say. There was no point in mentioning Greg's imagined fears about someone trying to deter her haphazard investigations. No point in mentioning the recent hints she had been receiving, remarks that were probably perfectly innocuous, bearing none of the ominous implications she had later read into them. And certainly no point in mentioning the effects of that lunchtime drink, any more than the wild idea that anyone might have tampered with the brakes of her car.

So, that was all that must be said. "With all best wishes to you and the twins," she wrote hastily, "Yours sincerely, Eugenia Andrews Potter."

In the quiet house, next day at midafternoon, the sudden sound of the telephone made her jump.

Muscles tensing, Mrs. Potter forced herself to pick up the receiver, then to speak calmly and pleasantly as Pete Felderkamp asked if he could come out to see her, saying that Greg had delivered her letter on his way to work early in the day and that he wanted to tell her how things stood.

With a few deep breaths to relax a tight spot somewhere in her chest, she went to the kitchen to put on a fresh kettle for tea. Were there any cookies?

Shortly, seated in Grandpa's brown leather Morris chair, Pete said that first of all he wanted her to know that nobody at the courthouse took any stock in that gossip of her taking a few too many drinks. Greg had told him about the brake fluid, and he'd even checked with the mechanic at Norton's. That could happen to anyone. Now, knockout drops in a cocktail, well, that was another kettle of fish. Still, there just didn't seem to be any way to check on that now, or to prove anything one way or another. Elsie didn't know any more about it than that if there had been a Mickey it hadn't come from her bar, she'd thank him to know, and he could search the place if he wanted to. To her surprise, he had done so.

Then, to Mrs. Potter's equal surprise, Pete said he had summoned his courage and rechecked all the alibis for that night of the stabbing, in spite of what people had to say about his being a stubborn Dutchman. And there wasn't a soul in that cooking class who had what he'd call cast-iron proof that he or she couldn't have been there in the parking lot and done the stabbing, except for the teacher, who had both the phone company and his Chicago secretary to back him up.

Pete had figured out the killer had to be right-handed, which ruled out Greg, at least. That was a comfort.

Pete had even included Mrs. Hofmeyer on his list of suspects and to Mrs. Potter's increasing amazement, he knew about the Florentine dagger in her recently acquired collection.

He had been in touch with the chief of police in that town in New York, Rhynesdorp, but that part of Jackie's past had come to a dead end. Seems that the old Morsback house had burned down just recently and someone found a burned half of an old hundred-dollar bill in the ashes. Apparently the old man had stashed away his hoard right there in his house, and his wife had sat on it like an egg all those years. Leastways, that's the way the fellow there had it.

And he now knew where both MacKay and Hoddy had come from before they showed up in Harrington. He really shouldn't give out information about this, but his checking had been thorough and there was no doubt it was completely *copacetic*.

Well, on second thought, maybe he'd better tell *her,* since he knew she wouldn't let it go any further.

167

MacKay Moore, Hoddy Hofmeyer either, hadn't ever been near any little town in upper New York State.

MacKay's family had a wood products mill up in Maine and that's where he grew up, town near Dover-Foxcroft. Went to Bowdoin College, then back to run the family company until one day he said he was fed up with it and sold out. Clothespins was their big business then, and he got a nice piece of change from the sale. Company still going strong, only it's toothpicks and golf tees now. No family left up there, but the town is on a pretty nice little lake, and the chief of police Pete talked to said he thought Mr. Moore wanted to get shed of the business, all right, but that he'd be pretty certain to live on a lake, wherever he ended up.

Pete looked at her uncertainly, obviously unhappy with his last two words, but Mrs. Potter gestured to him to go on.

About Hoddy—well, did Mrs. Potter know that there were more Germans in Oklahoma than anybody else out there? So Hoddy's father, Jacob Hofmeyer, went to live there in the twenties, settled in a little town near Bartlesville was what he did, and what do you think he did then?

Mrs. Potter could not guess.

Married him an Indian woman, Osage woman she was, just about the time the government was giving all that tribe so much money for the oil on their lands.

Well, who was to say why he married her, although Pete had talked on the phone with an old-timer there who said that it sure wasn't for her beauty. Said she had the fattest neck of any woman he ever did see—right straight down from her ears to her shoulders.

Anyway, Pete continued, no question about where Hoddy got his money after old Mr. Hofmeyer and White Cloud, or Fat Neck, or whatever her name was, both died. When he came to Harrington—leastways, this is the way it looked to Pete—he was just as well-heeled as MacKay was, and just about as closemouthed.

"Why do you suppose they were so secretive?" Mrs. Potter wondered aloud.

The Maine fellow said Mr. Moore's wife died—terrible thing—and maybe he wouldn't ever want to talk about it.

And about Hoddy, didn't it seem sort of likely he'd want to keep it secret about his mother? Hoddy maybe didn't want people to think his father married a squaw, and an ugly one at that, just for her oil money.

Pete had done all this checking by phone, and he was pretty pleased with the cooperation he'd got all around. He'd even braced the teacher Redmond with the name Rhynesdorp to see if he'd get any rise out of him, but that was a complete blank, too. He'd been in Paris, France, at the time of the Morsback bank scandal, going to a cooking school and working in some fancy restaurant.

So that was that on Rhynesdorp. And none of the other leads added up to enough to accuse anybody of murder.

Yes (Harrington's affirmative *yeah* always came out as *ja* to Mrs. Potter's ear, although she could never describe the exact difference in sound), yes, they'd all done a lot of speculating. He had talked it over with the county attorney, Melvin Dykstra was who he was. The two of them had gone down and spent a lot of time with Judge DeBoos to get his opinion. They'd all agreed, sort of informally, that their first solution was the right one.

MacKay stabbed Jackie. The suicide letter seemed pretty conclusive to him, and he was afraid she was letting old friendship influence her too much in her interpretation. They couldn't ignore the fact of the missing knife. Then there was what Elsie and Louie said about how MacKay behaved that night and how mad he looked and sounded when he and Jackie left the Inn, and what Bertha had told him about Jackie's making a fool of him in a way no man could take.

No, they were all agreed about it. MacKay killed the girl and then he did himself in. At his age, he didn't have much to live for, did he?

Mrs. Potter repressed her indignant retort to this and tried instead to focus on other questions. "What about Varlene's being at MacKay's house the night of the killing?" she asked.

Well, again Bertha had been a help about that. Seems she had a box of odd-colored hairpins herself, and while she usually stuck to the black ones, naturally, maybe she'd got a light one in her own hair by mistake. Mrs. Potter thought of Bertha's sleek, perfectly pinned French roll of heavy black hair, and could not imagine it with a brass hairpin. Then, flushing, she reminded herself of any of a procession of MacKay's girlfriends who might have dropped it. No matter; what else must she ask Pete about?

Without prompting, he disposed of her other questions. Sure, lots of people maybe had a reason to kill Jackie Morsback, but the fact was, only one of them could have done it, and it always came back to MacKay. No way Varlene could have been part of it. She had got herself drunk, floundered around in that little car out to the inlet. Threw up all over herself, went down the little old path to wash off, slipped, and that was that. That was the saddest part of the whole thing.

Mrs. Potter at last determined to call the whole unhappy story finished. She would mourn the three deaths but she would no longer prolong and intensify her sorrow by fretting over unanswered questions or loose ends. The official decision was in, and she would get on with her life.

She said good-bye to Pete with a sense of release, of a burden removed.

To start with, she would proceed with a half-considered earlier plan to invite a small group of young people to Indian Point for dinner. Now that Greg, obviously happy and busy with his new job, no longer mentioned returning to California, it was time he found a few more friends of his age in Harrington.

Mrs. Potter reached for a fresh yellow pad to write down a list of names and a possible menu.

The next afternoon, Pete stopped in again. "No tea today, thanks. I'm a coffee man myself. If you'd let me fix myself a cup of instant?"

At this moment Greg came into the driveway on his moped and the three sat companionably in front of the tiny sitting room fire.

At least all three deaths were now settled, the cases were closed, Pete repeated. Town can go back to life as normal.

Life in Harrington was not as peacefully bucolic as the casual outsider might assume, Mrs. Potter thought. She remembered the saying of an old friend from New York who had moved to a hamlet in Vermont. Everything that happens in New York happens here, he had told her. The only difference is that here *you know the people*.

Then Pete repeated, apparently as much for his own reassurance as for Mrs. Potter's: They had closed the books, no trial was needed; Pete hoped he never had another couple of weeks like this again in his life and his wife, Phyllis, hoped so too. He was going to take a week of vacation at the end of the month, go up in the Dakotas and shoot pheasant, and the twins could take charge.

Pete's surprise at seeing Greg again made sharply evident the changes Mrs. Potter had only gradually noticed during the past few weeks. She was delighted with his gain in weight, his new energy, his daily enthusiasm for his new job at the Dorrance factory.

Last week, moreover, Greg had gone to the small building between the bank and the Harrington Pool Hall, the shop formerly known as Tip Anderson, Barber Shop and Baths, now known as Hair and Happenings, run by Tip, Junior.

The old shop was where Mrs. Potter had her first haircut. She remembered the fragrant bay rum-scented hands of Tip himself, the frightening but exciting snip of his cold scissors on the back of her neck, the striped cotton bib that covered her to her toes, and the removable wooden seat he placed for her athwart the leather arms of the adult barber chair. She remembered the slap of Tip's straight-edged razor against the leather strop fixed to the side of the chair, a fearsome sight and sound as she awaited her turn for a haircut. She remembered the occasional shambling, discouraged-looking man who made his way through the double-shuttered doors over which Tip had lettered *"Baths 25¢."*

She remembered too how little she had known about those funny black people she had been brought up to speak of as "darkies." There had never been more than one in Harrington during all of her growing-up years, and he had shined shoes at Tip's barbershop. Maybe there had been a succession of these shoe-shining persons. She knew that Grandpa had called him, or them, "Uncle."

Now everyone under thirty in Harrington, male or female, had his hair cut, bleached, permed, styled, whatever, at Hair and Happenings. Everyone over fifty went either to Miss Bee, as Julie did, or did their own, as did Mrs. Potter. Presumably there were other arrangements available for the thirty-to-fifty group, with whom Mrs. Potter had very little contact.

As a result of Greg's new patronage of Tip's shop, his somewhat scruffy blond beard and long hair were, while still perhaps overabundant by Mrs. Potter's standards, now well-shaped and shining.

As Pete looked at him, she realized that her guest was no longer an invalid.

"Want to see my machine?" Greg asked, and the two went out together to inspect the moped on which Greg now regularly left for work at the factory each morning.

A few minutes later she decided to join them. In most respects a model guest, Greg had never taken on the job of closing the big barn doors at night, and she was convinced that doing so might discourage the raccoons or ground squirrels or whatever creatures were making themselves at home in the old playroom in the loft.

"Something running around up there," Pete remarked.

"I'll take care of it," Greg said reassuringly, "pick up some Hav-a-Heart traps next time I'm at the hardware."

Mrs. Potter reached out, in a familiar gesture, to roll the barn doors shut on their old smooth-running slides.

Greg intervened. "I'm ashamed that I always leave this for you, Aunt 'Genia," he said. "High time you had a man around the place instead of a boy to wait on."

Her talks with Pete had reminded Mrs. Potter of the one cooking class that had actually taken place. Consequently, a day or so later, when she had come again (for the fourth or fortieth time) to the conclusion that her stories had been stupid, insulting to her friends, and certainly valueless now that the murder investigation was closed, she thought about chicken breasts.

She had found herself feeling rather aimless after Greg left for work, taking her car rather than riding his moped because of the heavy rain. The early October morning was dark, but still almost summer-warm. The fields would be too muddy today, she thought, for the huge tractor combines that otherwise would soon be out harvesting soybeans.

The shaded hanging lamp over the kitchen table made a comfortable circle of light, and she sat down there with a cup of now-cooling tea.

When you don't know what else to do, cook something, she told herself. There is no point in brooding about MacKay's death any longer and there is nothing that any of your silly scenarios can do to help Jackie or Varlene. Get out your cookbooks and try something new!

The idea of novelty reminded her again of James Redmond's assignment to create a new dish using poached breasts of chicken.

Edward's Chicken Wellington had been delicious, but she was in no mood for the daylong, painstaking job of making puff paste that the pastry blanket would entail for her. She admitted only an amateurish grasp of the process. Besides, she wanted to try her hand at something of her own. Not that an original recipe was exactly possible. Every combination of foods and flavors and techniques had been tried sometime by somebody, and certainly most of the good ones, the ones that turned out well, had long since found their way into the cookbooks and repertories of the world's cooks.

However, as she leafed through her not inconsiderable pile of cookbooks, which included those of her mother and grandmother, she was surprised to find that cooking breasts by poaching—simmering them in liquid—was, as the instructor had suggested, not at all a usual procedure.

Undoubtedly this is a part of our new awareness of fats and calories, Mrs. Potter thought. "Brown in butter or in oil" seemed to be an initial step in all the old recipes. We all want to be much slimmer than our parents or grandparents ever considered possible or even desirable. Besides that, we're constantly told about the dangers of animal fats and cholesterol.

Whatever her inspiration was to be, she decided to keep it in this restricted field. It would be a really low-fat, low-calorie dish.

At that moment, the telephone rang. "It's Bertha, Mrs. Potter.

I'm home in town and I'm coming out to the house in a little while to pick up some clothes and things. Mrs. Dorrance told Alice that Greg had your car today, and I wondered, is there anything I could bring you?''

Mrs. Potter gratefully and hurriedly dictated a spur-of-the-moment shopping list. A half dozen whole chicken breasts (might as well do some experimenting with several dishes, she thought, or she could freeze what she decided not to use). Some unblanched almonds and a half pint of cream in case it wasn't possible to stay firm with those calories. Tomatoes, onions, celery, parsley—she had those in the house, along with seasonings and staples. *Celery*, she repeated with a sudden inspiration, more than the few stalks she had in the refrigerator. Two good big bunches of Pascal celery, she added, if it's nice. Mushrooms, if they looked good this morning. White grapes?

She settled down with the cookbooks until Bertha arrived. By then she knew pretty much what she was going to do.

First, she urged Bertha to have a cup of coffee, and was slightly relieved when this was declined. Bertha wanted to go through the closet and bureau in her old room and clear things out, bring back some of her old uniforms for Alice.

Mrs. Potter wanted to ask what was going to become of the house, but the words would not come. Later, maybe, but she could not yet think of MacKay's house with another owner.

Thank heaven for a job as absorbing, as pleasant as cooking, she thought after Bertha left. The rain outside just makes it all the cozier here in the big old kitchen. The pantry is stocked with a lot of good food, plus those few items Bertha brought. Whichever turns out best of my chicken recipes, Greg and I will have for dinner. Anything not so good is fairly sure to be edible, at least, as a base for some other dish or in sandwiches for Greg's lunch box.

With mild surprise she realized that while she had been cooking for—how long, forty years?—and while she had made a great many improvisations in that time, some quite good, some less so, this was the first time she had ever sat down and tried to make up a new recipe. A recipe that could be written down and possibly, in turn, cooked by someone else. The idea seemed significant. At the very least she would send it to her two daughters and her daughter-in-law.

174

It was tempting to begin by naming the dish. *Suprêmes de Volaille Pochés à la Eugénie* sounded very nice, and she said it aloud in her best college French accent. However, that should really wait until she had looked over the supplies. No mushrooms, too bad. Lovely, solid, big bunches of celery, however, and the chicken breasts were fresh, unfrozen, and unsplit.

Only for a brief second did she think of the horror of Jackie's death as she ran the sharpening stone in quick passes over the blade of her French boning knife. As she tackled the mound of chicken, she remembered most surely the procedure James Redmond had demonstrated, and with each breast she worked a little faster.

In a long baking tray, she assembled the twelve oval fillets, all of them creditably neat and shapely. I've never done this by removing that keel bone first, she realized. I've always tried to cut along either side of it from the top, then to separate the meat by working from the top side down.

A pile of bones and scraps filled a large bowl beside her. Whatever she made would probably want chicken stock for the poaching, she knew. So the contents of the bowl, along with some cut-off tops and outer stalks of the celery, went into the stockpot. She added an onion, peeled and thickly sliced, a couple of sliced carrots, a bit of salt (she measured this as always in the cup of her hand) and cold water to cover it all.

The mailman's car droned into place at the barn driveway, and she decided to postpone the rest of the cooking until after lunch.

As she covered the chicken with plastic and set the pan in the refrigerator, she was reminded again that the old monitor-top was too small and sounded ominously noisy. If she was going to stay much longer, they'd need a new one, hesitant as she had been about the decision that day at DeWitt's. This one had been bought long before Grandma died, but the freezer beside it was comparatively new; her parents had bought it only several years back.

On the other hand, the old icebox, now unused, presented another decision to be made. It was not in the kitchen at all, but instead occupied the outer wall of the pantry passage leading from the kitchen to the dining room. Its heavy oak-paneled doors were hung with great steel hinges and secured with big steel latch-handles, all still gleaming like silver. There were six large compartments, three above and three below, all but one lined with

175

white porcelain. The center compartment, for ice, was lined with a corrugated zinclike metal. From it a drain spout led to a drip pan concealed in its own paneled space at the bottom of the long wall.

This compartment had an outside door as well, so that the iceman could fill it without coming into the house. As she remembered, he would first mount the few steps to the little platform from which the outer door opened, look inside, and then judge the size of the ice block needed that day by the Andrews household. He would return to his wagon, lift the gunnysack coverings over the sawdust-encrusted ice, and with his long ice pick chip and split the right-sized block. Hoisting it with tongs to his leather-covered shoulder, he would deliver the ice to the outer icebox door.

If Will and Eugenia were in time to catch him, Grandma would provide them each with a torn square of muslin from an old sheet, and the iceman would give them a long daggerlike sliver of ice from his chippings. You were supposed to suck the ice through the clean white cotton to keep the sawdust bits out of your mouth, but as Mrs. Potter recalled, that sawdust taste itself was delicious as you raced around sucking ice on a hot summer morning.

As she opened each door, almost expecting to find the glass jars of Mr. Bjerke's cream and the tall bottles of milk with a layer of yellow cream rising to the top, Mrs. Potter sniffed slightly for the odor of mildew. She was relieved that previous energetic scrubbings, plus the presence of an opened box of baking soda in each compartment, had kept the old icebox still remarkably sweet-smelling. She considered the possibility of having it converted into a modern refrigerator. Its convenience, capacity, and its beauty would never be equaled by a present-day metal and plastic box.

Doing that would entail a compressor in the cellar, she thought. Which settles *that* good idea. Mrs. Potter had never in her life been in the cellar at Indian Point.

But the cyclone cellar outside the kitchen door was known to her. Apart from the slight delicious terror created by the wind overhead when the family sat waiting out the storms—very slight indeed when one sat on one's father's lap and listened to a wonderful long story made up especially for the occasion—she had always thought the old shelter a very good, sound, comfortable little cave.

The house cellar was different, but she did not intend to find out how or why. If there had to be a compressor there to turn the old icebox into a mechanically cooled refrigerator, she would have to go down to confer with whoever did the job. No. She would buy a new refrigerator to be placed in the kitchen whenever the old one finally gave up the ghost.

Mrs. Potter made herself a pot of tea and an omelet. Not as good as Greg's, but neither did she have the avocado and bacon on hand that went into his particular California specialty.

The chicken stock had simmered to a fairy satisfactory flavor by the time she had finished eating lunch and reading the mail.

By the end of the afternoon, some of the chicken breasts had been set aside, wrapped in foil, and frozen, being more than she needed for her experiments. Two trial batches were also set aside: combinations not sufficiently interesting to be served in their present state, but retrievable for chicken hash, maybe, another day.

Three good dishes had evolved. Greg is going to be pretty surprised, she thought, to have a first course tonight of cold chicken *en gelée* with cold braised celery vinaigrette. For this she had glazed the cold poached breasts with clear chicken jelly, brushed over the punctuation of a few slices of pitted ripe olives, to be served on a bed of the cold jelly, chopped and glistening. Alongside were chilled cooked quarters of well-trimmed celery that had been marinating all afternoon in a brisk vinaigrette sauce. A few strips of pimiento, if there was a jar in the pantry, would add color, and a little bouquet of parsley would finish the plate. Nice for a cold summer buffet, she thought, if you had one of those ice things underneath so the chopped jelly wouldn't soften.

Then she and Greg would go on to two dishes for a main course, she had decided—half servings of everything. The first was her version of chicken *amandine*. Several traditional steps had been eliminated from the classic recipe. The chicken was not browned in butter, and the breasts were not flamed with cognac before they received the creamy almond sauce. Instead, the chicken had been poached in a combination of chicken broth and white wine, then kept warm while the sauce was made from the same liquid. She had blanched a half cup of almonds and slipped off their brown skins, while the chicken stock boiled rapidly to reduce its volume. Taking about two thirds of the nutmeats, she had run them twice through Grandma's little nut grinder, which turned them almost to a smooth paste. A regular grinder would do, she thought, or a blender, or one of those new food-processing machines she didn't really want. The ground almonds, with a tablespoon of tomato paste, served to thicken the sauce slightly, but it still seemed to her to be too runny and she remedied the consistency with a little corn-starch stirred to a paste with stock. Finally, tasting, and realizing she had already lost the battle of the calories with the almonds, she stirred in what seemed a crucial two tablespoons of heavy cream, along with a bit more salt.

She arranged the chicken breasts in a shallow baking dish along with quarters of firm tomatoes, poured the sauce over them, then sprinkled the top with the rest of the blanched almonds, cut in sliv-ers. It would be an appealing dish, well browned later on under the broiler.

The third chicken dish was the best, she thought. The chicken for this had been poached simply in the well-seasoned chicken broth, then kept warm while she made a lemon dill sauce. She thickened a generous cup of the broth with a tablespoon of corn-starch (an earlier version of the dish called for three egg yolks in-stead, but she remembered her original Spartan intentions), then added a tablespoon of chopped fresh dill from the garden and a ta-blespoon of lemon juice. (Dried dillweed would be good, too, but one would only use half as much.) In serving, she would pour the hot lemony sauce over the chicken and little hot boiled new pota-toes. Really low-calorie, and really good!

When she had time tomorrow she would write down the recipes, copying accurately the measurements she had jotted down as she cooked, trying to make the directions sound professional.

Still vaguely uneasy, yet reassured by Greg and Pete that she had nothing to worry about, that she had no further responsibilities now that the three deaths were no longer considered mysteries, and increasingly convinced that the failing brakes and the inexplicably potent Bloody Mary had been only accidents that might happen to anybody, Mrs. Potter's mind and muscles began to relax.

In spite of the growing autumnal chill, most bright days she found it warm enough for a brief dip before lunch in the invigorating waters of the lake. She slept better, and she continued her daily walks through the still-flaming maples along the lakeshore.

And now, at the end of that first week in October, was the evening of her small dinner party for the Young.

(She had not yet completed plans for a celebration party for the DeWitts, which she now felt honor-bound to arrange, after her prying and suspicious questions about their business anniversary. The only thing she was sure about for that party was that she'd ask her guests to bring a white elephant—the awfulest, ugliest, most useless item they owned, of any size that could be gotten into a car for its transport—and to agree to take home whatever monstrosity fell to their lot in return. Even though a sop to her conscience, the evening might as well be fun.)

As planned, tonight she had invited a number of younger Harrington residents, both to celebrate Greg's new job at the Dorrance factory and his increasing satisfaction and success there and to further encourage him in new friendships among people his own age.

She had invited Pete Felderkamp and his wife, Phyllis, managing to get them before Pete left on his fall hunting vacation. She had also invited Roger Two and asked him to pick up Charlie-Charlotte.

She had invited the Hayenga twins and asked them each to bring a girl. These, she learned, were to be the shapely, ripely Italian Tressini twins, whose grandparents owned the Harrington Pizzeria and Frozen Yogurt Palace, formerly known as the Sweet Shoppe. (This had been the home of the Chocolate Teddy of Mrs. Potter's youth, as well as less frequent BLT lunches. She and Lynette and Julie had lived for their Friday afternoon treat of vanilla ice cream layered with chocolate sauce in a tall parfait glass and topped with a great scoop of salted Spanish peanuts, the little round red ones with the skins still on. Enough to last for at least three peanuts in every spoonful, if you were careful, right to the bottom of the glass.)

Sherri and Terri were, respectively, head of the data-processing department at the bank and office manager at the Dorrance plant, and they had never heard of a Chocolate Teddy.

Mrs. Potter then needed another young woman to even the number and had called Charlotte again to ask for suggestions. She had finally secured the pretty new nurse from Dubuque who had recently come to work at the (Dorrance-endowed) Harrington Community Health Center.

With the number evened (when entertaining people her own age, Mrs. Potter did not feel this was necessary, and due to the preponderance of widows and corresponding shortage of men among her usual circles of friends it was often impossible), a pinprick of conscience forced her to unbalance it again by telephoning another young man. Edward's gratitude at her invitation was overwhelming, and she did not regret the impulsive gesture.

However, he had promised the Hofmeyers he would go to Sioux City with them that day to bring home some things for the house in town and they would not be back until too late for her party.

Maybe he wouldn't have fitted in happily, she thought, but at least it was good for him to know he had been invited.

As is turned out, the evening was cheerful, the dinner simple but good. There was plenty of jug wine and beer (tomato juice for Greg); an enormous pot of her own special Five Star Bean Soup (she had kept the sausages and chunky bits of cooked ham separate, to be added at the sideboard, so that Charlie needn't try to eat around them); quantities of hot crusty rolls and butter and a good wheel of mellow Vermont cheese. For dessert she had decided upon a reprise of Grandma's green tomato pie, which really *was* better cold. This neatly used up all the remaining wrapped green tomatoes in the cyclone cellar.

Everyone had a good time, she thought with satisfaction after the party was over. "No thanks, Greg love, the dishes are all rinsed and stacked and I'll wash them in the morning after you've gone to work. Right now I'm ready for bed, aren't you?"

However, as always after any party, Mrs. Potter found herself replaying snatches of conversation in her mind before falling asleep.

Too bad the Ragsdale house had been marked for destruction now that the new junior college was going to take over all that block east of the courthouse. Good for Harrington to have the college here, to say nothing of all those construction jobs, but a blow to Charlie, who loved the house and who was used to spreading out, with lots of room for her plants and her painting.

Yes, Mrs. Potter did think there were rats, or maybe coons, in the old barn. Roger Two thought he had seen one as his headlights shone inside.

Yes, everyone would accept the Felderkamps' invitation to a pheasant dinner later on if Pete had good hunting. It came out that Greg had a strong aversion to guns used for any purpose at all. The Hayenga and Tressini twins quizzed him on this, in four-part chorus rather than the boys' usual duet. Would that include self-defense or protection of his family?

Charlie said that she, of course, would no longer shoot living creatures to eat (her father had been an ardent hunter and she had accompanied him enthusiastically as a girl) but that she was still a pretty good marksman with a target.

The new nurse said she was crazy about water-skiing and was it too late in the year?

Roger Two and Mrs. Potter both said that their docks would be brought in and their boats taken up in another few weeks, long before a chance of ice on the lake, but that there were several boats still in the water and that there should be a few more good days for skiing, if the sun was warm enough.

Roger Two offered the use of the Dorrances' speedy *Blue Lightning*.

Without thinking, Mrs. Potter had almost added that MacKay's *Blue Goose*, as well as her own *Blue Fish*, was still in the water. The words were choked back, but the painful reminder had plagued the latter part of her evening, as it did now in her wakeful postparty thoughts—MacKay, mustache twitching, brown eyes popping with pleasure, towing the pretty nurse on her water skis.

The next playback speaker was Greg. His new job was infinitely more meaningful (oh, that word again, she thought) than his research in behavioral science at Stanford. He really might stay on in Harrington. Anyway, he certainly planned to do so for the winter, since he could not leave the Saturday junior high classes in moped safety he had just begun teaching.

Yes, thanks, he'd love another glass of milk. This to Charlie, who was holding the old white Andrews milk pitcher in what

181

seemed a firm, possessive way, while the other tanned, beringed hand rested lightly upon his shoulder.

The Greg record continued. He had plans for a workshop in the barn, where he would work on a design to improve the hill-climbing power of a new moped model.

"Charlotte has a great idea," he kept adding proudly. "We're designing new double carrying-baskets to go over the rear wheel, and she wants to make sure these are the right size for supermarket shopping bags. Isn't that terrific?"

Terrific, *terrific,* terrific, *terrific,* agreed all the twins.

The next recording had to do with marriage. Pete and Phyllis, predictably, were all for it. The four twins held equally conservative views. Roger Two found the topic of little interest, one way or another.

The pretty nurse spoke admiringly about a couple she knew in Dubuque who lived together. In love and mutual trust, she said, but naturally avoiding "total commitment."

Charlie said she believed in complete honesty. Greg said he did, too.

Whatever that meant, it apparently did not mean marriage.

At this point, lying stiffly in the dark, enough of Mrs. Potter's conscious mind surfaced to reflect that Indian Point would be a wonderful place to raise a whole new generation of racing, driving, shouting, lake-loving little Andrews. But children certainly had no place in the world of two people who would avoid the word *commitment.*

Finally she went into fitful sleep, with antiphonal four-part responses echoing in her mind: Cary and Gary, Sherri and Terri, in continuing comment on all these and other matters.

Just before dawn, Mrs. Potter was again fully awake, feeling peevish and perverse—a state unusual for a woman of her usual good digestion and equable temperament.

I should have seen it, she told herself. Greg and Charlie have fallen in love and they've decided to live together. Charlie has to move out of her house, so that means they'd like to come here.

It's just too much, she thought. How can they expect me to give approval to an arrangement of "honesty and mutual trust," or whatever they call it, right here under my own roof? Me, a woman who can't even go to church without a hat?

182

Ordinarily Mrs. Potter would have enjoyed the leisurely job of washing the party dishes the next morning. The old kitchen was friendly and convenient and she found pleasure in using and handling Grandma's old tea leaf ironstone soup plates and tureen. Now, it just seemed a tedious job to be finished. She considered a trip to town, but found that for some reason her car would not start. Reluctantly she went to her desk, where the October bills and bank statement were waiting.

Finally, weary after her wakeful night, Mrs. Potter elected an early lunch and a nap. Prompted by an inner sense of unease, she sought a refuge in food, even though she was not really hungry. She reheated a generous portion of the rich bean soup, added some sausage and ham to it, toasted two of the leftover buttered rolls, and with it all finished off the last of the wine; then decided to eat the remaining sliver of Grandma's green tomato pie, since there was really not enough to save for Greg for dinner.

Both choices—the luncheon and the nap—proved disastrous. She fell into a sleep of horrors, distortions and dreams all the more dreadful because she knew she was dreaming, yet still unable to wake up. Only after a tremendous wrench of will was she free of them, and even after freshening her face, hair, and clothing she felt burdened and apprehensive.

The front door bell startled her as if it had been a spoken threat. When the hand-turned small brass bell key summoned her to the front hall, she knew the visitor was a stranger to the household. Any one of her friends, even the usual tradespeople, would simply have opened the big front door and called, loudly and cheerily, "Anybody home?"

Forcing herself to answer it, she was relieved (what *had* she been expecting?) to see again the pleasant pale face, the reassuring proper demeanor and dress, of James Redmond. In spite of his in-

183

sistence about fees in their telephone conversation a week or two earlier, he was harmless enough after the horrors of her dreams, and today he seemed almost as attractive as he'd appeared at their first meeting at the start of summer.

He had come, he said, to bring the refund they had agreed would be returned from his share of the cooking school fees. He wanted to apologize because he had, when they discussed this on the telephone, computed this on the basis of the ten remaining students, and he wanted to correct his unintentional error.

The check he was bringing, he went on formally, included refunds due for those three unfortunate class members who were no longer with us. Perhaps Mrs. Potter would be so good as to see that these three shares were distributed to the proper authorities, relatives, or estates?

And no thank you, he would not stay for tea, much as he would like to accept that kind invitation. He was packing, getting ready to depart for Chicago. The handyman was already there closing the cottage.

Mrs. Potter's good-bye was cut short by the ring of the telephone, which she answered as her caller went down the front steps.

"That you, 'Genia?" The voice was familiar, but Mrs. Potter was momentarily puzzled.

"I just want you to know I'm here at the lake," the woman's voice went on easily, "and I thought you might come over and have a cup of coffee with me. Or a drink maybe."

"*Bertha?* It's Bertha!" Mrs. Potter fumbled briefly for this recognition. "Why, yes, that would be nice, but I'm sorry, my car won't start." That part is truthful, she thought. "Maybe I can stop by tomorrow on my way to town, if Greg gets it started. Anyway, we had a small party here last night" (*yes*, Bertha replied, she had heard) "and now I'm feeling tired and upset and not fit company for anyone."

She hung up, still awkward with surprise at the invitation. "That you, 'Genia?" It had been a little startling. "*A drink maybe?*"

She wished she had asked Bertha what was going to become of the house. It was painful to think of the place with another owner, but perhaps less so than seeing it empty and neglected.

Anyway, she'd certainly stop by to see how Bertha was getting along. She knew the house would be spotless by the time Bertha left, and she briefly considered who among her friends might need a new housekeeper.

No, not for herself at the ranch. Not only was her household there functioning happily—with very little style, but comfortably—but it took a certain flexibility of spirit, perhaps more than Bertha would have, to transplant easily from Iowa small-town life to the open range, the vast ranch distances of southern Arizona.

Mrs. Potter drank half a glass of water with a teaspoon of soda. She still felt an uneasy pressure in some vague interior space, a feeling she could only define for herself as the knowledge that something was wrong.

She looked out over the lake. No sign of impending storm. No drop in the old brass barometer in the hall. Why this sense of impending disaster?

As always, Mrs. Potter felt that the best cure for any malaise was work.

Marshaling the necessary resolve, if not enthusiasm, she decided that this would be a good time, in the hour or so before Greg's return from work, to begin sorting a box of old papers in the upstairs south bedroom, the one that had been her mother and father's room when they all lived together with Grandpa.

She settled herself, feeling fat, in the faded armchair and looked out over the bare trees to the south. She pulled a dusty carton to her side and the endless afternoon wore on.

As she came to the faded document which was her father's honorable discharge from the Army in 1918, she was vaguely aware of the sound of a car, and she glanced at her watch. It was still too early for Greg, and besides he would be riding his moped.

She'd soon hear the questioning "*Anybody home?*" as whoever it was reached the door.

There was no sound, no call, and she resumed her perusal of the papers. The next was an old mining stock certificate, with "N.G." inscribed on its face in her father's neat, distinctive printing.

There was an old diary with her mother's initials on it, faded gold letters on faded red plush. She read the inscription on the flyleaf: "*Let not that day pass whose low descending sun sees not from thy hand some worthy action done.*" How accurately this principle had illuminated her mother's life.

Will future generations keep cassette diaries? she wondered idly. Tapes, cassettes were so much a part of business life now (she thought of James Redmond's dictated newspaper columns and book chapters) and of people's family communications as well. She put the faded volume back in the box, unread. If her mother had wanted her to read it, she would have given it to her long ago.

Then, startled, she put her papers aside. This was not imagination.

The door to the back porch and then the kitchen door had opened—all but silently, but with those faint sounds unmistakable to one who had known every creak, every thump, of the house from her earliest childhood.

She listened intently, unmoving.

There was a step, quiet and light. She knew each murmur, each soft complaint, of the old stair steps. Slowly, another. Someone was coming quietly up the back stairs.

Mrs. Potter's unease, her forebodings, her feelings of being enmeshed in a never-ending bad dream, all came together in sudden and terrible panic.

Who—pushed beyond caution, beyond reason—was coming up to ensure her permanent silence?

Who, moving stealthily, eyes flat and intent in the dim stair hall, might hold the final scenario poised on the blade of a thin, sharp knife?

No more endless, fruitless speculation about a murder, a suicide, a fatal accident. It had been three murders, and now it would be four. Whoever was there had come to finish the job at last.

As suddenly as she knew this, Mrs. Potter knew who was coming slowly, almost noiselessly, up those stairs to kill her.

In unreasoning, agonizing fear, she rose from her chair and fled into the hall, down the front stairs and out the front door, trying to decide which direction offered best hope of escape.

Sliding, stumbling down the grassy bank in front of the house to the long wooden dock, she saw her own two boats. Moored by its double lines at the dock was the *Blue Fish*, its strong outboard motors presumably ready, as always, for takeoff. Mrs. Potter ordinarily had no difficulty in starting it, in casting off, and in handling the boat on the lake.

She again momentarily lost her footing and almost fell on the last of the sloping pathway to the dock. What if the motor should not start at once, what would she do? Could she cast off the two lines quickly, flee without delay to the safety of the open lake? Would she have time to get away from the advancing threat in the old house?

She had a quick chilling recollection that the last time she had taken the boat out alone it had been slow to start. Could she risk delay?

The small red canoe, its paddle lying ready under the seats, offered an instant choice. The screen door of the porch behind and above her closed with its well-known throat-clearing rasp. There was no time for the *Blue Fish*. She grasped the canoe firmly, launched it in a single smooth motion and with the sureness born of long practice, seated herself in the stern.

Without wasted motion Mrs. Potter guided the canoe away from the dock, then swiftly and without a backward look, paddled toward the east, toward town and safety. But, suddenly she thought, even better and closer than town was MacKay's house, with a telephone, a car, and the sanity and safety of Bertha's solid presence.

As the small red canoe pulled out of sight beyond the first bend of shoreline, the shock of realization was complete. She knew the identity of that deadly, silent menace on the back stairs, the killer intent on destroying the final necessary victim.

What she had been wrong about, what Pete had so blindly accepted, was the validity of the one alibi he had been able to check. Impressed by the unfamiliar technology, he had accepted the proof that this suspect (so lightly regarded among all those possible others) had been on the telephone dictating to his office receiving set, his recording "tank," at the time of Jackie's murder.

They had overlooked one thing.

The murderer's dictation could have been recorded earlier. The tank, the receiver, could have been hearing the playback of a cassette rather than a live speaking voice.

There had been plenty of time for him to go to his cottage, dial the Chicago number, connect the cassette player, drive to Harrington, await the arrival of the girl in the parking lot of the Arms. Plenty of time for the sure sweep of the deadly knife blade, plenty of time to return to disconnect the telephone at the end of the recording.

The killer was James Redmond, and Jackie had recognized him as the man who framed her father.

When had he learned of her interest in Rhynesdorp? She knew now she had been right about that, if so very wrong in her unwilling suspicions of Hoddy and MacKay. Just as Pete had been wrong in accepting the story of Redmond's being in France. How could he *really* have checked those years and facts?

Even small details came into focus. There was the cancellation of Redmond's social life when he first saw Jackie at the early summer cocktail party, his shock at hearing the familiar name. There was his nearly incoherent recognition of her again at the cooking class (had she lisped as a five-year-old? Did he think a child might remember a broken little finger?) when he had undoubtedly thought she'd left town. And he had been right in his fears. Jackie's suspicions had in some way been roused, and for help and protection she had turned, that night, to MacKay.

How then had Redmond disposed of MacKay and Varlene after he stabbed Jackie? The reason was clear, if not the actual execution; in some way each had been a witness to his guilt.

Paddling yet more swiftly, breathing with difficulty, Mrs. Potter thought of the threats to her own safety. Redmond had arranged them all. It would have been easy to tamper with her car brakes in the old unlocked barn, and his presence on the road later in the day, after her near-brush with death, had been to make sure his work had been successful.

She remembered that Redmond had been one of those at their table before she joined Julie and Lynette for lunch, before she drank the cocktail that made her appear drunk and threatened her credibility.

Chilled now, even with the increasing exertion that caused her breath to come in deep painful gasps, Mrs. Potter summoned all her courage to look back over her shoulder.

At least he was not pursuing her in her own *Blue Fish*. There was no boat behind her. But that was small comfort, since Redmond could have driven ahead, could already be at MacKay's house, could have got Bertha out of the way, could be waiting for her there.

Could this small canoe, this one now-faltering paddle, find safety anywhere on Blue Lake before she was overtaken by the killer?

MacKay's dock was ahead, and the *Blue Goose* was alongside at its customary mooring.

A few steps above the dock was the railed deck that fronted the big stone and timber house. And there, to her overpowering relief, she saw MacKay's housekeeper stretched out easily in a deck chair in the sun.

She was not too late. Redmond had not yet arrived, or perhaps was even postponing his deadly attack for a time when she was again alone.

"Bertha," she shouted as loudly as her gasping breath would permit, "is Redmond here? Are you alone?"

"Nobody here, 'Genia. Glad you could come over after all."

Mrs. Potter pulled the red canoe in to the dock. She had reached her place of refuge. The terror was behind her, and Bertha's stolid calm would be her bulwark.

The reclining figure rose from the deck chair. The smooth upward twist of the black hair was familiar, the dark skin, the calm air of imperturbability were known to her. From the neck up, it was Bertha. From the neck down, Mrs. Potter could only stare in disbelief. No uniform, not even the neat striped blue shirtdress in which the housekeeper might be taking her ease on an off-duty afternoon.

Bertha, a Juno of dark curves, of large, firm breasts and swelling hips, of lavish belly and extravagant thighs, was wearing a stunning costume: a very small black bikini and a pair of high-heeled shiny black pumps.

Bertha's navel was a dark, downy hollow. Mrs. Potter resolutely looked away as she groped for suitable words of greeting and apology to explain her own unexpected, breathless appearance in the red canoe.

Bertha seemed to find nothing out of the way in their encounter. "I am so glad you could come, after all," she repeated calmly. "I was just having my afternoon sun, as you see."

As she spoke she pulled on a pair of tight silky black pants and patted them smoothly over the Rubenesque curves of her hips and legs. She picked up a flowered shirt, and knotted its pink, black and white ties snugly under the great round breasts. "You will have that coffee now, 'Genia?" she asked.

Mrs. Potter did not know how or where to begin. Her terrified arrival at the dock was blurred by this unexpected apparition. Momentarily, she found it difficult to explain her own flight from Indian Point and her fear of the furtive threatening footsteps on the back stairs, the complicated details that had revealed the identity of the assailant and had proved him a murderer. "I'm just going in to town," she offered lamely, "and since my car wouldn't start I thought I'd take the canoe."

Embarrassed, unable to continue her explanation in all its complexities, she decided at least to pursue her goal of a ride to town. To the courthouse, the library, the bank, any place she'd find the reassuring presence of people, of protection from those quiet footsteps. "I don't suppose you'll be going back into town soon?"

"My car is having a little work done," Bertha told her easily. "I know it's old, but it's worth another forty thousand miles. That's what they tell me at Norton's. I've given the little car to Alice, now, and my Mercedes isn't back yet. Tomorrow, maybe."

Bertha, smiling, then looked at her caller more closely. "It's important? You look upset, Mrs. Potter. 'Genia. You got to get into town right away?" As she spoke, she smoothed her bare midriff below the knot of the flowered blouse and tucked the end of the long gold chain she was wearing around her neck more securely into the swelling curve of the black bikini top underneath. "You're sure you won't have that coffee now? Or a drink with me? Now that we're neighbors, 'Genia. Now we're old friends and neighbors, no?"

"Yes, of course, but I really don't think I have time to stay for coffee. I'll just be on my way—" Mrs. Potter turned awkwardly to return to the canoe.

She reconsidered. "Bertha, I'm not being honest with you. I think I now know who killed Jackie and MacKay and I've got to get away. I've got to get to town and find Pete."

Bertha jumped up. "In that case we'll go in a jiffy in my own boat." She came down the four steps from the deck quickly, balanced and secure on the high black heels. "I insist, plenty of gas, it's all ready to go. See, the cushions are already out? You will sit here, please," and she put a large capable hand under Mrs. Potter's elbow and propelled her into the *Blue Goose*. "I will have you there at the town dock before you know it." She lifted the red canoe easily and placed it in the bow of the boat.

Mrs. Potter felt she had lost her usual sense of command. Bertha leaned over the motor and the outboard responded instantly to her skillful touch. The boat roared away from the dock.

As Bertha turned from the motor and seated herself with easy confidence at the tiller, Mrs. Potter's eyes were caught by a flash of brilliance. Loosened by her movement, the gold chain swung free against the generous cleavage of Bertha's breasts. Suspended there, momentarily blinding in the reflected light of the late afternoon sun, was an electric flash of a bright blue gem, surrounded by a dazzle of diamonds.

Quickly Bertha quenched the flash of color and light in her large smooth hand, and slipped the suspended jewel back under the snug edge of the narrow black bra. Again only the chain was visible beneath the open neck of the flowered shirt.

Mrs. Potter said nothing, but looked up in doubt and disbelief. Bertha stared back in challenge.

The noise of the boat discouraged conversation and in any case, Mrs. Potter could think of nothing to say. It was impossible to voice her question, to demand what Bertha was doing with MacKay's grandmother's sapphire and diamond ring. Bertha had said my car, my boat. Those claims had been phrased in unmistakable terms. Now was it *my* ring as well?

The boat veered right, turning in an abrupt flare of white water toward the western end of the lake, away from town. Mrs. Potter found her voice. "Oh, the other way, please. Bertha, remember, I'm going to town, to Harrington, not back to Indian Point."

Bertha's face was expressionless and Mrs. Potter repeated her statement more loudly, pointing vigorously toward the east.

The dock at Indian Point was on their right, but the *Blue Goose* did not enter the small, gentle bay with its double-scalloped point. Without pause and with its throttle full open, the boat roared toward the lowering sun in the autumn sky.

The small guest cabin of James Redmond came into sight, in its own cushioned shell of evergreens on the shorefront, blank and shuttered, its summer occupant departed.

The Pink House loomed above them, its flat face expressionless behind long white winter shutters.

Beyond the silent house, the *Blue Goose* whirled into the small, quiet cove at the end of the lake, the one part of Blue Lake not yet lined with houses and cottages, and almost completely obscured from the rest of the lake by the indentation of its shoreline and the encirclement of its wooded verge.

For the first time, Mrs. Potter knew real fear. Not the earlier frenzied, thoughtless panic she had felt when she heard the quiet footsteps on the stairs. This time it was cold, real fear.

Bertha stilled the roar of the motor and the boat slowed almost to a halt, rocking quietly in the light breeze and clear rippling water.

Mrs. Potter looked at the heavy, powerful figure facing her, the strong hands firmly planted on flexed knees in shiny black pants. "Bertha?" she questioned. "*Bertha*. What's this all about? What are you doing? What's happened?"

192

"Mrs. Eugenia big-shot high-muckety-muck Andrews Potter. You need me to tell you?"

There was no misunderstanding that hard blue gaze and the ferocity, the anger, the hate that lay behind it.

"You hate me. Is that what you're saying? You've always hated me?" Mrs. Potter was incredulous.

"From the day I saw you, I hated you, little girls we were then. We went to you and Alice's graduation, I hated you then, too. You there with your folks and your brother all dressed up so nice in white. You and your prizes and your roses and the rest of it. Sure I hated you."

The cold voice went on. "Elsie didn't hate you. Alice always kept saying that was just the way it was. The Andrews and the Dorrances and the Vermeers and the Vanderpools, it was right they should have the best of it."

Briefly, the voice softened. "I hated you . . . I wanted to *be* you. I don't know."

Bertha shifted her weight and touched the gold chain at her neck. "My mother hated you folks too. She had a bad time, poor, left alone on the farm. She worked in your grandma's kitchen, for old lady Vermeer, for old lady Vanderpool, for everybody. Twenty-five cents an hour."

Mrs. Potter was silent, knowing that a dollar for a half day of cleaning had indeed been the going rate. She also remembered that Grandpa had always bought the Walters' winter supply of coal and had paid their doctor's bills. She thought of the baskets of food—vegetables, eggs, canned goods, with which Mrs. Walters was sent home at the end of the cleaning day. She refused to feel guilty for Grandma Andrews.

"You and your gang were too busy out playing with your boats and tennis rackets to notice," Bertha spoke again. "But I got even with you, didn't I? *I'm* the lady now. I'm the one to say, come have a drink with me, 'Genia. I've got the big house on the lake and the Mercedes car and I've got this."

The big sapphire ring swung free. "See it? He was going to give it to me, how do you like that? I know he was. And he was going to marry me—you hear that, too?"

Bertha held the ring, twisted the blue fire into the sunlight. "For a while there, I was crazy. I thought we could be friends, you and

193

me. You know, friends like you three used to be with your little club and your playhouse in the barn.''

The big gem swung again on the golden chain. ''But I saw your face when the ring slipped out. I knew right then you'd never believe me if I said he was going to give it to *me*.''

Bertha's face was now almost black against the late afternoon sun. ''You don't believe he was going to marry me, do you? They said you wouldn't believe it.''

''Who said?'' Mrs. Potter asked quietly, hoping that her voice did not quaver.

''Alice, Elsie, Louie. They all said you'd never let me be one of the crowd. They told me I was crazy thinking I could get by with it and that you'd never say, '*Bertha, come by for dinner, just the old gang,*' things like that. Oh, they were right, all right.''

Mrs. Potter thought of Louie and Alice and Elsie, of the loosened valve on the brake system, of the drugged drink at the Blue Room. All of them had known, all except Bertha, that whatever Bertha did in her attempt to change the social pattern that dominated their very small town, it wasn't going to work.

Moreover, as Bertha had not, the three of them had perceived that Mrs. Potter's earlier questions could lead only to one inevitable conclusion: Bertha's guilt. However they had learned of this, and however—apparently without her knowledge—they tried to protect her, it was clear that the Walters family had closed ranks in their sister's defense.

And they had very nearly succeeded.

The *Blue Goose* had long passed any points—her own dock, the closed Pink House, the shuttered cottage—from which she might possibly have summoned help, had there been anyone to signal.

The only other chance now was to go overboard and swim for it.

Bertha read her mind. ''No chance of getting away,'' she said. ''These outboards would chop you to sausage meat before you made it halfway to shore.''

Mrs. Potter knew she was right.

''Anyway, I got this much, no matter what,'' Bertha spoke again. ''No matter what Alice and Elsie and Louie said, I got you to see that I made it. Without you to see that I made it, all I did wasn't worth it, wasn't worth it at all.''

Mrs. Potter was unable to answer. At last, hoping to restore some pretense of normality, she tried to smile, tried to speak gently. "I'm so sorry about all of this, Bertha. But now we should head back to town, and then we can talk about it another time."

"Giving me orders again, are you? Always so polite, always taking charge. The lady tells the housekeeper what to do, yes?" A last blaze of sunset disappeared behind the trees. "No, Mrs. Muckety-Muck Potter. *I'm* the one does the saying now."

"Jackie?" Mrs. Potter's question was almost a whisper. "You thought Jackie was going to take all this away from you?"

Bertha's hands tightened on the sleek black knees. "*She* didn't get him. I fixed her wagon, all right."

The voice became less certain. "He didn't even thank me. He told me I did wrong, he said he wasn't ever going to marry me anyway, no matter did I get rid of that girl for him. He said he'd have to tell the police."

"You killed MacKay, too?" Mrs. Potter asked in horrified disbelief.

"No, that Varlene was the one. She was the one killed him, that's for sure. Drunken little no-good came to the house right after I got back from Jackie's. He put her in his car to try to take her home, then she opened the door and fell out. I was watching from the stairs. He started back around his side of the car, going to pick her up, I guess, when he slipped, looked like, maybe on that little piece of pipe. *She* killed him. It was all her fault."

"But you turned on the car? You left him there unconscious and closed the doors?" Mrs. Potter knew she had guessed this right as she watched Bertha's face.

"I got rid of that Varlene, all right. I fixed her up, just the same way I'm going to fix you right now."

Bertha's voice became plaintive. "I told them not to hurt you. I told Louie and the girls. I didn't want to fix you too, 'Genia, not until you saw how good I'd made it for myself."

The boat rocked gently and now Bertha spoke with a new intensity. "But you wouldn't have it that way, would you? You looked at that ring and I knew you wouldn't have it for us to be friends."

Frozen, uncomprehending, Mrs. Potter watched as Bertha reached forward and slid out one of the heavy wooden oars stored for emergencies along the length of the boat. She watched without moving until the Valkyrie figure rose in front of her.

In a wide arc, steady in the powerful hands, the swinging oar aimed at the side of her head.

Mrs. Potter's reflexes were slow to remember the water games of her youth. At first awkward, she ducked her head between her knees and twisted away from the blow.

Then, with dexterity programmed long ago, she drew her knees to her chest, doubled her body into a ball and rolled herself over the side of the boat. With the best surface dive her sixty-year-old body could manage, she aimed at the bottom of Blue Lake, deathly cold, as she had never known it before.

Kicking off her shoes as she went down, she struggled for control, and for recollection of what should be the next gambit from when this kind of horseplay was the stuff of her teenage life on the lake.

Up, yes, when it was impossible to stay down longer. But *look* up, young 'Genia, she told herself, remember to look up for the boat above you. Try to surface as quietly as possible, close to the boat, just under the bow. It would be far safer there than swimming away and coming up where she could be seen and run down by the knifelike motor blades.

Maybe a place at the waterline to breathe again, and not be detected?

She had not reckoned with the utter quiet of the cove and the sound of her own labored breathing. Above her head there was again the heavy upraised oar, the heavy-breathing voice.

"Next time you come up, I get you for sure," Bertha was saying. "The canoe and the paddle go after you when it's all over. When they find those things floating, they'll know. No marks on you to show. You tipped over, they'll see it plain as day, and you couldn't make it to shore."

Underwater again, but this time she knew it would not work. She could not swim deep enough, fast enough, in that clear water to evade her killer. Maybe I can do it once more, she thought, but that will be the last one.

In the water, her ears picked up the sound of a motor entering the cove, seconds before a rifle shot cracked across the water. As she surfaced she saw Bertha, a new design flowering the patterned shoulder, turning to face the sound.

Coming into the cove with a great white fishtail of wake behind the twin outboards was her own *Blue Fish*. Greg was at the tiller, and in the bow stood Charlie, rifle ready at her shoulder.

A rescued heroine should behave with more dignity, thought Mrs. Potter. Throwing up is not dignified. But then neither am I much of a heroine, and I am a *terrible* detective.

Over and over, early that evening, back in her own old-fashioned bathroom, Eugenia Potter was very sick to her stomach and almost numb of other feelings. She remembered a cool hand on her forehead (Charlie? Greg?) and a comforting rumble of voice that must mean Doc was there. Pete and the twins were in and out of her bedroom, or so she thought, between the times she was in and out of the bathroom being sick.

"Tell me, Greg," Mrs. Potter asked weakly at one point, "how did you and Charlie know I needed you?"

Their worry, it seemed, had built up in stages. Charlie had come into the house by the back door (quietly, in case Mrs. Potter was resting), had started up the back stairs to the bathroom, and had been surprised at the sudden clatter of steps down the front stairs and the porch steps. Baffled, Charlie had watched the flight to the dock and the hurried launching of the canoe.

When Greg came home they discussed, over milk and cookies in the kitchen, what could possibly have caused this abrupt departure. Suddenly, they were startled by the sound of the *Blue Goose* roaring past the house. It was too late in the day, too late in the season, for it to be out. They went to the porch in time to recognize Mrs. Potter as one of the two figures aboard, and to see the boat disappear, heading for the deserted end of the lake.

Whatever was going on, Greg knew at once that something was wrong. There had been too many accidents, too many near-misses in the attempts on his aunt's life.

"But the gun, Greg, the gun? Whose idea was that?"

"Well, Charlotte brought it to shoot rats in the barn. But believe it or not, Aunt 'Genia, right then and there I knew there were some things that would justify using one. Sort of an answer to what the twins were bugging me about last night at dinner.

"Only thing is," he went on, "I can't shoot for sour apples, and Charlotte is a whiz. So you might say I aimed the thought and she pulled the trigger."

"Great shot," was Pete's professional comment. "Hope I do as well next week in Dakota."

Then she and Pete, Greg and Charlie put the story together, all the pieces fitting at last.

Bertha, already furious over the two evenings Jackie had spent alone with MacKay at his house, and having seen the ring (it just matched her eyes, she told Pete in her jail room), considered the girl the final intolerable threat to her hopes to marry MacKay.

(You should have seen her bedroom over the garage, Pete told them. Pink lampshades, white fur rug, black satin sheets. She must have been trying to get him any way she could.)

MacKay came home from the class just before Bertha left for the night. She listened in on Jackie's call, asking him to meet her at the Inn.

After he left, she looked in his room and his desk for the ring, which she knew he had taken from the bank vault earlier. Not finding it, she was convinced that he planned to give it to Jackie that night.

When Jackie returned to her apartment from the Blue Room, Bertha was waiting for her in the tree-shaded darkness of the parking lot, the thin-bladed knife from the kitchen rack in her hand.

"Of course I know how to stick a pig," she had told Pete. "Who doesn't, around here? It was too good for her."

Unable to find the ring on Jackie's hand or in her purse, yet sure

198

she had done the right thing, Bertha went back to the house on the lakeshore.

"I know what MacKay told her," Mrs. Potter put in. "She thought he would be grateful to be saved from a scheming woman, which Jackie undoubtedly was. What she couldn't believe was that he would consider it murder."

Pete resumed his recital. Just as Bertha had shocked MacKay by announcing that she had solved his problem with Jackie, Varlene, drunk and sentimental, arrived in her little flowered car. "I just wanted to thank you for being so nice to me"—that was what Bertha remembered hearing her say.

Then he sent me to my room, Bertha said. He told Varlene she was in no shape to drive herself home. He pushed her to the garage, shoved her into his own car, opened the garage doors, and went back to start the motor.

Varlene, sick and dizzy, opened her car door just then and began to slide out. Watching from the door of her room above, Bertha saw MacKay start back around his side of the car to try to grab her before she fell. And then he slipped and came down hard on the concrete.

"I expect she pushed Varlene out the open garage doors toward her own car," Mrs. Potter said, "then followed her, closing the doors behind her. Leaving the motor running."

"What did she mean when she told Aunt 'Genia she took care of Varlene?" Greg asked Pete.

"I got this much out of her," he said, "that she got in Varlene's old car with her and that Varlene drove out the old road.

"I guess Varlene was sobering up some when she saw the old bridge. 'How'd we get here?' she probably asked Bertha, who had been the one to point the way, and then she was uncontrollably sick.

" 'You made a mess of both of us,' Bertha told her. 'You can't go home until we get you washed up.' " Pete paused.

"I can imagine what happened then," Mrs. Potter added. "They probably left the car by the road and went down the path to the inlet. Varlene knelt by the water, at Bertha's direction. Bertha pushed her head down and held it until the struggle was over."

"I know what she told Varlene, right at the last," Pete said.

199

"Told her it served her right, that she was turning out bad, just like her mother."

The four of them sat silent for several minutes.

Then Bertha walked back to MacKay's house, Pete continued. She drove her own car back home to Harrington. Nobody thought to ask Alice or Elsie or Louie what time she got home that night.

Of course the three of them knew. They saw the blood on Bertha's uniform, the mud on her neat white oxfords. Naturally they're denying the whole business now, but the twins are with them and we'll see about them later.

"We sure slipped up there," Pete admitted, after another pause, "but most of what we did find out was right. We just added it up wrong, is what we did."

Mrs. Potter didn't see how she could explain about Redmond now, and like Louie and the Walters girls, that could wait until later. Whatever proved to be the true story of Rhynesdorp (and Pete could pursue this or not as he chose) she now knew Redmond was innocent of the Harrington murders. By now he was back in his Chicago office tower, beside another larger, less placid lake, writing his columns, and he could be forgotten.

And what I'm going to do, I'm going back to bed, thought Mrs. Potter, somewhat dizzily.

A few minutes later there was a light knock at her door and Charlie appeared with a tray. "Just a cup of tea, Aunt 'Genia, and some of my raisin toast. Sleep well."

Soothed by the comforting, sweet milky tea, drowsy with whatever Doc's pills contained, Mrs. Potter let a brief, happy preview of the ranch cross her mind. Shirt-sleeve fall weather. Calves to gather, cowboys to ride with. Good tequila *puro* and chili beans to share with the brand inspector and the stock-truck drivers before the year's calf crop, bawling wildly, was driven off to the feedlots.

The lovely ease of a swim in a heated pool (Mrs. Potter favored a sybaritic 80 degrees) after peeling out of blue jeans and boots.

Doc's pills asserted more authority. She next imagined herself in that new (well, not new, but *current*) violet coatdress, on her way to church in Harrington. No hat (what? that faded red summer straw? that thousand-year-old black velvet bow thing that had served its ecclesiastic purpose for so many of her Sundays? *never!*) on her bared and shining silver-gilt head.

Instead, she was wearing a pair of amethyst earrings, repeating the color of the suede. These, she realized happily, were just what St. Paul would have approved.

"By the way," she was saying to Lynette and the rector and a circle of raised eyebrows on the sandstone steps after church, "I know you'll all be delighted. Dear Charlie is moving out to Indian Point to be with Greg there after I go home."

The next slide—her thoughts had the quality of movie stills— was that of a wedding invitation very much like one she had recently received.

The face of the invitation, instead of bearing the formal engraved tidings of custom, was covered by a soft, sepia-tinted photograph. Mrs. Potter now saw in this, not the original actual senders of the invitation, but a picture of Greg and Charlie.

Smiling confidently through a luxuriant blond mustache, plaid shirt open to show a now-strong, thick young neck, was her nephew. Turning slightly to face him, eyes crinkled and lips softly parted, her dandelion head framed by the leafy background behind them, was Charlie.

Printed in a dark raised script over the lower part of the photograph, over the two clasped hands and the blue-jeaned legs, was the following:

Charlotte Anne Ragsdale
and
Gregory Willard Andrews
invite you to share in the joy
when they exchange marriage vows
and begin their new life together

The church and the date followed, and the fact that the reception would be held at Indian Point directly after the ceremony.

Whenever Mrs. Potter felt feverish and disoriented, as she now knew herself to be, she remembered an old song their mother used to sing to her and Will when they were sick, as children.

How did it go? "Frog went a-courting, he did ride, umhm, *huhm.* Sword and a pistol by his side, to ask Miss Mouse to be his bride, umhm, *huhm.*"

A slightly altered next verse came into her mind: "And what will the wedding supper be, *umhm, huhm?*"

What indeed? "Two dried prunes and a black-eyed pea?"

That simply will not do, Mrs. Potter decided firmly, as she envisioned Charlie's possible vegetarian repast of health food. Fresh fruits, trays of figs and nuts, pitchers of healthful juices. Maybe yogurt. Maybe pompandums or pappadums or whatever those bread things are called. Anyway, *impossible.*

Click. Another frame slid into Mrs. Potter's projector. A mountain of lovely, lively lobsters (the co-op near the Maine cottage responding with a noble airborne shipment in answer to her telephoned request) to be made into her own rather perfect lobster Newburg.

Patty shells by Edward, of course, made with his lightest puff pastry. And naturally he could be counted on to see to opening the cases of champagne she would summon, to arrange for the twins to help with the pouring and passing, and even to be sure there were enough stemmed glasses.

Finally, one dreamy blurred daguerreotype. Aunt Hillie, in shirtwaist-collar, black hair piled on top of her proud young head. And she was saying, "I hope you'll see how easily a skylight could be added to that north bedroom, Charlotte. You've seen my watercolors in the parlor. Now when you see my painted china, you'll know how much I'd like that room made into a real artist's studio."

White clouds and occasional sunlit snow flurries obscured the view from the plane window beside Mrs. Potter's seat on the Minneapolis-Denver leg of her flight to Tucson.

Smiling slightly, she eased back to look out at the changing white light as she sipped her icy prelunch martini.

The little airline bottles labeled ''dry martini'' held too much vermouth for Mrs. Potter's taste. Some now-forgotten fellow passenger had long ago taught her his secret: Order one martini-mix miniature and one of straight gin; combine half of each over ice, with a twist of lemon peel if you can get it, to make one good martini. Combine the remaining two halves later, he told her, over fresh ice (again if you can get it) for a second even better one.

Waving away the airline luncheon tray, Mrs. Potter went to sleep.

ABOUT THE AUTHOR

Virginia Rich, making her debut as a mystery writer with THE COOKING SCHOOL MURDERS, was born in Sibley, Iowa, a small Midwestern town similar to Harrington. At one time, Mrs. Rich wrote a food column for *The Chicago Tribune*, under the continuing *Tribune* name of Mary Meade. She has also served as food editor for *Sunset* magazine. Presently, Mrs. Rich divides her time between her working cattle ranch in Arizona, and spending some months each year at her home in a small town in Maine, not unlike the town where Mrs. Potter will next appear in THE BAKED BEAN SUPPER MURDERS.